Advance Praise for *Coded to Kill*

"A beautifully written, complex mix of medical drama, espionage story and high-tech skulduggery, *Coded to Kill* is a thrilling read under the guidance of someone who knows what he is talking about, and never fails to enthrall with its detail and deft plotting."

—Iain Pears, author of *An Instance of the Fingerpost* and *The Dream of Scipio*

"Dr. Marschall Runge gives us both a heart-stopping thriller and a searing indictment of the degree to which technology has sapped the soul of medicine and handed it to the technocracy."

—Holden Thorp, Editor-in-Chief, Science Family of Journals

CODED
TO KILL

CODED TO KILL

A TECHNO-MEDICAL THRILLER

MARSCHALL RUNGE, M.D.

A POST HILL PRESS BOOK

ISBN: 978-1-63758-927-4
ISBN (eBook): 978-1-63758-926-7

Coded to Kill:
A Techno-Medical Thriller
© 2023 by Marschall Runge, M.D.
All Rights Reserved

Cover design by Jim Villaflores

Post Hill Press
New York • Nashville
posthillpress.com

Published in the United States of America

For centuries, doctors have pledged to "Do no harm" as they receive their medical diploma. The *Oath of Hippocrates* drew upon the wisdom and power of the great Greek gods Apollo, the Physician, and Asclepius, the God of Medicine. The twenty-first century witnessed the emergence of a new god—a god of human creation. That god was the *Electronic Health Record* (EHR). The promise was to unleash the power of artificial intelligence and a machine learning to end preventable harm to patients. Like all human creations, it was not infallible. Its power was awesome.

CHAPTER

1

Jesse Gutierrez was the last man standing from the construction crew, now almost as invisible as the high-tech bunker they had built. But his time was running out—a team in that underground facility was recording his every move.

Gutierrez's commute to Drexel Memorial Hospital took him over a backcountry two-lane bridge that spanned a stretch of deep water. The investigators would find multiple contributing factors. Gutierrez worked long hours and was probably fatigued. His cell phone would show that he had received a robocall which would appear to have originated from Malaysia just moments before impact. The accident reconstruction team would conclude that the curving road, dew-slickened pavement, sun in his eyes, and distraction of his phone caused Gutierrez to crash into the guardrail.

1

What they wouldn't find was that the guardrail had been modified to crumble through the application of organic acids and other reactants.

And they would never learn of the panel truck, commanded by an expert driver who knew how to force another vehicle off the road without making contact. The computer models said that as long as the truck swerved at just the right time, Gutierrez's car would crash through the weakened guardrail, clear the bridge, and fall into the water, sinking to the deep bottom in ninety-three seconds.

The highly choreographed attack on Jesse Gutierrez was complicated, but worth it given the enormous stakes.

~

A satellite 430 miles above beamed real-time images to the underground conference room with large monitors on the walls. Hugh Torrence rarely attended terminations. His presence was further evidence of its importance.

Decades of experience in the military—and later the NSA—had honed Torrence's attention to detail. He considered every possible outcome of an operation, analyzed the results, then rethought the plan. There was no substitute for disaster awareness and disaster mitigation in his line of work. Evil abounded. On this brisk Sunday morning, he was ready, as always.

Twenty-three-year-old IT wunderkind Benny Rasinko adjusted the images on the screen from his black Aeron chair. Beside him stood Torrence's unflappable second in command, Hasan Saied.

At precisely 6 AM, a muscular man wearing a brown Drexel Memorial Hospital polo and blue jeans appeared on the screen. He exited the front door of his small townhouse and climbed into a blue Honda Civic.

"Subject is en route to Drexel," Benny announced.

Two minutes later, Gutierrez pulled onto a two-lane blacktop. He had so many questions, and the peaceful drive down a rural highway gave him time to think. His mind kept returning to the construction job he'd worked on a year ago, building a tricked-out underground bunker in southern Virginia.

His misgivings intensified as he learned that other workers—all, like him, unmarried Spanish-speaking men—had been meeting untimely ends. Drunk-driving accidents, barroom fights, drownings and drug overdoses. Each one seemed legit, but so many? A year ago, he wouldn't have cared. He hadn't cared much about anything after the meaningless carnage he'd seen in Afghanistan as a member of the Special Forces. But he had slowly rebuilt his life after leaving the service, taking on any job or opportunity that came his way, and his old instincts began to kick in. Building an underground bunker in the middle of nowhere made no sense. Nor did the passing mention of Drexel Hospital and electronic health records by the boss of that job—a sixty-something man known as El Jefe. He wondered, *is that the key to those deaths?* and his own fate.

His antennae started pinging on high alert a few days before when he sighted a familiar face across the hospital parking lot: Dr. Mason Fischer. They went way back. *No way Fischer was at Drexel by accident.*

"Subject is two miles from Jordan Lake Bridge," Benny called out. Torrence glanced at Benny, saw the boy's energy drink sitting nakedly on the workstation, and placed it on a coaster before looking back to the screen.

~

On any other day, the oversized panel truck tailgating his car would have irritated Gutierrez. Damned civilians. But not today. He considered slowing down just to annoy the jerk, but decided, *Why bother?* His phone rang. As he looked down to grab it, the panel truck whipped out across the double yellow line. *What the hell?* The truck was beside him in the oncoming lane as they crossed a bridge.

Suddenly it swerved toward him once, then twice. Gutierrez was all instinct and adrenaline now. The guardrail would save him. He'd slide into it at twenty-five-miles-per-hour, puncture the airbag, grab his Sig Sauer P226, and see if the bastard wanted to dance.

He slammed on the brakes, but instead of stopping his motion, the guardrail gave way like a bullfighter's cape.

His head hit the steering wheel, and the Honda plunged into the water.

The guardrail on the north side of the bridge, where the acid had been applied, was in shambles. The Honda Civic was no longer in sight, sinking to the bottom of the lake. The panel truck moved slowly, then accelerated off the bridge. A mile away, an empty eighteen-wheeler waited to swallow it. No record of it would ever exist. "Operation complete," Benny declared. Torrence smiled.

~

What Torrence and crew couldn't see was the small boat underneath the bridge, where a man was sleeping amidst the sloshing remnants of a Coors Light twelve-pack and a fifth of Old Crow before a violent splash awakened him. The man considered doing nothing; every movement caused a ripple of pain that intensified the throbbing in his head. He heard a car door slam, an engine rev, and tires squeal from above. *They're going for help*, he thought, *and don't need me.*

Then he saw the black car beginning to sink and the outline of a man, solid and immobile. His conscience kicked in. He jumped in the water, swam to the car, unlocked the door, and grabbed for the seat belt. He found the latch and unsnapped it. The victim slid out with little effort. The strength that comes with panic enabled him to drag the victim towards the shore. Another creaking movement and the car turned downward. In five seconds, it was gone. The vortex nearly sucked them both down.

The victim was badly injured. His right leg dragged at an awkward angle. He moaned indecipherable words. The deep gash on his forehead gushed. His savior gently laid him on a flat spot that some fisherman had cleared out. He removed his shirt, ripping off a sleeve to make a bandage for the man's head. He couldn't find his cell phone. He scrabbled up the bank in time to see a car speed by. So did another, and another, until an elderly farmer in a pickup full of vegetables pulled over. The farmer had a phone. In minutes, the ambulance arrived and soon raced away, its lights flashing and sirens screaming.

CHAPTER

2

"Shit."

"Chief," Benny called out to Torrence, who was heading back up the stairs. "We got a problem."

Torrence looked at the screen where a wet old man stood on the bridge frantically waving his arms, the body of another man dressed in a brown shirt and jeans laid out below, next to the lake.

This is impossible, Torrence thought. *My plan was flawless; my team was the best.* Yet this laborer had somehow cheated death. His savior, some dripping wet bum, had appeared out of nowhere and dragged him to safety. He'd also have to be attended to. But completing the Gutierrez termination was job number one, and time was of the essence. Torrence considered the options. The panel truck was safely packed in the eighteen-wheeler, rendering it useless. The trip to Drexel was too short to put the ambulance in play. Gutierrez looked done for, but what if he survived? What did he know? What would he suspect? Whom would he tell? No matter, for now. Torrence had Tyler Jensen, his man on the scene at Drexel. Jensen left no loose ends.

"Set up a secure call with Jensen," Torrence barked while massaging the St. Christopher's medal he always kept in his right-hand pants pocket. "Then get into Gutierrez's medical record. We'll feed Jensen whatever you find."

Benny froze for a moment. "Got it?" Torrence yelled. "Tell me you can do this without screwing it up."

"Yes sir," Benny replied, his voice a slightly higher pitch than normal.

"Jensen better be on top of his game," Torrence said to everyone and no one. "Dead means dead!"

"Thought you said the plan was perfect," said Tyler Jensen, his words clipped and caustic.

Jensen knew he was treading on dangerous ground, but he didn't care. He never cared what anyone thought of him. A graduate of Annapolis, he'd had a decorated career as a Navy SEAL and seen action in Afghanistan, Iraq, and other hotspots on missions so highly classified that his very existence would be denied if the shit went south.

But Jensen's missions never did and never would.

He could pass for a linebacker—an inch over six feet tall, two hundred thirty pounds of muscle, short-clipped red hair, a tribute to his maternal gene line that also made him favor violent solutions for most problems, and an angular, unsmiling face. But tackling people wasn't as satisfying as watching that last flicker of life in their eyes extinguish. He was smart and lethal. That came with the SEAL training.

Few had the balls to deal with the complications—the ethical lines and moral dilemmas, the rules that arose in civilian operations and civilian life. Jensen did. He knew he was a tool for Torrence, but a sharp one Torrence needed. Who cared if Torrence, or anyone else, liked him?

An hour before, he had received the coded text message—the number "48" ("HT" on the telephone's keypad)—that told him to call Hugh Torrence on a secure line. He knew instantly the plan to kill Gutierrez had failed. There was no other reason Torrence would call him now. They needed him to clean up a mess, again.

If Torrence had only listened to me in the first place, Jensen thought with satisfaction. *A bullet to the brain from eight hundred yards, the man's dead, and no one's the wiser.*

He'd made the argument five days earlier. Of the many ways he killed, he preferred the sniper's bullet. Its elegance sent an unforgettable message to anyone left behind: stand down. The target's compadres would get the message and bug out. No one wants to spend the rest of his life wondering when a faceless killer was taking aim.

In all likelihood, killing Gutierrez was another of Torrence's absurd, bootless errands. Nothing suggested that Gutierrez was onto them. He was just another poor son of a bitch who took the wrong job at the wrong time.

Jensen agreed with Torrence that those deaths were necessary. But he suspected that Torrence was crossing the line between caution and paranoia as his obsession spread to all those others at Drexel, from that dumb-ass jock, Dr. Mason Fischer, to Bud Burgess, Drexel's supposed IT genius, and his top lieutenant, RT. The only thing they had in common was that they worked at Drexel, along with twenty-five thousand other losers, and they might know each other.

Jensen said none of this to Torrence. There was work to be done. Jensen, whose badge identified him as a representative for National Health Care Insurance, was already in the hospital when Torrence called.

"Determine if Gutierrez is conscious and if he is going to make it. If he's done, slip away. But if it looks like the bastard will even be able to blink the alphabet, call me. Got it?" Torrence said.

"You're going to do it remotely?" Jensen asked.

"That's my decision, not yours," Torrence said, shifting into the tone that said it wasn't a discussion but an order. Torrence glanced at Saied, who nodded in agreement. Drexel's Electronic Health Records system [EHR] provided the means to take out Gutierrez without Jensen's iron touch.

Jensen remained silent. He might have disagreed with Torrence, but he knew the bastard could bring a world of hurt down on him. With the Drexel gig drawing to a close, it was about time to get the hell out of Torrence's world. No need to set a bounty on his own head.

~

Gutierrez was still unconscious when the ambulance reached Drexel's emergency room. His heart was racing, his blood pressure perilously low. His ribs were broken, his femur shattered. Doctors, nurses, and technicians descended upon him in Trauma Room One, working with crisp efficiency.

In an instant, his clothes were cut off, and the blood-soaked bandages were removed. The cuts on his forehead and deep wounds on his right leg were scrubbed clean with

Betadine and re-bandaged. Anxious residents and nurses who weren't assigned to his case peered into the room before huddling in the corridor as they talked about his accident. It was a bad one.

"He works in Physical Plant," said one nurse. "One of the guys down there said he's working full time and trying to get a voc-tech degree. Now this."

"Scary," said Dr. Carrie Mumsford, a resident physician. "Could be any of us, as little rest as we get. I was still half asleep when I hit the road this morning."

An emergency medicine resident rushed out of Trauma Room One and was immediately collared by the others.

"What's the story?" Carrie demanded.

"Bad. The attending says it's touch and go. He's bleeding internally, but they can't figure out where. His leg is mangled, maybe an artery was severed. The EHR shows some sort of weird rhythm on his EKG. Are any of the cardiologists down here?"

"There's an acute MI in Critical Care Room Four, Mas …." She stopped herself. "Dr. Fischer's there," said Carrie, referring to one of the newer cardiologists, Mason Fischer.

The emergency room resident hurried down the hall, an EKG in hand.

Tyler Jensen, now in green scrubs, his National Health Care ID in his pocket and a Drexel badge declaring him an EMT, listened in on their conversation, then wandered down the hall. He pulled a cell phone from his pocket and dialed a secure line to Torrence.

"They say he's fifty-fifty," Jensen whispered.

~

The emergency room crew threw everything at Gutierrez, but for each step forward, he took two steps back, toward the grave. Within ten minutes, Gutierrez had his third cardiac arrest.

"It's got to be the damned ventricular tachycardia," yelled the ER attending physician. "Get a cardiologist. Now!"

"He's here!" shouted the nurse in charge.

Dr. Mason Fischer read the initial EKG as he ran down the hall to Trauma Room One. It did not show ventricular tachycardia or any dangerous cardiac rhythm, just the very fast heart rate of a very stressed man with multiple injuries. A path to Gutierrez's side cleared as he rushed into the room.

He took one look at the man and did a double-take. The EHR data record open on the computer and the hospital ID band on his wrist read Jesse Gutierrez. *No way.* The man on the stretcher was an old friend, Longorio Cabreja.

They'd met at Fort Bragg. At 251 square miles and a population that ranges up to fifty thousand, it was the largest military installation in the world. Cabreja was a Delta Force commander when Fischer was assigned there, fresh out of medical school. They weren't quite twins—both were about six feet tall, with neatly cropped hair and lean, athletic frames. Maybe brothers from another mother. Fischer was fair with blue eyes and sandy-colored hair. Cabreja, his parents from Mexico, had brown eyes and dark brown, nearly black, hair.

They'd bonded over ice-cold bottles of Pabst Blue Ribbon and stories at the local dive bar. It turned out that Cabreja had grown up about an hour from Mason—little more than a stone's throw in central-west Texas, where goats and cattle far outnumbered people and the mesquite, live oaks and prickly pears coexisted with native grasses, at least in the years when there was enough rain to sustain something besides the scrub brush. After about six months, Cabreja shipped out for another tour in Afghanistan. That was a dozen years ago. Mason hadn't heard from him since. He'd assumed his friend was still in the game, or dead. That was the life of Delta Force soldiers.

The EHR said that the man on the ER table worked in Physical Plant. If that was all there was to it, Mason thought, what a terrible waste of the singular skills of a pinnacle warrior. Cabreja was clearly in extremis. A cursory exam revealed significant lung congestion, particularly on the left side, and crepitus, a grating sound consistent with rib fractures. He glanced again at the huge monitor hanging above the bed. The chest X-ray and CT scan were normal. No fluid, no fractures. That couldn't be right. Vital seconds ticked by.

"This guy's problem isn't cardiac," Mason said. "This looks like a severe deceleration injury. Rib fractures, fluid… probably blood in his left lung. He may have a torn aorta. He needs to be in the trauma OR, not here!"

The attending physician was confused. "The chest X-ray and CT were normal."

"Those imaging studies have to be from another patient." Mason grabbed the other doctor's hand and pressed down on the broken ribs.

"Get the trauma team here," yelled the emergency medicine doctor. "Use the overhead. Where the hell are they?"

"Three minutes," was the response.

Mason looked back at the man. Was it really Cabreja? His friend had identifying marks. Not unique, but close to it in combination. Mason saw all three: the faintest outline where the tattoo had been, a coiled rattler ready to strike that had been lasered off, per Delta protocol to prevent enemy identification; a jagged appendectomy scar from a surgery done by a Delta medic in the mountains of Afghanistan; and a long scar along his left upper arm, a sign of his trade. *It's him*, Mason thought.

Then he heard a loud beep. Cabreja's blood pressure dropped again.

"Hang two more units," Mason instructed. "He's bleeding out."

Cabreja's eyes snapped open. He was awake and confused. A breathing tube connected to a ventilator precluded clear speech. Still, he tried.

Mason looked at him intently. Even in his critical condition, Cabreja's eyes smiled. Mason smiled as well as he grasped his shoulder.

"You're hurt bad, man. Broken ribs, bleeding...."

Cabreja waved him off and tried to quickly speak—which was impossible with the endotracheal tube. When Mason shook his head, Cabreja slowly mouthed several words. It was clear Mason didn't understand what he was trying to say, but before Cabreja could continue, the monitors blared again. Mason looked up. The heart rhythm was unchanged, but the blood pressure had dropped again.

Cabreja was fading fast. He had to get the message to Mason. He tightened his jaw and slowly mouthed short syllables.

"Guv op..." Guiterrez then mouthed the last two words of his life while holding up a single finger, "our north."

"Government operation an hour north?" asked Mason. Cabreja gave a short nod, and then was out.

"Flatline. Defibrillate!" shouted the ER attending. "All clear."

14

Mason stepped back. The defibrillator fired. Cabreja's body jolted. The monitor was unchanged.

The trauma team arrived in force. "OR One is open," said the lead surgeon, "but I'm going to have to open him here." If Cabreja had any luck this day, it was that Drexel was one of the few hospitals that had a highly specialized critical care facility within the emergency room. Critical Care Room One was as fully equipped as any ICU room, anywhere. It could even be used as an operating room.

In less than a minute, Cabreja's chest cavity was visible. The surgeon recognized an enlarged and misshapen aorta, indicating that the accident had caused a tear between the layers of the aorta. The injury led to nearly 100 percent mortality within hours.

"He's got a big dissection. Jesus Christ, how did that get missed? And how did he hang on so long? He's dumped ten units of blood in his chest."

It was too little, too late. Half an hour later, they called it.

"Time of death is 8:38 AM."

Jesse Gutierrez, or Longorio Cabreja, was dead.

~

Benny's secure line buzzed.

"You better not have compromised our status, you little shit!" Torrence yelled into the phone as he always did when pissed.

Maybe it wasn't that big a deal. Maybe Saied was right that the chance of detection was infinitesimal. But Torrence's antennae were up.

"W-what do you mean?" Benny stammered.

"Don't give me that innocent act. Changing out the chest X-ray and CT scan. Jensen told me all about it. Saied confirmed it."

"No worries, boss. Yeah, I used the EHR to replace Gutierrez's imaging studies with normals. I was watching everything in real-time, and when the computer read all kinds of problems, I just switched them out. Made it look like the radiology tech uploaded the wrong study. Poor sucker will be lucky if he only gets fired, what with the dude dying. But nothing more. We're clean."

"We'd better damned well be," Torrence said. "And put that goddamn drink on a coaster."

~

Mason Fischer scrolled through the messages on his pager but his mind was elsewhere. What was Cabreja doing at Drexel? Did it have anything to do with the cryptic text message he received two days ago that simply said, "Things are warming up"?

For all he knew, it was a coincidence. Or maybe he and Cabreja were working on different sides of a problem, or different sides altogether. Stranger things had happened.

What do I really know? he asked himself. In the months since coming to Durham, he'd learned everything that a non-techie could about the Drexel EHR. He'd gotten to know the hospital's IT genius, Bud Burgess, befriended Burgess's right-hand man, RT, and established a perhaps too-close relationship with the daughter of the hospital's president, Carrie Mumsford. All remained just bits and pieces.

Now Cabreja's death and garbled comments. It had to mean something.

There was only one conclusion possible. Trouble was lurking, but where? He'd needed to dig deeper and be mighty damned careful to leave no trail.

CHAPTER

4

Derrick Mumsford cut a sleek image in his dark blue pin-striped bespoke Brioni suit, 100 percent Egyptian cotton shirt and Carolina-blue tie. Strong features, burning blue eyes, and a square jaw to match. Without his streaks of gray, he could still pass for the fraternity president he once had been. The high intensity lighting and the CNBC cameras might have thrown a lesser man into a fit of nerves, but not Mumsford. He'd carefully cultivated the image of grace under pressure— and between his iron will and a milligram of Xanax taken twenty minutes before, he was.

Mumsford was in particularly high spirits as he looked out over the audience. Just three hours before, Charles Richmond, an old friend from the Cap and Gown Club at Princeton who had helped recruit him to Drexel and now led the powerful National Institute for Medical Safety, had called with good news. The joint review process of Drexel's EHR with federal agencies, including the Centers for Medicare and Medicaid Services (CMS) and the Food and Drug Administration (FDA), was nearing completion. Everything was on track. Drexel's apparently impenetrable encryption system had enabled it to swat down the last-minute Hail Mary pass thrown by Drexel's main competitors, which played on the fears that the system's core benefit—the ability to collect and analyze every medical record in America to devise new treatments—would compromise patient privacy. "At this point," Richmond told Mumsford, "no major obstacles remain. My sources tell me that Elvin Walters might make one more show of resistance, but it's all theater—a final chance him to champion privacy in public before the inevitable."

"I hope he knows not to be too convincing," Mumsford said with a laugh. "He's not just one of our state's senators, but he also receives treatment from us."

"I'm sure it won't come to that," Richmond responded playfully. "A few minor details need to be hammered out. The typical regulatory rigmarole. A week or two at most before our hard work pays off and Drexel's EHR is named the national standard."

Of course, no one in the auditorium—not even Mumsford—had ever heard of Jesse Gutierrez (a.k.a. Longorio Cabreja) and those familiar with Mason Fischer knew him only as an up-and-coming cardiologist new to the staff.

Today's presentation was the latest—and hopefully the last—in a long road show that had taken Mumsford across the country. Key politicians were in attendance, including North Carolina's governor. The rest of the nearly two hundred attendees included some of the wealthiest men and women in the Southeast as well as the CEOs of the biggest hospital systems—early sales targets. The most important had already been given private demonstrations by Drexel's IT guru, Bud Burgess. Many already had equity stakes in DrexelMed, the umbrella corporation that would market the Drexel EHR, which would instantly be worth multiple millions when the stock was taken public. That, more than anything else, made it a done deal.

Mumsford took a deep breath, straightened his back, and walked from behind the podium.

"I want to thank you all for delaying your tee times on this beautiful day to be with us here today. I promise it will be worth it. It's hard to believe that just a few years ago, our nation, and our world, was at the mercy of COVID-19. Before we start, let's take a moment to remember those who perished in that awful pandemic and salute the heroic health care providers, who delivered the care that saved even more lives."

Mumsford bowed his head and silently counted to thirty.

"Thankfully, we humans are not only resilient, but ingenious. Today, we'll see more evidence of those wondrous qualities as we demonstrate mankind's next great step in the battle to control the forces of nature: the Drexel Electronic Health Records System. Our EHR is so robust that I cannot display all its capabilities to you today. In earlier presentations, I have shown how our real-time centralized data collection will allow public health officials to identify the next COVID-19 as it emerges—to spot and link the first cases seen in hospitals and doctor's offices so we can nip epidemics in the bud. A few random fevers in Boston and Seattle suddenly form a lifesaving pattern. This central database will also provide researchers with the rich troves of data they need to quickly develop vaccines and other new treatments. A recent editorial in the *New England Journal of Medicine* recognized that our EHR could have spotted the coronavirus in December 2019, saving hundreds of thousands of lives. You can, of course, watch me detail these wonders on YouTube. Please follow us on Instagram, Twitter, TikTok, Facebook, and Pinterest, and ask your ChatGPT to leave ringing comments on all our posts."

The audience laughed.

"The Drexel EHR is much more than a national database. It utilizes state-of-the-art artificial intelligence and machine learning advances to quickly and accurately diagnose every human malady," Mumsford paused for emphasis, "and select the very best evidence-based therapy in seconds.

"Today, you will have a truly unique experience, something we have never done in a public setting: a real-time demonstration of the Drexel EHR in a clinical setting. I will show you how it makes our care of patients better, safer, and less expensive. By connecting all the medical devices we use for care, we increase the efficiency and speed of treatment, thereby reducing the amount of time any of us or our loved ones spend in the hospital. The Drexel EHR reduces the chance of complications that occur the longer you're in the hospital which, in turn, lowers the cost of health care."

Heads nodded throughout the audience.

"I have asked Dr. Robert 'Bud' Burgess to demonstrate to you how the Drexel EHR is truly an extension of our medical staff. Our 'patient' has recently had a heart attack and is critically ill. As you will see, with instant access to specialists twenty-four-seven and the ability to activate cutting-edge medical technology remotely, we speed treatment. Our own comparisons have demonstrated a 40 percent reduction of hospital days in the ICU and reduced our harm events to nearly zero.

"Dr. Burgess," he continued with a sweep of his arm, welcoming him to the stage.

Burgess attached a microphone to his lapel.

"Sign in. My name is Bud Burgess," he said while pressing all five fingers on his right hand on a keypad.

A computerized voice replied. "Voice and fingerprint confirmed. Welcome, Dr. Burgess."

Mumsford spoke to the audience. "As skilled as he is, Dr. Burgess is not the only physician with us. Dr. Roberts in Greenville, are you there?"

"Yes, good morning."

A woman appeared on the screen.

"Dr. Roberts is one of our leading kidney experts. Dr. Smithee, in Statesville, are you there?"

Another woman appeared in a box on the screen next to Dr. Roberts.

"Yes, how are you?" asked Smithee, who was a pulmonologist.

"Just fine," replied Mumsford, "and hoping our patient won't have breathing problems. Thank you both." Robert's and Smithee's thumbprint photographs disappeared from the screen and the image of a patient in an ICU bed filled the screen.

"The Drexel EHR enables doctors even in the most remote rural facilities to tap the expertise of specialists in an instant. Now, the right doctor is not only on call, but in the house."

"Status?" Burgess said to the screen.

"Myocardial infarction confirmed, at 9:45 AM, ninety minutes ago. Oxygen saturation is ninety-five percent, normal.

Blood pressure is ninety over sixty, and heart rate is 110 beats per minute. Vital signs and laboratory data suggest dehydration vs cardiac insufficiency. The patient continues to have chest pain, despite receiving morphine twelve minutes ago."

The numbers and a small graph changed on one panel of the screen.

"Stethoscope?"

Burgess now spoke to the audience. "The patient has tiny monitors on her back and chest that allow me to listen to her heart, lungs, and intestinal tract with every bit the fidelity of my examining her in person, using my own, old-fashioned stethoscope."

Burgess proceeded through a physical examination using the computerized system. Some of the findings were displayed in writing. Others appeared as pictures on the screen—images of the woman's mouth and throat, her ears, and the retina of her eye, all in ultra-high definition.

"Let's see what her labs look like." Burgess pushed a series of buttons and the patient's lab values appeared. "Cardiac enzymes elevated, consistent with her heart attack. Her renal tests are a bit off. What do you think, Dr. Roberts?"

"The lab data are consistent with mild dehydration, in the setting of a recent heart attack, of course," replied Roberts.

"Time for treatment," Burgess told the audience. "From all the information we've gathered, while never entering her hospital room nearly a hundred miles away, the most likely explanation for her low blood pressure and high heart rate is dehydration or heart failure. Doctors in rural hospitals face this kind of conundrum on a daily basis and have to make treatment decisions entirely on their own. With the Drexel EHR, a specialist is always on site."

He looked at the large projection screen where both doctors were reviewing data.

"I'm thinking dehydration, not heart failure, when you put everything together. There was no fluid in her lungs by my examination. Doctors, do you agree?" Both nodded affirmatively. "I'd recommend increased fluid replacement," added Dr. Roberts, the kidney specialist.

"Increase IV rate to 150 ccs per minute." Burgess watched as the IV pump, now shown in the center of the frame, gradually increased its rate. "Under normal circumstances, what you're seeing would involve several steps: an order would be entered, the nurse would see that order when he checked the medical record, and then he'd have to walk into the room to reprogram the IV machine. With the Drexel EHR, we can do everything remotely, and instantaneously."

"Now," he continued, "we still haven't treated her for pain. In heart attack victims, treatment for pain can improve outcomes." Burgess turned to the computer in front of him. Morphine, three hundred milligrams IV, stat."

"Repeat order?" replied the computer.

"Morphine, three hundred milligrams IV, stat."

"This order is not recommended at the present time. The dosage is outside recommended range."

"That's bogus," mumbled Burgess, loud enough to be picked up by his clip-on mic. "She didn't respond to the lower dose."

"Morphine, three hundred milligrams IV, stat," repeated Burgess, an edge in his voice. "Override EHR."

"EHR time out. Bedside assistance being requested."

Mumsford stepped up to the podium, a look of amusement on his face.

"Dr. Burgess ordered enough IV morphine to treat a horse, and the computer called him out. Based on the large amount of data we have on this patient, Dr. Burgess's order was categorized by the Drexel EHR as *contraindicated*. He tried to override the system, and it called for backup. The system is not locking out him or his order. As a safety feature, however, it will require on-site confirmation that the order is correct. There is always a nurse or doctor with whom our remote doctor can converse and explain his rationale."

Mumsford looked at Burgess, who shrugged.

"Dr. Burgess, of course, is not only the brains behind our revolutionary EHR but also a practicing internist with an encyclopedic knowledge of medicine. He agreed to play along with our demonstration to give you a glimpse of the power of Drexel's EHR to control connected devices, the IV pump in this case, and to make things right if a distracted doctor issues an errant order."

Burgess smiled broadly, waved with both hands, then bent at the waist in an exaggerated bow as the audience applauded.

Mumsford turned back to the screen and touched a small button that looked like a microphone.

"Gladys, thank you as well," he said while returning his attention to the audience. "This is Gladys O'Neill, one of our volunteers. Gladys fortunately is not having a heart attack. In fact, she will be returning to the fourth floor where she circulates with magazines and books for patients, family members, and friends."

Several in the audience chuckled. A long round of applause followed.

Beth Peskol, CEO of Tri-State Medical, a consortium of seventy hospitals with locations across the Carolinas and

Virginia, looked again at the numbers she had written over two legal-sized pages. At the bottom of her second sheet was written, "$350k/year." The number was circled. She drew a line out of the circle and added the notation, "per hospital." Joe Mangoli, Midwest Regional VP for HealthTrust, a national for-profit consortium of over three hundred hospitals, leaned over with his pen and added a second circle around the $350k/year figure and a question mark.

Peskol leaned over to Mangoli. "That's twenty million dollars per year for our system, at a minimum, more for yours," she whispered. Mangoli smiled. "More for us."

~

Dr. Justine Peterman, a revered sixty-ish internist, had a very different reaction to Mumsford's address. She leaned over to Mason Fischer, whom she had come to rely on for his cardiology expertise, and said, "This all makes me ill. They talk about costs, but what they're really talking is profits. What about the human toll?"

Mason nodded but said nothing, so she continued.

"Now we're a doctor, a transcriptionist, a billing clerk—the whole shebang. I know I'm preaching to the choir, but I spend nearly two hours filling out paperwork every damned day when I get home. Two years ago, I was finished before I was in my car. Everyone talks about how the EHR produces better patient care...."

"Every talking head, anyway...."

"—but I've yet to see a study showing that these so-called innovations have decreased medical errors or improved health care. And you've got to wonder how many more lives we might have saved during COVID."

Mason nodded but said nothing. If anyone had earned the right—and had the authority—to complain, it was Peterman. A "doctor's doctor," she was admired as much for the way she could connect with people as for her voluminous knowledge of medicine. She could talk finance with Drexel's biggest philanthropists, the sorrow of death and loss to the poorest of the poor, and, when it fitted the situation, pepper her comments with locker room talk that was so pervasive in the largely male world she trained in. Her critique of the EHR was not old-school opposition to change, but deep concern about how it could compromise the delivery of patient care and physician health.

"Does anybody think requiring us to spend fifty percent more time personally typing in every medical order and every abnormal test finding on our patients is somehow, magically, going to improve patient care? There are plenty of reasons why physicians suffer more burnout than anyone else, why more than half of us feel depressed or overwhelmed, and why our suicide rates are twice the national average."

"EHRs," Mason muttered. "With the glitz Mumsford showed today, the CNBC news feed will go into overdrive and Mumsford and Burgess and the EHR gang will cash in."

Peterman jumped on his statement.

"Exactly. I used to wonder about the profit motive in medicine, but not anymore. During the height of the COVID pandemic, everyone was afraid to go to the doctor, much less to the hospital. Insurance companies made out like bandits. They kept premiums the same but didn't have to pay for half of what they would have paid for in a usual year. Did they refund anything? Hell no. They didn't even reduce premiums the next year."

"I know, I know," responded Mason, hoping Peterman would calm down.

"Now it's the same shit but a different flavor. Doctors are getting pushed aside by this marvelous technology. Jesus, now they are tracking our "screen time," with vague comments about compliance. Study after study has shown that stressed, overworked people make mistakes. I'd like to see the real data, not a fancy dog and pony show. A lot of good people are leaving medicine, and I almost followed them out the door. I was the dumb one—thinking I could do more by working from the inside, trying to help people understand not only the benefits of the EHR—and there could be plenty—but its problems. I'm telling you, I've about had it myself."

Mason, trying to smile but his face showing anything but, replied, "Hang in there, Justine. This isn't over yet."

~

In Washington, D.C., two bright young staffers who had watched the live-stream feed hustled back to the office of Senator Elvin Walters to pull together their notes and observations. The boss would want a full report by evening.

A four-term senator from North Carolina and a pillar of the mainstream Republican party, Walters was warming up for whatever came next. Even after losing the 2020 election, Trump maintained a powerful grip on the party. But Walters was convinced that Agent Orange would get his ass handed to him sooner or later. The GOP needed a new standard-bearer to heal the party's fractures and unite its warring factions. The party, and the nation, needed Elvin Walters.

Walter's plan was to thread the partisan needle on health care under the slogan "America Cares." First, he would appease the left by supporting universal coverage through government subsidies to private companies. Basically, Obamacare on steroids. When Walters talked about the "Denmark" model, he'd get an instant 10 percent boost in his popularity from the MSNBC crowd, and that would be all he needed to garner the presidency.

At the same time, he would appeal to the right by ramping up his attacks on the "Big Brother police state" being created by surveillance technology. He'd made it his signature issue—and become a fierce enemy of the NSA—a decade before he both condemned Edward Snowden as a traitorous spy and trumpeted his purloined documents as proof the nation's intelligence services were spying on ordinary Americans. But that was yesterday's news. He needed something fresh to cast himself as a leader for tomorrow. The national EHR was a ripe target. He'd already written a good line for his speeches: "They want to know everything about you—the most private details of your private parts."

Demonstrating a rare caution in the face of tremendous opportunity, Walters shocked his staff members when he said he couldn't go ahead with the winning strategy unless he was convinced the EHR, as he put it in his southern drawl, "at least might could" pose a real threat. His hesitancy had less to do with conscience than it did self-interest; he'd been receiving secret treatments at Drexel for decades. But what the hell—he could always find a new doctor, and this was the presidency!

CHAPTER

5

Aleksandre Torchilov pumped his fist. He was in!

He glanced nervously around the small internet café—he knew his business was dangerous. For the tenth night in a row, Aleks had chosen a different place in his quest to hack the Drexel Electronic Health Record. Except for the café's posh address, on glitzy Rustaveli Avenue with its hotels, bars, and sulfuric hot springs that had been the inspiration for King Vahktang to found Tbilisi, this one was no different. A haze from the heavy, unfiltered cigarettes hung over the room. The place stank from too many cancer sticks, which were ubiquitous in the capital city of Georgia. In the corner, a garbage can overflowed with paper coffee cups and fast-food containers. Everything except the terminals looked like it had been there since before the Revolution.

At this desolate hour, he was alone, except for an agitated man in the far corner typing furiously while cursing quietly in a language Aleks did not recognize. Maybe a terrorist. Maybe a jilted lover. Maybe…who knew? Who cared, as long as he didn't care about Aleks?

The closer he got to cracking the source code for Drexel's EHR security, the more carefully Aleks selected his location for the evening. Mainly the tiny, overpriced internet cafés the tourists frequented. A library one day, a Starbucks the next. As long as he kept on the move, he was safe. Someone from the other end might get as far as Georgia or even Tbilisi. His best protection was the thousands of hackers working twenty-four-seven in Tbilisi. It was an industry and would make picking him out of the horde nearly impossible. Even if they located him, what could the Americans do?

He was anonymous. He'd never get caught.

Aleks was a naïve young man.

He wanted more, much more than the two other hackers in his small flat. Their main line was selling stolen credit card numbers to the Russian Mafia. They were trying to grab what they could when they could. The way they saw it, they had the misfortune of being born smart in a poor, backward country. This wasn't fair. It wasn't fair that others were born in rich countries and got more than they deserved. In the beginning, when they thought about it at all, they tried to justify their actions, make themselves the heroes in the story of their lives. They considered themselves Robin Hoods, gangsters rather than criminals, forces of the laws of nature working to restore equilibrium. After a while though, they didn't care about the why, just the what: the money.

Aleks was different. Russian by heritage, his blond hair and blue eyes distinguished Aleks as a minority in Georgia. The Muslims, mainly Turks and Armenian, were taking over Tbilisi. His parents were both dead—alcohol got his father, cigarettes, his mom. They'd done the best they could rearing their only child. They had loved him deeply and recognized he was gifted when, at age three, he took apart and reassembled their alarm clock. As bad as it was, the old Soviet system would have identified and nurtured Aleks. Instead, he sat, bored, in one school after another.

He'd quit school three years ago, at seventeen, after his mother followed his father to the grave. He had gotten, and kept, a legitimate job, flipping burgers at McDonald's. It was legal, and he was paid forty lari a month. It was just enough to pay his third of the rent. He had three squares a day at McDonald's—if you considered French fries a vegetable— and, if it didn't kill him, he could keep eating there until he landed somewhere better.

His fascination with computers was, he had to admit, all thanks to his crooked roommates. From the first day he saw them in action, saw those lovely lines of code, so simple, powerful, and pure, he knew he'd found something that could inspire and challenge him. Maybe there was a way out.

Crime was the price of freedom. While Aleks wanted to explore the wonders of cyberspace, his roommates insisted he help them steal credit card numbers.

So he became a hacker. He started with public entities. Rustava 2 and Imedi TV, the local television stations. Their personnel files were a treasure trove of remunerative data. But they were too easy. So Aleks moved on. Universities sounded interesting, so he accessed Tbilisi State University. It was child's play. Aleks briefly considered inserting himself as a student with sparkling grades and a PhD in computer science. He went so far as to plug in the information but chickened out before finalizing it. His next stop was the Tbilisi State Medical University. It linked directly to the hospital. There, it had taken him all of five minutes to overwhelm their self-proclaimed "state-of-the-art" password-protected system. With practically no effort, he had been able to bring up patient records. Igor, one of his roommates, quickly claimed the patient database as his own and was busily selling off patient information. With their birth date, address, and phone number, his pals in the underworld could create fake credit cards. Sadly for Igor, no bank in the world wanted to give a credit card to an unemployed Georgian, which described most of the patients. It was more a mirage than gold mine.

His ticket out of Tbilisi was money, and Aleks had decided that America—especially American health care—was his golden goose. The patients were rich, at least compared with the typical Tbilisi resident. Their medical records would likely have all the identification needed to set up a credit card account with a five-thousand-dollar limit. The combination of an American birth date, phone number, address, and social security number was worth something. The information was available in various hospital databases, but the most easily hacked information treasures were in hospital electronic health records.

American hospitals were paralyzed by the thought of their patient's health information showing up on the web. A hospital in Hollywood and then another in Florida had paid big bucks in ransom. He was sure it was the GRU—Russian intelligence. Igor was sleeping with a GRU hacker and had the straight shit. The GRU group demanded $3.6 million from Hollywood Presbyterian Hospital. The news stories said the hospital admitted to a seventeen-thousand-dollar bitcoin payment. The real number was closer to half a million. The bloggers claimed there had been more, many more. In each case, it had been kept quiet, and the hospitals had banded together to enhance security. Only a handful of the elite hospitals had yet to join with the others. Their security was even better.

If he could only get that one big payday. He'd be out in an instant. Go legit. Work for an IT company or go to Germany and get a degree. The future was there for the taking. No more barely getting by in Georgia.

He picked Drexel Memorial. They claimed theirs was one of the most comprehensive and advanced EHRs in the world. They purported to have four million patient records and the most secure firewall in the world. Better than Bank of America. The web was full of talk that the Drexel EHR was on the verge of becoming the national standard in the states.

It would be a great challenge, and, if he succeeded, a great payoff.

For a solid month, as soon as his shift at McDonald's ended, Aleks had focused on accessing Drexel's EHR. As advertised, security was intense. Over and over, he ran into dead ends, each with its own warning of doom: he was committing a felony, punishable by up to twenty years in prison and a hundred-thousand-dollar fine. *Blah, blah, blah.*

Tonight, he struck pay dirt—or so he thought. He had found a way into Burgess's system. His first target: the records for every woman who had had a mammogram in the state of North Carolina during the last fifteen years. Problem was, they had all been de-identified, stripped of all the juicy bits of information that Aleks needed. He was so close.

Then his screen went blank. He had tripped an alarm with his mammogram search.

Unbeknownst to Aleks, he was being watched by an enigmatic group operating from an underground facility in southern Virginia that its denizens called "the Cellar." Part of Benny's job was to thwart the more experienced hackers who might make Burgess worry about his precious EHR and do a deep dive back into his code. The idea was to let Burgess think he was as brilliant and his system was as perfect as he'd imagined it. They needed the Drexel EHR to appear impenetrable. And most hackers weren't a threat; Burgess was good. But this Georgian had mad skills, so Benny—with the approval of Saied and Torrence—let him play on, not on Drexel's actual site, of course, which might raise alarms, but a clone site to which Benny redirected all the traffic from Tbilisi to Drexel. Aleks never knew he was in a house of mirrors. Benny knew it was time to figure out who this phantom foreigner was— and up the ante.

6

The two men sat silently on the veranda of the white clapboard Colonial-style manor on a centuries-old estate the locals had always called "the Plantation." Located off tiny Virginia Highway 92 between Boyden and Chase, it had been in grave disrepair when Torrence had arranged its purchase. Their vision, combined with the skill and hard work of Mexican laborers who called their employer El Jefe, had returned the place to its former glory, and then some.

At first glance, they were unlikely pair, their differences so stark that the idea they might be working together was inconceivable. But they were, in fact, two sides of the same coin.

Charles Richmond, sixty-two, the suave and devious head of the National Institute for Medical Safety, was a renowned figure, celebrated for his brilliance, integrity, and devoted public service. His greatest gift was keeping secrets—especially his own. He was distinguished-looking, tall, with a small slightly-upturned nose, light blue eyes, and a thick head of dark hair greying along the edges, not movie-star handsome, but memorable. Never seen in public wearing anything but a custom-fitted suit with shoulder padding to augment his narrow shoulders, he radiated confidence. The implant he had back in 2000 to strengthen his weak chin didn't hurt, either. Hugh Torrence, by contrast, had spent his life working in the shadows. From his clothes to his manner, every detail was calibrated to discourage attention. Rather than confidence, of which he had plenty, Torrence radiated a thinly veiled sense of aggression.

If there were an official record of his government service, which there was not, it would show twenty-eight years at the "Puzzle Palace," better known as "No Such Agency." The son of a devoutly Catholic auto mechanic and a homemaker from Dayton, Torrence was a brilliant only child with a chip on his shoulder. He loved ideas—God, patriotism, righteousness— far more than people, who usually betrayed them. After graduating Phi Betta Kappa from The Ohio State University, he cut his teeth as an army ranger in the 1980s, clandestinely supporting Osama bin Laden and other Mujahedeen fighting the Soviets in Afghanistan. "Their faith," he'd written his mother, "is something to behold." During the 1990s, he saw that computers would control the future and transferred into cyber intelligence. He was a driving force behind ThinThread, the NSA's first foray into advanced data mining, and later, PRISM, the agency's clandestine surveillance program that collected metadata from multiple internet providers. He was married to his work, but through the years, he became increasingly frustrated by the orders of Ivy League-educated elected officials who thwarted his ever more aggressive desire and designs to make the world a better place. When Charles Richmond of the National Institute for Medical Safety asked him to run a covert project involving the cutting-edge electronic health records system being developed at Drexel Memorial Hospital in Durham, he jumped at the chance to leave the NSA. This operation would not just be his crowning glory, but the start of something beyond his wildest dreams.

His attire was always the same; a light blue button-down shirt, dark tie, and well-tailored suit. Fine, but forgettable. If it was anyone else, his uniform might have been a topic of conversation or gentle ribbing. Not so with Hugh Torrence. He was definitely not the kind of person one joked about.

Six feet even with combed-back salt and pepper hair, he could pass for a Wall Street executive or lawyer. To Torrence, such comparisons were an insult. He didn't lounge around a big office playing with other people's money. His work mattered.

In their own way, both men were bastions of an establishment that required both light and dark to survive. Both burned with ambition—Torrence, fiercely, Richmond, quietly beneath a calm facade. Now, after a few years of working toward their common goal of transforming Drexel's EHR from regional success to the one and only national leader, their fates and fortunes were inexorably tied together.

Richmond was driven in *almost* equal measure by the desire to do good and to do well; his idealism was always slightly less powerful than his ambition. Early in his tenure, he had elevated the National Institute to national prominence with a shocking report—*"Preventable Harm: Building a Safer Health System"*—which found that almost one hundred thousand people die each year from medical errors. Overnight, policymakers, politicians, and the public began looking to the National Institute for the answers to America's health care woes.

That was how Richmond came to imagine a national EHR that could reduce errors and costs, something all the necessary stakeholders cared about. With health care consuming nearly 18 percent of the United States' GDP and rising, the nation was on the verge of a crisis. Controlling health care costs had been the country's most pressing domestic issue before the COVID-19 pandemic and still was. Drexel's EHR—which Richmond had recruited Bud Burgess to build and his Princeton classmate Derrick Mumsford to oversee—promised to solve it. COVID-19 provided the national emergency he needed to secure the funding required. Working his congressional friends behind the scenes, he made sure the $1.2 trillion Health Information Technology for Economic and Clinical Health Act ("HITECH") mandated that all of the nation's health records be housed in a single database. It was the HITECH Act that provided the money to build the Drexel EHR—and gave it a secret edge.

Richmond might have realized his plan without Torrence's expertise in sabotage, but he needed more than just a good plan and good luck. It was always a long shot that Drexel could beat out the big boys. Of course, his ability to steer a massive flow of COVID dollars to the Cellar crew, who could cripple competitors through cyber-subterfuge while simultaneously protecting Drexel's system from attack, was not a simple plan. But it was done, and here they were.

If the Drexel EHR went national, as planned, the deal with the devil he had struck with Torrence would be worth it. The Senate seat he had long prized would be his; maybe that would just be a stepping stone. At first, Richmond worried about how Torrence would use the EHR, but he quickly convinced himself the man was a patriot, not a psychopath. Torrence might use the EHR to kill and blackmail, but there would be nothing random about it. At least that was what he'd told himself. Still, he had to handle their relationship with care. There was no denying that they knew each other. That was easy to establish. But no one could prove anything more. And Richmond, of course, had a backup plan including his own deep cover assets just in case everything went south.

From his perch at the National Institute, the major organization working with Drexel, he was being recognized as a prime architect of the breakthrough that would save health care. The plan was working.

As they sipped their coffees on the veranda, listening to the gentle breeze caress a stand of loblolly pines, Torrence finally broke the silence. "Mumsford seemed to get the job done."

"He was magnificent," Richmond responded, offering the mindless flattery that had become a habit. "Who would have thought that the COVID-19 pandemic would give us such an opportunity?"

"Wars, famine and plague have always been the strange bedfellows of progress," Torrence responded.

Torrence felt his watch vibrate. It was Saied.

"It's time," Torrence said, rising from his chair. "Down we go."

~

Hugh Torrence loved everything about the Plantation—but he adored its Cellar. He had engineered every detail of its design and construction, thirty feet below ground to specifications for withstanding a nuclear attack. It was remote and impenetrable yet connected to the world, like few other places. It was almost completely off the grid it was built to conquer.

Opening the door to the room's wide metal staircase, Torrence immediately heard the hum from supercomputers—five rows, each with five, five-foot-tall machines, details only a numerologist could fully appreciate. He felt the slight chill of the room that was kept at sixty-nine degrees. Simulated sunshine shone from walls programmed with thousands of potential backgrounds—Paris, Rome, New York. As he got to the bottom of the stairs, Torrence saw the sun was setting over Istanbul, giving the Hagia Sophia a sepia tone.

The main room, one thousand square feet with a ten-foot ceiling, housed the servers and the twelve cyber savants who labored there, six to a shift, twelve hours a day, 365 days a year, before the bank of widescreen 4K monitors. One hallway led to a dozen small rooms with beds. Another hallway led to a small kitchen with three Moccamaster coffee makers and cases of Red Bull. Bowls of M&Ms, gummy bears, pretzels, mixed nuts, and Doritos Late Night All Nighter Cheeseburger chips were placed throughout the rooms. More substantial fare was brought in under the cover of darkness. There was also a seldom-used gym, a multi-media room with huge screens for video games or movies and other multipurpose rooms for distraction from the reality that they lived in a hole. The Cellar had everything a geek could want—everything but freedom. The young men—they were all men, on Torrence's insistence, to avoid what he called "funny business"—had been carefully vetted for their desire to stare at a screen endlessly. And the pay was extraordinary. It was easy to pay the talent well from the federal COVID money Richmond had siphoned from Drexel. The irony struck Richmond every time he visited. The Cellar embodied the COVID experience—isolation, fear, and new, often secret methods for organizing society.

Fitting their age and station in life, the four geeks in attendance wore dark, hooded sweatshirts emblazoned with the names of prestigious universities or hardcore rap groups. They were the core team of programmers led by Benny Rasinko, who, at the tender age of thirteen, had already become a legendary hacker known as Shadow Wolf, operating out of the attic of his parent's home outside San Jose. It made Benny feel special. It was also great fun to float through the tiniest holes in any firewall, leaving untraceable cyber carnage in his wake. That reckless skill had finally brought him to the NSA's attention. Torrence had made the final call between killing him or redirecting his talent. He'd never regretted his choice.

The twelve had varying expertise. All were world-class hackers. Some were capable of writing software most experts didn't understand. Others had solved bandwidth speed and data storage retrieval. All of the twelve—Torrence loved that number—were hand-picked, thoroughly vetted, and fully aware of the dire consequences should they ever compromise the operation.

The geeks were bleary-eyed. Torrence had ordered them to run facial recognition on everyone at Mumsford's talk and present the latest information on possible threats to the EHR. Overnight, they had confirmed almost all of their previous research. This was hardly the first time they had run background checks for the man they called "our fearful leader" who, nevertheless, demanded that they run through it all again as a test of their precision and willingness to take orders. But they also discovered surprising connections linked to a relatively new Drexel hire: Mason Fischer. Torrence, as always, turned to Saied, who, at thirty-five years of age, was his most senior and trusted associate. "Saied," ordered Torrence, "get started."

Egyptian by birth, he was just four when he was brought to the U.S. by his parents—who constantly reminded him that he hailed from the same region of the northern Egypt delta that produced Ramses II, the great Pharaoh. Saied was groomed for greatness. A mathematics prodigy fluent in six languages, he graduated from Harvard Law School after earning a master's in data analytics from the University of Chicago. He had his choice of high-paying jobs from America's best firms, but he wanted more: the beating heart action he could only find in intelligence work. He possessed what Torrence had more than once called an extraordinary mind: focused and unflappable, able to synthesize vast amounts of data into spot-on judgments with an uncanny ability to see around every corner. He was rocketing to the upper echelon of the NSA before he left to work for Torrence for reasons he sometimes still questioned. Each time, his analysis was the same: the power, the toys, the challenge. A tough trio to ignore. The team he and Torrence had assembled, including Benny, the other Cellar geeks, and the proven assets who had rid the world of Jesse Gutierrez, were the best of the best.

As the geeks settled into their chairs, Charles Richmond experienced a moment of clarity. The effort *would* succeed. Should they hit bumps in the road, he had an ace in reserve: a still powerful political figure now living in Florida who had spent his lifetime in combat. The man, whose name he could never mention, not even to Torrence, might not be book smart, but his predatory IQ was at least two hundred. It took about half a second for him to see the EHR's full potential, the multitude of ways in which the Drexel EHR, including manipulating medical records, doctors' orders and the whole caboodle, would prove uniquely useful. He would protect and reward Richmond.

"Let's get started," Torrence commanded.

Benny ran the keyboard and Saied narrated.

"When Derrick Mumsford spoke, we found some interesting people in the audience."

A panel of faces was projected. Saied focused on a familiar-looking one, a doughy man in his mid-fifties wearing an off-the-shelf gray suit, most likely because Mumsford made him dress up for the presentation. His hair was grayer than not, and he needed a haircut. "Frederick 'Bud' Burgess. Director of Informatics at Drexel. We all know him. Formidable intellect. Winner of the Westinghouse Prize in Science and Math at sixteen. Among the other Westinghouse awardees, six have been Nobel Prize winners, two Field's Medal winners, and thirty National Academy of Sciences members. Burgess's IQ is 181. Top 0.001 percent in the world."

"Not top 0.0001 percent, like you?" said Torrence with a smirk to Saied.

"Finished college at nineteen," Saied continued, "earned both an MD at Harvard and a PhD in bio-computing at MIT in just five years." He advanced to the next slide that showed Burgess in his usual uniform of worn khaki pants, a short-sleeved white dress shirt, and a shirt pocket full of pens and note cards to match his thick black-rimmed glasses. "Not much of a dresser."

"Looks more like a stock room clerk at Walmart than one of the smartest guys on the planet," Benny interjected.

"He's got the smarts," Torrence added.

"No doubt, the dude's got mad skills, though not enough to find the master code we embedded in his glorious creation," Benny said with a note of triumph. "It's kinda weird that he's never wondered why his EHR is the only system that hasn't suffered devastating cyber-attacks or ransomware holdups."

"Excellent point," Richmond responded in that easy way successful people have of lavishing gratuitous praise to soften up their audience. "As the man who recruited Burgess into this project, I think I can provide an answer. Like so many gifted people, he suffers from both grandiosity *and* insecurity." Richmond paused and smiled as he looked around the room. "I picked Burgess because, as you put it so eloquently, he has mad skills. There would be no EHR without him. Before I gave him this opportunity, he'd had a fine, but not stellar, career. Burgess rightly thinks the EHR is his baby, his purpose, and his destiny—no one is more invested in believing it is foolproof. This is good for us. It means he doesn't want to ask questions that could raise doubts about his own achievement. If he just keeps quiet and goes about his business, he gets to build the world's finest EHR and earn the recognition he craves. And just as important," Richmond said, glancing at Torrence, "he's reliable."

"Agreed?" Saied looked around the room. No one else spoke.

"Next," directed Torrence.

Benny's keyboard erupted with a blast of typed commands. A slender, young black man appeared on the screen.

Saied continued his narration. "Reginald Taylor. Age twenty-six and goes by RT. Closest person to Burgess at

Drexel. He's their version of Benny—a super-geek." A tiny smile crossed his face as he glanced at Benny out of the corner of his eye.

"He lacks all of Burgess's credentials—barely made it through high school, where his brilliance made him bored; he worked for the Geek Squad at Best Buy before attending Guilford Tech in Greensboro where he became a star student."

"At a community college?" Torrence sniffed. "Why the hell would Burgess hire him?"

"Funny you should ask," Saied replied. "RT was also a hacker, and one of his favorite targets was Drexel. Most of the portals, especially human resources and food services, should have had huge welcome banners; the EHR, which Burgess was just developing, was more of a challenge, which he respected. As graduation neared, RT put on a shirt and tie and applied for an entry-level position. Emails show it didn't go well. Burgess said he'd never hired someone from Guilford Tech but promised to keep his resume on file. RT knew that was an empty promise. A week later, Burgess received this email," Saied said, as the screen showed this exchange:

Doc. Looks like you've got some serious medical problems. Check it and call me if I can of any help.

"Burgess immediately opened his medical record which had several additions."

Employee suffers from erectile dysfunction despite fondness for boy geniuses from MIT and Caltech.

Everyone in the Cellar laughed; Torrence almost cracked a smile.

"Then Burgess searched for patients with the name Reginald Taylor. Knowing he had no right to look at RT's medical record, he opened it anyway. There were only two diagnoses on the problem list. The first, 'Extreme brilliance.' The second, 'Looking for a job.' Our telephonic monitoring watched him dial up RT's cell phone and recorded this conversation."

"You little bastard. Do you have any idea how much trouble you can get into hacking into protected records?"

"You and me both, boss."

"If you can patch the hole you found, you're hired."

"Very uplifting," Torrence said. "Makes a great movie, but you didn't answer the question: does he suspect anything about the EHR?"

"No," Saied said. "RT's as pleased as Burgess that the Drexel system seems foolproof. But, unfortunately for us, he's young, has an open mind, and is not invested in outcomes. He'll need watching."

Torrence had already moved on.

"Who's the kid talking to in the auditorium?" he gestured towards a photo too small to decipher.

Benny responded with another blast of keystrokes. As the image enlarged, Mason Fischer came into view, flanked on one side by RT, on his right, by Justine Peterman.

"That's goddamn Fischer," Torrence complained, gesturing at the screen. "He keeps showing up. What the hell is he doing there, sitting next to the Taylor kid? Jesus, I don't know what Fischer is up to, but he's been on our radar from day one, asking questions about the EHR. And isn't he connected to Tom Birck?"

"Yes," Saied replied.

"Birck was major league. Smart, effective, a true genius when it came to medical technology, but also a sanctimonious pain in the ass who always stuck his conscience where it didn't belong. I wasn't sad when his name came off the board."

Then Torrence felt his intuition screaming. "Fischer's connection to Birck feels like a loose end. Maybe he should receive a visit from Jensen."

Jensen was a blunt instrument whose visits always ended the same.

"You might change your mind after you hear what we've learned," Saied said.

Saied was careful with his words. As always. He was the voice of caution in a group more inclined to act first. He was not just a paranoia Geiger counter, but someone whose vast intelligence could calm those tick-tock clicks that whirred in Torrence's mind. Other people's deaths didn't bother him—otherwise, he wouldn't be here—but logic told him that death was merely one arrow in the quiver, to be used, like the others, only when it was the most effective tool. Torrence was smart enough to know he needed to hear this voice.

"Fischer can be an asset, an insurance policy for these final days."

"Enlighten me," Torrence said.

"Fischer and RT are no strangers. He drops by to ask RT about different Drexel IT issues. We occasionally capture bits and pieces, but nothing damning. You also need to know that Fischer is friendly with Carrie Mumsford, Derrick Mumsford's daughter. She's a resident at Drexel."

"You're telling me," Torrence thundered, "not to worry that the mysterious new doctor who studied under Birck is asking lots of questions and has befriended the hospital president's daughter, as well as the number two guy in IT?"

"There are mitigating factors that, I think, you will find useful. Part of the reason I am not as concerned," Saied explained, "is that RT and Carrie Mumsford are at cross purposes. RT owes everything to Burgess, who has everything riding on the EHR's success. Carrie is obsessed with patient safety and has real concerns about the EHR. If anything, RT would see Carrie as a threat rather than an ally, someone to keep tabs on. Don't get me wrong, Carrie Mumsford could be a problem. She's tough and tenacious. We need to keep an eye on her," he said, nodding to Torrence.

"But her interest in Fischer doesn't involve the EHR," he said definitively. "She's not a danger."

"How could you possibly know what her interests are?" demanded Torrence.

Saied's thin smile returned. "We ran the total physiologic response package we brought in from the Agency. Analyzed her body language, changes in her voice, the color of her cheeks."

Torrence glared at Saied. It was unnerving. "And…."

"She's got the hots for him. Biological urges. You remember those."

Torrence raised an eyebrow.

"What about Fischer?"

"There are good reasons for concern, but what you see on the surface is just part of the picture," Saied said as he glanced toward Benny, who filled the screen once more with a photograph of the sandy-haired Fischer in his dark blue Drexel scrubs.

"Talk to me."

"Mason Fischer. Forty years old. Born in rural Texas, mother died when he was three, father died ten years ago.

Football star at the University of Texas. Big man on campus. Could have gone pro but decided on medicine. Medical training at Vanderbilt, paid for by Uncle Sam, graduated number one in his class. Specialized in cardiology. When his seven-year debt to the Army was paid, he left to join the staff at the University of Texas Medical Branch at Galveston, where he could make real money. Everywhere he went, A-plus performance through and through."

"Can he really be that boring?" responded Torrence.

Saied smiled. "But there's a hitch. Fischer was on the fast track for academic stardom. Then, suddenly, he was on the outs and had to leave town in a hurry."

"Because?"

"Because the doctor has a little problem. He picks patients with a past. Real scumbags. And he bumps them off. No one cries. No one cares. The world is a better place."

"Evidence?"

"It begins with three unexpected deaths in two months. All three had big-time medical problems. The coincidence was not that they died. It was the timing. The first was an old man, a former Mafioso, Marco "the Chin" Chinzano, who was serving twenty to life in a Texas State Prison. The prison sent him to Galveston to have his gallbladder removed, a one-day procedure. Now that they use a laparoscope, mortality is next to zero. Easy, low risk, right? Except Chinzano croaks. How? Maybe he was a heart attack waiting to happen. He was an old Italian who'd eaten too much cheese, drunk too much booze, and smoked too many cigarettes. Or maybe he was offed and it was made to look like a heart attack. We had our man, Dr. Van der Graf, look over his record. The most likely cause would have been a heart attack. But it didn't fit.

No chest pain or trouble breathing, nothing. Chinzano was sleeping like a baby. It could have been any of a dozen reasons, but Van der Graf's number one? Someone injected his IV with potassium. It would stop his heart in minutes, but with enough time for the killer to leave the scene. And potassium is undetectable after death. Nothing showed up on tox screens or the quickie autopsy he had. One case like that and no one cares."

Another slide appeared on the screen showing a thirty-year-old white male with a brown mullet and a poisonous look in his black eyes.

"Three weeks later, another bad dude, Adam John Williams—in for life after killing his girlfriend's toddler because the kid 'cried too much'—dies suddenly. He was a cancer patient whose heart also just stopped. Same deal, in for chemotherapy and sleeping and dies suddenly. No more Adam Williams."

A third image, of a handsome black man in his early fifties standing in front of a silver Jaguar XJ 358, appeared on the screen.

"Then another piece of work, Orage Galloway, a shady banker who ran shell companies for third-world despots who wanted to hide the money they weren't spending on drugs for their child soldiers. Came in for a routine appendectomy…."

"…and went out with a heart attack."

"Exactly. People die in hospitals all the time. We don't know why the higher-ups in Galveston connected these cases, but they did. And they were very worried. They feared they had a killer in their midst, one who never left a trace."

"Sounds familiar," Benny joked.

"Fischer was definitely on their list, but not because they had any evidence. He was fingered by a pissed-off colleague, a loudmouthed drunk, Dr. Richard Henderson, who couldn't prove anything except that Fischer was screwing *his* mistress. You can't make this up."

Torrence was starting to feel better already, as he always did when he saw Saied at work.

"Benny hacked into the Galveston servers and found 'deleted' emails on the hospital president's servers. They are vague, probably written under the advice of counsel, but express 'concern about unfortunate patient outcomes' and 'unexpected responses to treatment.'" They never mentioned Fischer by name, but included Henderson's concerns about an unnamed colleague. The next week, Fischer's gone. A month later, he's working at Drexel."

"Don't tell me that just happens," demanded Torrence.

"Sure it does. Like all big institutions, hospitals are good at hiding difficult information, especially when there's a chance Fischer was innocent and might sue them if they ruined his career. Giving Fischer a clean bill of health was the path of least resistance. What do you do when you have someone only you know is toxic? Write him a good recommendation—if you really want to get rid of him, make it great."

Torrence nodded his head side-to-side violently. "Point taken. Still, someone high-up must have helped. It smells like something Birck would have done."

Saied replied in his most calming voice. "Birck may well have pulled some strings before his death, but we haven't found any. And if Birck were as much of a straight-shooter as you say, what we found out about Fischer would make it especially hard to believe he helped him."

"This better be good," Torrence scowled.

"Fischer is a clever guy. Fortunately, Benny is even sharper. He came up with the bright idea of hacking into the stored digital images from two convenience stores located near a side entrance to the hospital. Guess who he finds entering the hospital about twenty minutes before Chinzano dies and hauling ass out immediately afterwards? Fischer. Same for the other two. Even better, Benny aligned hospital security footage with records showing magnetic card use to enter certain hospital units. There's Fischer, using someone else's card to swipe himself in each time."

"You're sure?" asked Torrence.

"As close as we can get without getting Jensen to inspire a confession," he deadpanned.

"Why would Fischer kill people?" Torrence continued without so much as a smile.

"Fischer is a perfectionist," Saied continued, fully aware that he was also describing Torrence. "Just look at his life. He's excelled at everything—small-town hero, football star, accomplished cardiologist, real success story. That's the view everyone sees."

"And..." interrupted Torrence.

"That's the outside. Inside...he's a mess. His mother drove her car into a tree off a dirt road when he was three. He was in the front seat. He was belted. She wasn't. It could have been an accident. It could have been a suicide or even a murder-suicide, which would be quite the mindfuck for Fischer. She suffered from depression. So did Fischer's aunt. When this happens to a kid, more often than not, he feels like he could have prevented it, the crash, or that he even caused it. They can have nightmares for the rest of their life.

Psychotherapists make a living out of trying to help people get over it. There are no drugs that can fix it and, mostly, there is no fixing it. The question is, how does the kid adapt as an adult?"

"Since when are you the expert in psychobabble?"

Saied glared at Torrence for a nanosecond before proceeding. "Most people are crushed by this burden. A few manage to turn it into a strength. Fischer found a way forward by harnessing his negative emotions and self-loathing. At first, he had football, which allowed him to use his aggression to defeat enemies. After he almost killed a player from the University of Oklahoma during the Red River showdown, he turned to medicine. For a time, he channeled his aggression more subtly, toward saving the world. But he couldn't, of course. No one can. And somehow, somewhere along the line, something snapped—he started to ruffle at the imperfection of the world around him. Outwardly, he was and still is perfect."

Torrence shook his head, muttering, "What does this have to do with his killing patients?"

"Fischer doesn't kill just any patient. He kills those that don't deserve to live. Drug dealers, murderers, victimizers. It's quite common among the nurses and doctors who work on the other side of the street. They all think they are better, smarter, and purer than everyone else, and they are ridding the world of modern-day lepers. Donald Harvey, an orderly, claimed to have killed eighty-seven patients. He told the judge that he was doing what needed to be done, right before he was slapped with twenty-eight consecutive life sentences. He was a self-proclaimed angel of death."

"Fifty years later, the world has gotten a lot more sophisticated, and Harvey's favorite potions, arsenic and cyanide, are screened for routinely, so today's killer angels have to up their game. Put it all together and voila! For Fischer, there couldn't be a better place than Drexel."

"Because?" asked Torrence, fully knowing the answer.

"Because if you like killing patients, what better way to do it than remotely."

Laughter filled the room.

"That's why Fischer is not a problem, but an opportunity for us."

"Go on," demanded Torrence.

"I'm seeing Fischer as a fall guy. A diversion."

"Yes."

"We're confident that we can complete our final run throughs of the EHR without leaving a trace. But, if the need arises, all signs will point to Fischer."

Saied noticed that Torrence had his right hand in his pocket, where he was undoubtedly rubbing his St. Christopher medal, a telltale sign of doom. It was an odd tic. Maybe Torrence was not so different than Fischer—seeing himself as an avenging angel, praying for and then delivering death.

With a gleeful smirk, Torrence commanded, "Get a list of his patients, give it to Van der Graf, and present me with a plan ASAP."

Benny looked at Saied questioningly. Saied responded with a barely perceptible nod. The game plan was clear. Torrence's medical mastermind, the infamous Dr. Christian Van der Graf, would craft a death plan for one of Fischer's patients based on that patient's unique vulnerabilities. The EHR would carry out the murder. The cause of death would be undetectable. But, if something went wrong, they had a fall guy. Dr. Mason Fischer. Sick, but brilliant.

CHAPTER

7

The AT&T van heading south on the small rural highway near the Plantation set off an electronic tracking system in the Cellar. The same van had passed earlier, at 12:03 PM. It was one of the new eco-friendly E-series Ford vans whose side windows were emblazoned with the AT&T logo—a blue and white striped globe. A ladder was strapped to the roof rack, along with several large polyethylene tubes and a thick coil of heavy black rubber-coated wiring. The driver was an African-American man in his forties, wearing a dark blue AT&T polo shirt.

It was just another repair van traversing this quiet stretch of highway since last Wednesday's thunderstorm knocked out power, phone, and internet service to about four thousand customers. That was the *look*, but not the case. Behind the driver was a metal door that hid two other black men with open laptops. Data streams flashed on the monitors mounted to the walls, alerts sounding on a regular basis.

One of the men, Alphonse Witherspoon, headed an IT outfit that did black-op missions for the Department of Defense, almost always as a stealth asset for Thomas Birck. Alphonse had noted the high-octane power grid in the middle of nowhere a few months ago, on a routine surveillance drive. Given the uptick in EHR oddities at Drexel, it was time for a little investigating.

It was a beautiful late spring day for a drive, and with the recent storms, there were many power outages in rural southern Virginia.

The power grid was still blasting away with an occasional highly encrypted note. The mere presence of the facility—it had to be underground—was a mystery. Alphonse and one of the guys had hung around the local Waffle House and Hardees, just listening. Occasionally there would be talk of "that big-ass project" but it was clear none of the men they overheard had been part of the construction project. In fact, it was impossible to track down anyone who had. Weird. Weirder still, satellite photos from Google Maps showed nothing—the current images looked like repeats of those from five years ago, except that the trees had grown taller. Could someone have hacked the databases? Even the Russians and the Chinese would be hard-pressed to pull that off. Could the chatter just be local gossip?

Alphonse was about to call it a dead end. But Lady Luck is fickle, and she was smiling on him this fine day in May. A black Lincoln Town Car Limousine barreling north down the two-lane state road toward D.C. caught Alphonse's attention. It was the third of these vehicles he had seen in the area. The nearest town in that direction was Red Oak, Virginia, a forgotten place that was piss-poor with no economy and practically no residents. Its best restaurant was Shoney's, and its biggest news was who was shacking up with whom at the local Motel 8. It was a highway to nowhere. Not exactly the kind of place frequented by those who could afford fancy limos. Alphonse snapped a picture of the plate and sent it to their command center in Greensboro.

~

Alphonse's IT business had moved around during the last ten years, depending on where Thomas Birck needed him to run off-the-books projects.

For the last two years, he had set up less than a mile from the Morningside housing development in Greensboro. It was a perfect location: close to Drexel, but way under the radar. Alphonse, a wiry man with a shaved head in his mid-50s who almost always wore jeans and a button-down shirt, lived on a vegan diet and had a special intuition about computers, much like his nephew, RT.

With the money he made—and with the government, there was plenty—he'd taken care of his immediate family, his mother and brothers, a vast array of aunts and cousins, and more of the people of the Ebenezer Baptist Church than he could count. He also acted on his core belief that untapped genius was present in low-income communities. Driven by a powerful faith and a keen eye for talent, he plucked people, mainly from his old neighborhood in Durham, and let them, for the first time, operate at full capacity.

He employed nearly a dozen found souls—former drug addicts and dealers, hustlers and prostitutes, all of whom had done hard time. They jokingly called themselves his disciples. Unlike the geeks in the Cellar, none of them had advanced degrees, but they were smart and tenacious. "God helps those who help themselves," Alphonse would say, "and the best way to help ourselves is by helping others."

~

The next morning, one of Alphonse's star operatives, LaToya, gave him some intriguing news.

"Your limo photo hit pay dirt. It's the favored service of the CIA and NSA. The car you saw dropped off its passenger at the home of Charles Richmond."

"Head of the National Institute for Medical Safety and wizard behind the curtain of the Drexel EHR. Damn, girl. Nice work."

"It's possible the National Institute just happens to use the same car service as the agencies, but unlikely. It's not a service you look up on the internet. I contacted our old friend Barney."

"Bagman Barney's still working sanitation in the district?"

"One and the same. He's sending the latest haul from the National Institute's confidential recycling bin. It'll take some time, but we can reassemble the pieces."

"Excellent. Keep me posted, LaToya."

Alphonse reached out to his second-in-command, Jefferson "the Jet" Jenkins. Jet was tinkering with the new microfluidic cooling system they had recently imported to reduce thermal resistance in the high-powered microchips that drove their computing system.

"Jet, remember that place in Virginia, where our satellite feeds crashed from a big power surge?"

"Right between no-how and nowhere."

"Looks like there may be a there, there," Alphonse said, filling him in on what LaToya had found, including the shredded documents.

"One man's trash," Jet quipped, "is another man's treasure."

CHAPTER

8

SUNDAY, MAY 8
4:36 PM *[MONDAY, MAY 9, 12:36 AM GEORGIAN TIME]*
INTERNET CAFÉ #32, RUSTAVELI AVENUE
TBILISI, REPUBLIC OF GEORGIA

Aleks was playing Resident Evil 9 when the message popped up on the screen.

"We know what you did at Drexel Hospital."

The hacker's heart shot through his throat as his pulse topped 130.

The next message came exactly one minute later, after Aleks had sufficient time to feel the fear. "Relax, friend. We want to reward you." Following a quick negotiation, five thousand dollars was placed in his Bitcoin account, which Torrence considered a bargain price to learn his identity. Aleks was promised another forty-five thousand dollars if he could crack Drexel's encryption program.

Benny and the Cellar crew knew the answer—they had the code. Their fear was another hacking genius might be able to crack the encryption program, even without the code.

One massive intrusion into Drexel's system and their project, and probably their lives, would be over.

Patient privacy was, of course, the Achilles' Heel of all EHRs. Insurance companies, pharmaceutical manufacturers and pharmacies, quality-review organizations, and federal regulatory agencies were just some of the outside groups who examined medical records that many patients thought only their doctors and nurses could see. If Drexel became the national standard, the demand for data would be multiplied geometrically. There was no way around this. The great promise of a national EHR hinged on the ability to collect and analyze millions of records from across the country. But a central repository of so much personal information also raised fears of a privacy nightmare—one-stop shopping to find anything about anybody.

To protect privacy, medical record developers had created encryption protocols to de-identify and anonymize the patient records viewed by outside entities—the goal was to share the data but not the personal information. This usually involved converting patient names and other personal information into random numbers generated by computers, a tough code to break.

One of Drexel's main selling points was the unmatched strength of its proprietary encryption code that, it claimed, protected patient privacy by keeping the data anonymous while simultaneously making it easy to search and analyze. "Always anonymous, always safe," was how Mumsford pitched it at his roadshows.

Benny laughed when he heard that one—he even thought of changing his name to "Anonymous."

Now, Benny wanted to see if this talented Georgian hacker, who had clearly been working on the problem for months, could find a hole that needed to be plugged. The promise of a sweet payday would sharpen the boy's mind. After sending Aleks to a mirror site, so the real IT people at Drexel wouldn't notice any funny business, Benny watched as the hacker ran custom scans of Drexel's data. Aleks only saw long strings of anonymized numbers and letters. Each was unique, representing a patient who had been anonymized. Names, birthdates, social security numbers, dates of visits, and all identifiers were unavailable. Without an algorithm to decode the tantalizing strings—or a warehouse full of supercomputers to try to solve the problem through the brute force method of running quintillions of combinations—they remained suggestive gibberish.

One of Aleks' efforts did catch Benny's eye—something Benny hadn't noticed. Many records had similar numbers in the names field. This was not unusual. There were plenty of Jerome Garcias and Emily Joneses in the world. After running several sorting algorithms, Benny found something intriguing: 652 records that shared a single name: John Doe or Jane Doe. All had the same identifying numerical sequence that translated into the name—135-24681-A for the Johns, 135-24681-B, for the Janes—followed by an extra number, usually a single digit, linking to one specific person; John Doe 1, 2, and so on. It raised the question of whether there was a back door to identifying John Doe 1. Maybe it was something else entirely. Benny knew he had discovered something important, but what, he had no idea.

He had gotten more from Aleks than he had expected.

A message suddenly appeared on Aleks' screen: "Very good start, but we must end our session. An additional five thousand dollars has been deposited in your Bitcoin account. DO NOT REENTER THE SYSTEM. You will receive another message shortly."

Aleks was thrilled. He must have been making more progress than he thought. He was ten thousand dollars ahead of the game. With a little more time, the rest would be his. He could start his new life. But right now, it was almost time for his shift at McDonald's.

Mason Fischer sat in his 1995 Ford Bronco, waiting for Carrie Mumsford in the circle drive in front of the hospital. It was time for a little relationship building. There just wasn't any easy way to get the information he needed about the Drexel EHR as a casual acquaintance. They needed to be closer.

He'd promised her a nice evening while providing himself a chance to learn more about her insights on the EHR. She'd been there when Cabreja died. What did she think?

A short drive later, he pulled into the gravel parking lot behind Bullock's. Stepping out of the old Bronco, Carrie looked back at him.

"This is your idea of the perfect date? Barbecue?" Carrie said with a smile.

"All part of my plan," quipped Mason with a smile that masked his wordplay. Get closer to Carrie, but not too close, get information about her father and his goals for the Drexel EHR, and get out. A delicate dance.

Bullock's Bar-B-Cue was a landmark Durham institution. Started by the family patriarch in the 1950s, it remained family-run with worn cushion seats in the booths and plain wooden tables. Smoked pig—chopped or sliced—was served on white ceramic plates with hush puppies, slaw, and shoulder skins; the chicken was also first-rate. Clear glass bottles filled with its tangy vinegar-based sauce adorned every table, along with, of course, Texas Pete. There was one dessert, banana pudding, and one drink, sweet tea (though, in deference to the Yankees, with a "pretty please," one could get a glass of unsweet tea). No beer or wine. The walls showcased photos of famous actors (Andy Griffith), musicians (Randy Travis), NASCAR drivers (the Terminator himself), and local politicians (Elvin Walters), holding plates of barbecue as big as their smiles.

As Mason and Carrie walked into the restaurant, a booming voice called out, "Sit wherever you want, folks."

The man waving them in was the owner, Tommy Bullock, a robust man in his sixties with powerful arms, a broad smile, and a solid white beard.

Mason led Carrie to a well-worn booth in the corner. Moments later, Tommy appeared with two large glasses of tea and two menus.

"Mason, I barely recognized you thanks to your lovely companion. Whole different look than those guys in scrubs you usually bring here."

"You saying I'm moving up in the world?"

"Nah, just the company you keep," he laughed, a long, full-throated laugh. "Folks, we've got everything on the menu. And, if you aren't in too big a hurry, I've got a brisket just coming off the pit. I do believe it can meet even your high standards."

After Tommy headed back to the kitchen, Carrie looked at Mason curiously. "What was that about?"

"Tommy and I are men of the world who talk about things that matter. On my first visit here, I explained that, as a Texan, I grew up eating the finest cuts of meat grilled or smoked to perfection. That's why I am a fully accredited doctor of brisket. He answered with a plate that almost felt like home."

"You and Texas. What was the name of that little town you're from?"

"Castell."

"Now I get it. You brought me here to show Tommy and his friends that you do have a life, and to impress me with your cowboy knowledge of barbecue."

Mason smiled. "Kind of a 'big hat, no cattle' situation?"

Carrie laughed out loud. "I hadn't heard that one, but it fits the circumstances."

"Ya got me," Mason said, holding up his hands.

"I'm glad we're here," said Carrie. "It reminds me of the places my mother and dad used to take me on Fridays when I was a kid. Which is silly, because, I don't know. Maybe it's more...the feeling. My dad and I still get together. It's nice. But it's never been the same since Mom died."

"How old were you?"

"Twelve."

Mason gazed in the distance, recalling something he could not share.

"She was supposed to have a hysterectomy and come home the next day. But…" Carrie trailed off and was silent for a few seconds, "she didn't. It took me years to stop hoping she would walk through the door."

The image of a tree flashed in Mason's mind. His face showed nothing. Carrie stiffened as she absorbed her memories. A look of strength seemed to rise within her where there might have been tears. Mason slid over and firmly put his arm around her shoulders.

A moment later, Tommy returned with two heaping plates.

"Eat up folks, it doesn't get any better than this, anywhere," he said with a nod to Mason.

For the next half-hour, they laughed and joked and enjoyed their food.

"I took a risk bringing you here," Mason said. "I wasn't sure if you were a diner girl."

"Because I'm a Mumsford?"

"Guilty as charged on that count."

Carrie smiled.

"You obviously have a great sense of humor. You're here with me after all," he laughed. "Maybe I was unsure, because you're so together, so focused, so on top of everything. You're smart…"

"And beautiful."

"*That* is too obvious to say."

"I get it. It may seem like I'm above it all, but I sure don't feel that way. After my mother died, I wanted to be perfect. Perfect for her memory, perfect for my father. It wasn't easy."

"Like…"

"Like I constantly felt like I'm letting someone down. That's a feeling that has never gone away. And it is not all that easy to form lasting friendships, or any kind of relationship, when you feel that kind of pressure."

"Not to speak out of turn, but maybe the person putting this pressure on you is you."

Carrie paused. He was clearly right.

"Okay, Dr. Freud. Here's one for you. You've heard me talk about patient safety and worrying that I'll do the wrong thing. That's one I have figured out. It all goes back to my mother."

"Let's hear it."

"During my first year in medical school, my father decided it was time for me to know the whole truth about my mother. She'd had a series of abnormal pap smears and a hysterectomy seemed the best course. On the night before surgery, the only private room available was on the OB floor. Since it was basically the same doctors, it seemed fine. The next morning, she had routine orders for pre-op medications. One of those was for IV Valium. It was a small dose, just enough to relax, and she didn't need to be monitored. When the resident returned, five minutes later, my mother was blue and pulseless. They couldn't resuscitate her."

"I don't get it. A small dose of IV Valium?" asked Mason, shaking his head.

"The postmortem revealed that instead of Valium in her IV, she was given succinylcholine."

"What?" asked Mason.

"A resident was running behind and no nurse was available, so she took it upon herself to administer the Valium. She took a pre-drawn syringe from the cart they use for emergency C-sections. But instead of Valium she grabbed a syringe of succinylcholine. At the time, the syringes looked almost identical."

There was a brief silence before Carrie continued.

"Five minutes was all it took. My mother died the most horrible death imaginable—wide awake, but unable to breathe or move or call for help. That's why I'm so concerned about patient safety. I'm happy that technology, like the EHR, will help reduce human error, but even the world's best EHR can't cover everything."

Mason's look of gentle compassion hid his roiling emotions. Life wasn't fair. Carrie's pain was real, he could see that much, and there was nothing he, or anyone else, could do about it.

Carrie's pain touched his psyche. Twice in the last week, he'd had nightmares about his mother's death when he was three years old. As always, he saw himself in the car beside her; she was wearing her light-yellow cotton dress, clutching the brown steering wheel. He felt a dreamlike surety that he could save her. But then he didn't. He awoke, as always, with a mix of guilt and anger, at the world and at himself.

For a time, he could take out that anger on the football field. That ended with the injury he had dealt out to Oklahoma's star wide-out in the annual Red River Classic. Then there was medical school and his plans to save the world. As that faded, his punishing early morning runs dissipated some of the anger, at least temporarily. There was more, but he wasn't going to let himself go there.

He felt Carrie's pain. At the same time, however, he was able to assess the situation with cold clinical detachment. *Interesting*, he thought. *A tragic story. Most people would have had trouble getting through it without their eyes watering or their voices quavering. Not Carrie. She had channeled her grief instead of drowning in it.*

"My mother's death was the pivot point in my life," continued Carrie. "I became a different person, more alone, more self-reliant, and more caring for others. I used to dream that she was there, that the good old days were back. Eventually, those dreams stopped. My dad did all he could, but some holes can never be filled—and probably shouldn't be. I just figured I had to get on with my life, kind of like you."

She's as transparent as a polished pane of glass, thought Mason, something he could never be.

They sat quietly before Carrie finally spoke.

"Do you realize we've spent two hours at Bullock's? Wonder if we broke a record. Now, you promised to tell me why barbecue is the best setting for a fabulous date." She stood and turned to the door, Mason right behind her.

"Be glad it wasn't a fishing date. I wanted to do a little test, see if you're the right kind of woman."

"And what would that be?" asked Carrie.

"I have the very highest standards: the three Bs."

"Which are?"

"Brilliant, beautiful, and loves BBQ," said Mason. "You knocked it out of the park. Now, there is a fourth B, for extra credit: Black Bass fishing."

Carrie laughed. "Did you minor in alliteration at Vanderbilt?"

"What makes you think I went to college?"

Carrie yanked Mason's hand, making him stop. She turned to face him, so close that their noses almost touched.

"I don't know many cardiologists who didn't go to college."

"Ever heard of Ferdinand Demara, the Great Imposter? He performed surgery from a textbook."

"Well, you don't seem *that* smart. And how about being the big man on campus?"

Mason looked at her quizzically.

"Sure, act like you don't know what I'm talking about. Of course, I am a top-notch investigator with secret technology." She paused, then whispered, "It's called Google."

"I doubt you found much."

"Two-time All-America defensive back at Texas."

"There've been lots of good football players at Texas," Mason protested.

"Should have gone pro," she continued. "I read the Sports Illustrated article. Good move, losing the moustache."

"I've got lots better secrets," Mason heard himself saying. *Control yourself.*

Carrie gave him a surprisingly powerful shove with her foot hooked behind his left ankle and then grabbed his arm so he didn't fall. With a feigned look of anger on her face, she said, "I've got my secrets too."

"Hidden man-hating?"

"No, Shotokan, dummy." She hopped up on the short brick wall lining the sidewalk and offered her hand but then just as quickly withdrew it as he reached. "Featuring quickness and strength," she laughed as Mason stumbled. "A form of karate I've studied since I was fourteen. So watch it, bub."

Carrie remained stationed in front of Mason. "Here at dinner, I tell you all about me, but you remain a mystery."

"I thought women liked mysterious men," said Mason.

She laughed. It had been a great evening, despite—or maybe because of—the emotional roller coaster. She'd only told a few close friends the entirety of her mother's story. But clearly, Mason wasn't about to cough up anything personal. There was no point in pushing things. That could wait.

10

Benny zeroed in on Mason Fischer's patients at the highest risk of dying. But more specifically, any patient selected for EHR-based death had to be sick enough so their deaths wouldn't raise questions, but healthy enough so that the Cellar crew knew that their intervention was the cause. Like all major hospitals, Drexel used a *severity index* for billing. The higher the severity index, the more likely that patient would have a life-threatening event, or even die, in the hospital. Six of Fischer's patients were in the top tier of the severity index.

Benny forwarded the complete medical records of all six to the disturbed and so extremely useful genius, Dr. Christian Van der Graf. Tall and handsome, people said he looked like the actor Bradley Cooper, with the patrician accent cultivated by National Public Radio announcers. He combined the wind-swept Ivy League look of brains and privilege that made one think he was born on third base. His eyes told a different story: they were almost black, inky pools that didn't look out but seemed to draw one into depraved and remorseless depths. Benny had only seen him remotely; he had no interest in getting any closer.

Van der Graf graduated from Harvard at sixteen with a degree in neurosciences. He completed the famed Harvard-MIT combined MD-PhD program in five years. Just like Burgess, but there the similarities ended. He became a neuropsychiatrist, and within three years of completing his residency, he became the youngest Harvard Medical School associate professor ever. Van der Graf was a force destined for greatness. For those who would listen, he told them it would only be a year or two before he'd be on the cover of Time magazine. Then, things began to unwind. He took shortcuts, started a love affair with cocaine, and slept with assistants, nurses, and even two patients. People began asking questions.

An investigative reporter for the Boston Globe discovered that he had ignored common clinical trial rules, leading to the deaths of at least three subjects. She died in a boating accident before she could write that story, taking her evidence with her to the bottom of the lake.

Not everyone was in the dark. The NSA knew. Seeing a chance to corral a rare talent, Hugh Torrence offered Van der Graf a deal. The Agency's technical wizards would scrub his murderous record if he became an agency asset. Van Der Graf leaped at the chance to create combinations of psychotropic drugs, no FDA review required, that made hard-bitten terrorists wish they were being water-boarded. He traveled the world—from Guantanamo to Pakistan, Afghanistan to Uzbekistan, Nigeria to Honduras—earning the moniker

Dr. Feel Bad. Maybe not the garden spots of the world, but better than bunking with Michael Swango in the Colorado Supermax. Whatever he came up with for the next Drexel patient would be inventive—and deadly.

After reviewing the six patients in Benny's dossier, Van der Graf picked a winner: Aaron Goldstein, whose serious but treatable heart disease hit the sweet spot. He was scheduled for a procedure in the cardiac catheterization laboratory first thing in the morning. "This is very promising," Van der Graf said. A problem in the cath lab could be dealt with. In the hours after the procedure, almost anything could happen, and it would. "A real name, a solid medical record, nothing to hide—sometimes I wonder why they make it so easy. Honesty and trust. We couldn't do our work without them."

~

Van der Graf's chilling comment reminded Benny of the discovery the Georgian hacker Aleks had led him to—Drexel's cache of masked John and Jane Doe records. His initial research, however, deflated his enthusiasm. Instead of subterfuge, he'd found a rational and much less interesting explanation. Many patients showed up at the hospital unwilling or unable to provide their name—they were in a car accident or suffered a gunshot wound and didn't have an ID or didn't want to say. The hospital system, even the new EHR, required a name to initiate care, at least until the wizards in billing could track down the real one.

Most John and Jane Does were eventually replaced with their real and proper names. But a few cases on either end of the spectrum, the very poor who died at the hospital or the very rich who insisted on anonymity, retained the generic name. Benny grabbed a Red Bull and a twenty-ounce Coke from the refrigerator, along with a handful of M&Ms, and brought up the Drexel list. There were hundreds of records. Twenty-one of them stood out. Where most of the numbers were used by one-time admissions and recycled—this year's John Doe 1 was not the same as last year's—the twenty-one numbers were tied to specific records: the same people using the same anonymous ID. People who wanted to keep their care secret.

Who? *Why*? Benny wondered. There had to be a reason, and it was likely important.

Benny had another brainstorm. He could synch a patient's time of admission with the recorded video from the hospital's closed-circuit TV monitors and use facial-recognition software to unmask the power player with something to hide. Joining those data streams worked like a charm. He was able to identify all twenty-one. There were athletes, entertainers, and business people; none was of any immediate interest or use—though maybe down the road.

Except for John Doe 17. He was the jackpot. Finally, he had something Torrence wanted and had not been able to get.

MONDAY, MAY 9
8:36 AM *[MONDAY, MAY 9, 4:36 PM GEORGIAN TIME]*
INTERNET CAFÉ #32, RUSTAVELI AVENUE
TBILISI, REPUBLIC OF GEORGIA

For the first time, the future seemed bright for Aleksandre Torchilov. He still didn't know who had hired him, but he was sure when they said "DO NOT REENTER THE SYSTEM," they meant it. He'd keep the money close to the chest; if not, his roommates would smell opportunity and demand their cut. After more work and waiting—in Tbilisi that was practically an Olympic sport—he might bring in the full fifty thousand dollars from his secret source. Enough to leave quietly and never return. In Europe, or maybe even the US, he'd live a different life than would ever be possible in Georgia. When he closed his eyes, he saw a beautiful girl with shoulder-length brown hair, children, a yellow house, two dogs (a pit bull and a Rottweiler), and a tree by a brook. That was his dream: a decent, normal life.

For the moment, however, he was in his second home, under the mighty Golden Arches. Today, he was in charge of French fries; he preferred grilling burgers, but every day can't be pierogies and vodka, as his mother used to say.

~

When Aleks' shift came to an end, the sun was setting on Tbilisi. A man of habit, he clocked out when his shift ended and then went to the grill to assemble his own combo: a double quarter pounder with cheese topped with a crispy McChicken patty, lettuce, pickles, and Big Mac special sauce on a sesame seed bun. His co-worker, Lado, looked at him and shook his head.

"You know that stuff will kill you," Lado said.

"I'm drinking Diet Coke. That should offset the burger and is healthier than a milkshake or vodka."

Aleks took his tray to his favorite corner seat by the window near the door. There were only a handful of people there at this time of night. The pensioners had left hours ago, and the young hipsters wouldn't show up until later, after they'd had so much to drink that Mickey D's seemed like a good idea.

He sat down and carefully removed each item from his tray. He laid them on the table with care, as if he were having a real meal in a real home. He brought the sandwich to his mouth. He smelled the salty aroma before taking a bite. It was delicious. He was happy.

Soon he was on his way back to the apartment. When he walked into the tiny living room, he saw a new, deep red stain on the carpet. Igor, it had to be. The guy was a total slob. Probably spilled an entire bottle of wine.

He headed down the dark hall to the bathroom and nearly fell after his foot hit a heavy object. He reached over and turned on the light. His two roommates were lying face down, the back of their heads now bowls of brain stew. There was no holding down the two thousand calories from McDonald's. Vomit spewed as Aleks turned back to the tiny living room.

The door to the hallway swung open. It revealed a very fit man, about thirty, wearing brown slacks, a black turtleneck, leather gloves, and an expensive-looking long winter coat with flecks of snow on his shoulders. "Aleksandre Torchilov?" he asked in a sweet, mild voice.

"Yes?"

"This is the message you were promised."

The man pulled out a gun, placed it on Aleks' right temple, and pulled the trigger. The only sounds were the wisp of the silenced weapon and the thunk of Aleks' head on the floor. A pool of blood spread across the table. Aleks' eyes were vacant. His dream of leaving Tbilisi had come true.

The man methodically checked for any evidence that he had been there. There was none, so he silently slipped out the door.

Torrence only used the best.

CHAPTER

12

MONDAY, MAY 9
10 AM
CARDIAC CATHETERIZATION SUITE, DREXEL MEMORIAL HOSPITAL

Mason's day started early. By 6 AM, he was in his scrubs, rounding in the CCU. At seven, he entered the cardiac catheterization suite—patients often found its mix of antiseptic smells, humming high-tech equipment, and bright overhead lights off-putting; for Mason, it was almost intoxicating. "I love the smell of Betadine in the morning," he'd joke sometimes, riffing off one of his favorite movies, *Apocalypse Now*.

His first two procedures went off without a hitch. His third patient, a genial, balding sixty-eight-year-old local hero named Aaron Goldstein, arrived at eleven. Goldstein had been a leader his entire life, building bridges between Durham's Jewish community and other minority groups, especially African Americans and recent immigrants. His three children and large extended family adored him. His beloved wife, Rachel, had died two years before. After his sorrow lifted, Goldstein had resumed his community work while handing over his custom clothing business to his eldest son. His internist, Justine Peterman, had determined that Goldstein had a blocked artery in his heart and asked Mason to perform the catheterization.

"The patient is prepped and ready," a nurse said.

Mason smiled as he backed through the swinging doors in his gown with freshly-scrubbed hands held high. He carefully tugged on a pair of sterile latex gloves and turned toward the table, where Goldstein lay covered to his neck in green cloth with only a small area over the right side of his groin exposed.

"Good morning, Mr. Goldstein. We'll start your catheterization after a bit more sedation." Then he turned to the nurse at Goldstein's side. "Two milligrams of morphine, please."

He turned back to Goldstein. "Once the medication is in your system, we'll use some lidocaine to numb you up before we put in the catheters. We should be done in less than an hour, and I'll let Dr. Peterman know the results as soon as we get that artery unblocked."

"This isn't my first rodeo, Doc."

"It's my accent, right?" asked Mason.

Goldstein smiled, raising his index finger and pinkie. "Hook 'em horns, eh, Doc?"

"Always and forever."

In fifteen minutes, the procedure was at a critical point as Mason manipulated the catheters near the groin area, watching each movement intently on overhead monitors. He spoke in a muted voice to the cardiology fellow in the room. "This is where it gets tricky. He's got a one-in-a-hundred twist in the left anterior descending coronary artery. I'll advance the catheter very slowly while turning just a little clockwise…. Bam!" He smiled.

But the chief technician in the control room, Samuel Thacker, was not happy. He was seeing the same pattern as a few weeks ago, just before the entire lab shut down without warning.

He jumped out of his chair and grabbed the microphone.

"Doc! Everything okay?"

Mason's head shot up at the sudden interruption, but his hands and voice remained steady.

"No problems."

"The monitors are getting jumpy again."

"What?"

"Looking just like the last time we lost power."

Moments later, the monitors displaying Goldstein's blocked artery from different views, as well as his blood pressure, heart rate, and other measurements, went blank.

"Reset, reset!" Sam shouted.

Goldstein's eyes popped open. "Is there a problem?"

"Just checking the equipment," Mason replied lightly.

He pushed the reset button. Nothing happened.

"Did you reset? I said reset!" Sam yelled again.

"Sam. I'm resetting. Why don't you come in the room so we can talk more easily," Mason suggested. Anything to get Sam off the microphone.

Sam entered the room, looking grim. He sidled up to Mason. "Doc, we gotta stop. Just take him off the table. We can get him back on when we are certain everything's back and working."

"Give it a minute, Sam."

Almost magically, the four monitors simultaneously crackled and came back to life.

"We're back up. Let's give the monitors a couple of minutes to stabilize and we can continue," said Mason. He leaned over Aaron Goldstein.

"Mr. Goldstein, everything is fine. We will take a short break to recalibrate, and we'll be back in business."

"Whatever you say, Doc," replied a woozy Goldstein.

To the side, Sam shook his head vigorously from side to side. "Too risky," he mouthed to Mason, so that the patient couldn't hear. Mason intentionally looked back at Goldstein, ignoring Sam's concern. He wasn't going to let a machine determine his care; he had everything under control.

Three minutes later, Sam said, "We're back up."

Mason pushed a pedal on the floor. An X-ray image appeared instantly. The two large X-ray tubes rotated in tandem as he manipulated a joystick attached to the table.

"Everything looks good," Mason said. "Fifteen minutes and we'll be done. You okay with continuing?"

Goldstein, groggy from the sedation he had just received, mumbled, "Git 'er done."

Thirty minutes later, the blocked artery was open, and blood flowed briskly to Goldstein's heart. All was well, except for the look Sam shot Mason.

~

Fifty miles north, Benny and Saied were following the drama with growing excitement.

They were pleased to have good news when Torrence checked in.

"How are we doing?"

"Everything's on track," Saied responded. "Fischer just finished his procedure; Goldstein's in recovery. But we threw in a little wrinkle from Van der Graf. We shut down the cath lab power briefly. The tech running the monitors was freaking out and wanted to stop, but Fischer proceeded, which is bold, but not quite by the book. If the need arises, the technician will say the good doctor doesn't always put his patients' welfare first."

Benny jumped in. "Van der Graf came up with a grand finale for Goldstein, which will be happening pronto. Dude may be whack, but that's just the medicine we need."

Torrence did not laugh.

Saied continued. "Every patient who goes through the procedure receives intravenous fluids to flush the catheterization dye out of their system. Standard practice. Goldstein's IV will contain sodium, glucose, and an added bonus—a sky-high amount of potassium."

"Is Jensen delivering the goods?" Torrence smiled.

"No need. The EHR controls all the machines, making it quicker and easier to order tests, review results...."

"And order drugs from the pharmacy..." Torrence added.

"...that are mixed," Saied continued.

"...by robots," they both said at the same time.

"Ya gotta love machines," Benny said. "Your wish is their command, no questions asked."

"Like you," Torrence said, finally showing a hint of a smile.

Saied continued: "All those promises about checks and safeguards fly out the window with a few key strokes. In fairness, our high-tech assassin asked if we really wanted to put that much potassium in the IV-bag. We assured it we did—so it did. Then we went back into the EHR and altered the record to reflect a normal amount. To the nurse, the labeled bag will look no different than any other. The machine that measures and reports blood electrolyte levels in blood samples is also a connected device working for us. Using Van der Graf's calculations, I've had Benny put in a temporary setting that will make Goldstein's potassium level appear to be absolutely normal."

"So Goldstein gets an overdose of potassium, but it doesn't show up in the label on the bag of fluids, and even though his blood level of potassium is way high, it's reported as normal. Am I getting that right?" asked Torrence.

"Precisely. The beauty of it all is that the attending physicians won't have any idea what's wrong. They'll just see that Goldstein is dying before their eyes and that there's nothing they can do about it."

"The potassium will be untraceable?"

"One hundred percent. Nice, right?" Benny said. Torrence's lack of a response was no surprise.

Feeling like they were on a roll, Benny decided to share his recent discovery. "Hey boss, want to know something really special?"

Torrence rolled his eyes. Humoring Rasinko was his least favorite pastime, but it came with the territory.

"I can't wait."

After Benny told him that Elvin Walters was John Doe 17, Torrence laughed out loud. "For once, you didn't oversell. That *is* something special."

Saied and Benny were all smiles. It was turning out to be a banner day.

Torrence being Torrence, never satisfied, switched topics. "The guy from Tbilisi," he said. "The one you let prowl around in the system. Aleksandre Torchilov. What's the status?"

"He's aces," Benny said. "He got the ball rolling on John Doe 17 and is awaiting further instructions."

From the cold look in Torrence's eye, he knew he'd said too much. "He knows about John Doe 17?"

"Nah. He figured the pattern in the common names. It took our facial recognition program to unmask John Doe 17."

"What if he was connected to the GRU? They have the tools."

"I've got a program that alerts me to anyone looking at the closed-circuit feeds. No alert came across, but give me a second."

The room was silent but for the clack of Benny's keyboard. "No one has looked at the closed-circuit feeds in the last two weeks. Hard to imagine the GRU is smart enough to get in, get the info, and get out, not knowing that I'm monitoring access."

Just as Torrence began to speak, Saied jumped in. "We could speculate about known unknowns for hours. The chance that the Georgian hacker communicated to anyone is less than 0.01 percent. We were watching him the entire time. There is less than a one in a hundred chance the GRU had time to act on it. That makes it a one-in-ten-thousand chance the GRU could know if they are even involved. Benny can keep watching, but I can live with those odds."

Benny felt queasy when he saw Torrence's hand slip into his right pants pocket. He glanced at Saied, who gave the tiniest knowing nod. Hugh Torrence, the destroyer of lives, was once again caressing the St. Christopher's medallion he kept in his right pocket. This once infrequent appeal for other-worldly help was becoming a weekly, if not daily, occurrence. Benny knew Torrence was a devout Catholic, but he had not understood this habit's fearsome meaning until Saied explained it.

Torrence glowered at them both with his *I am death* look.

"Aleks Torchilov is no longer a problem."

Benny and Saied knew no one was safe.

CHAPTER

13

A sudden eruption of alarms and monitor squawks exploded the tranquility of the Coronary Care Unit. Nurses ran down the hall to Room 14. Carrie Mumsford was close behind.

Forty-five minutes after his procedure, Aaron Goldstein's face was beginning to turn blue. He wasn't breathing. His heart had stopped. The first nurse in checked his vitals. Finding no pulse, she started CPR, loudly counting out chest pumps. A second nurse grabbed an Ambu bag, an inflatable resuscitation device that forces oxygen-enriched air into the lungs.

Carrie quickly arrived and took charge of the resuscitation effort.

"Call a code and get anesthesia stat. He needs to be intubated. I need an EKG, arterial blood gas, and chem panel, all of them stat," Carrie commanded.

Alerted by a page that his patient was in trouble, Mason sprinted down the hall of the CCU, where a small crowd of medical students and residents who had been on rounds observing patients were getting more than they had bargained for.

"Coming through," he said to one of the students at the edge of the room.

The student ignored him, talking loudly to his classmate.

"Yeah, they were in there on rounds, and the guy freakin' codes."

"No shit," said the other medical student.

"Move. Now."

As Mason pushed his way through, he paused for a split second. Looking in from the gaggle was a muscular, dark-haired guy in scrubs with a stern face. By now, Mason knew all the CCU staff, and this guy looked more like he belonged in the gym than in the CCU. Then he remembered; it was the same guy in the emergency room when Longorio Cabreja died.

In the room, Carrie was performing CPR while an anesthesiologist at the head of the bed peered down Goldstein's throat with a laryngoscope, preparing to intubate him.

"What happened?" yelled Mason over the commotion.

"Cardiac arrest," Carrie answered. "It's heading south. Lidocaine, one hundred milligrams IV, stat!"

As the nurse at the bedside reached into the code cart, Mason gripped her arm.

"Hold up a second," he said. "Lidocaine isn't going to help this guy."

Carrie stared at him, her eyes showing irritation and confusion.

"Repeat an EKG please."

The technician standing next to the EKG machine pushed a button. Pink paper with three parallel, wiggly lines began to scroll out of the machine.

"Send a potassium level, stat."

With that, a nurse rushed out of the room with a tube of blood.

"What was the last potassium level?" Mason asked Carrie.

"Normal. Stat sample was sent just a couple of minutes ago."

"I guarantee it's not normal now. Push an amp of D50, five units of insulin, and an amp of calcium," Mason said to the nurse at the code cart.

"You're treating him for high potassium?" asked Carrie.

Mason ripped the EKG off the machine.

"What the…"

"What?" Carrie asked, as she pumped Goldstein's chest.

The EHR read-out showed Goldstein had developed a lethal abnormal heart rhythm, ventricular tachycardia, or VT. In a man with known heart disease having had an artery opened up earlier in the day, 99 percent of the time a catastrophic collapse was due to VT.

But the EKG showed hyperkalemia.

"It looks like VT, but it isn't," Mason lowered his voice. "It's not responding to lidocaine or other drugs or electrical cardioversion. The EKG is classic for a sky-high potassium level. That's gotta be it."

Carrie looked at Mason.

Just then, the nurse who had taken the blood sample bulled her way back into the crowded room. "Potassium is 4.1. Normal."

"Just give glucose, insulin and calcium," Mason ordered. "If his potassium is really normal, it won't hurt him. If it is a lab error, and everything else points at hyperkalemia, the glucose, insulin, and calcium could save him."

"Getting it now," said another nurse.

Carrie continued administering CPR for another thirty seconds until the anesthesiologist shouted out.

"I think I can feel a pulse."

Mason cut him off, looking directly at the nurse monitoring vital signs. "See if his blood pressure has responded."

"One-fifteen over fifty, and pulse is getting stronger," she replied.

"Good. Now we've got to get Mr. Goldstein stabilized," Mason said. "Get another potassium, stat. Call nephrology. He may need to be dialyzed soon. Then call Dr. Peterman and bring me the phone."

With Goldstein stable, at least from the cardiac standpoint, the crowd gradually dispersed, leaving Mason and Carrie standing at the bedside. Carrie was pale, her confidence shattered.

"Listen," Mason said. "I don't have any idea what happened here. Goldstein is a sick guy, but his pre-cath labs showed normal renal function. You sure he didn't get any potassium?"

Carrie scrolled through the electronic order entry system. "No, no one ordered potassium. His morning level was normal."

"I don't know," said Mason. "His EKG is classic for hyperkalemia and he responded to therapy. How could he have developed hyperkalemia in three hours?"

"Peterman?" asked Mason to no one in particular.

"She's on her way," said Carrie. "I've never seen anything like this."

Mason put his hand on her shoulder. "Something strange is going on here."

"There is no way the stat lab, showing a normal potassium, could be right."

"Let's just get him stabilized. We can try to figure out what happened later."

~

Justine Peterman entered the room breathlessly. "What happened? The stent you put in this morning looked perfect. His labs were normal. I don't get it."

"He must have received potassium somewhere along the line, but there weren't any orders. He's making urine normally." He pointed to the bag hung on the side of the bed, bulging with light yellow urine.

Mason pulled Peterman aside, just outside the room. "Justine, Goldstein's resuscitation took too long. He coded at least five minutes before I arrived and it took us another few minutes to get him stabilized. That's a long time for CPR. At his age, his risk of hypoxic brain injury is high."

"The damned EHR," said Peterman. "How do we know that it didn't screw something up? Taking control—and accountability—away from doctors is an invitation to chaos. Like some office dwelling Neanderthal or whiz kid computer programmer understands medicine. I'm going to get to the bottom of this. Aaron Goldstein was more than a patient. He was a friend, and I don't have many left."

"Maybe he'll recover," offered Mason.

"Doubtful."

They both looked up to see Carrie holding a laptop. "I've checked every lab, every vital sign, every X-ray. Up until he arrested, there was *nothing* abnormal, top to bottom."

"Carrie, are you okay?" asked Peterman.

Carrie nodded without conviction.

"Listen, I'll give you a page later in the day. Let's have a cup of coffee."

A wash of relief came over Carrie, visibly. Peterman was a strong woman who had deep compassion, especially for fellow women in medicine. She was not just her role model but a friend.

"But right now," Peterman said, slightly slumped and deflated, "I have to call Aaron's family."

~

There was a firestorm in the Cellar.

"Christ, Benny," Torrence complained, "what the hell is going on here? First that Mexican Gutierrez, and now Goldstein? I thought Van der Graf said it was a lock. Now you tell me Goldstein isn't dead?"

Benny knew better than to say anything.

"Get Jensen on the phone. He *was* there, right?"

Torrence had instructed Jensen to be sure his ass was in the CCU, just in case. It seemed that "just in case" was their new reality.

Jensen answered on the first ring. Before Torrence could speak, he said,

"I'll clean up the mess."

"Meaning?"

"I'll make sure Goldstein is planted. The good news is Fischer thinks he's already brain dead."

93

Torrence mulled that for a moment.

"We might have a bigger problem," said Jensen. "Fischer correctly suspects that Goldstein got too much potassium but can't figure out how. He told Goldstein's doc, Justine Peterman, a smart and tenacious pain in the ass, who promised to get to the bottom of it. She'll try. She hates the EHR."

Torrence said nothing.

"Want me to deal with that too?"

"You mean with Peterman?" asked Torrence.

Silence.

"Perhaps, in time," Torrence responded. "I'll let you know. Do nothing without a direct command from me." Torrence clicked off and glared at Benny.

"Goldstein was moments away from his permanent dirt nap when Fischer showed up and pulled a rabbit out of his ass," Benny said. "It was like he knew exactly what was going on. Van der Graf says he was too late. He's betting they'll pull the plug as soon as they can get the family together. He said it was a one-in-a-million chance that someone like Fischer would show up and figure it out. Said Fischer was pretty smart to figure that one out. Or maybe Fischer has seen more than his share of high potassium levels."

Hasan Saied spoke up. "Fischer's heroism may be a stroke of luck. Remember our Plan B. We know that Fischer likes to play with potassium from his Galveston days. Easy enough to pin this on him. Just give us the word."

Torrence frowned as he rubbed his St. Christopher medal. "Plan B. Plan Z. Maybe we're going to need an altogether new game plan."

Saied and Benny glanced at each other. With Hugh Torrence, new plans invariably featured his old standby: murder.

CHAPTER

14

MONDAY, MAY 9
6:59 PM
FIOLA MARE RESTAURANT, WASHINGTON, DC

Senator Elvin Walters wasn't feeling so hot. Well, actually, he *was* feeling *very* hot, as in bathing in a clammy sweat. He couldn't catch his breath either. Whenever he raised his head to look out at the small group of well-heeled donors convened at Fiola Mare—a "your expense account better be paying for this" Italian seafood place on the Potomac—the room went in and out of focus. He felt a bead of sweat trickle down his back. It wasn't the first time. In the last few weeks, the light-headedness and nausea had come on several times, but only for a minute or two. Now it wasn't going away.

His campaign manager, not noticing his discomfort, whispered, "It's time."

"Got it," Walters replied. Given the small crowd, he could speak from his seat, thank God. If he kept feeling the way he did, walking up the stairs to a podium could have done him in.

95

Suck it up man, Walters told himself. *Ten minutes, that's all.*

His cardiologist at Drexel told him that his past heart attacks had put him at risk for irregular heart rhythms. He had pressed Walters to have a defibrillator implanted to protect against the arrhythmias, which can be fatal. But even with the promise of total anonymity, he'd be in deep trouble if the reporters found out. His hope of being the GOP nominee would die before it ever got off the ground.

As far as the public knew, he was in perfect health. Following his annual check-up at Walter Reed Hospital, he'd proclaim himself to be in "tip-top shape." He had no problem with deception; he was a pro. He had convinced himself that his ruse was for a noble cause. He was hiding his health problems *for his party, for his country*. Following the 2020 election, both needed him now more than ever. Sure, transparency was his mantra, but that didn't apply to his protected health information. The fear was that someone, somewhere, would figure out why he went to Durham so often—and disappeared for several hours. And if that goddamned Drexel EHR went national, it would only make it easier for enemies to pry into his affairs.

Although Drexel harbored his deepest secret, he was bound to the hospital because its doctors had treated him for most of his whole life. The son of mill workers, he was the first in his family to go to college, much less law school. Having graduated from Duke, it made sense to practice corporate law in Durham, mostly serving large corporations with offices in the nearby Research Triangle Park. His heart problems arose then. Nothing serious—at first. Then, as he entered politics and his profile became more public, his health records became more private. Years ago, the name Elvin Walters had been removed from Drexel's medical records. He was assigned a permanent pseudonym: John Doe 17.

Thanks to a Georgian he would never meet, Walters's identity was not as secret as he thought.

Walters had been a natural in politics, quickly gaining acclaim as a man of the people, as a straight-talking, God-fearing Republican. That used to be enough. But following Trump's victory, and then defeat, his conservatism was bending toward populism with a slight progressive edge. As he held his hand up to speak, the one hundred or so folks attending the two-thousand-dollar-a-plate event put down their forks and wine glasses. Walters felt a sudden surge of energy as he began.

"Do you know how many people could be employed and have health insurance if not for our oil wars and trade wars?" he asked, then paused before answering: "Everybody. That's right, *everybody*. We can do that. Not with Medicare for all, by God, but with an American system. One that finally delivers truly affordable universal care by maximizing freedom and choice while eliminating the maze of duplication and administrative overhead that is strangling today's health care system."

It brought down the house.

But before he could exploit the response, his dizziness suddenly returned with a vengeance. He leaned over to his campaign manager.

"I'm going to cut it short. I really don't feel soooo…"

Before he could finish his sentence, it happened. His lights went out. When he opened his eyes ten seconds later, he was surrounded by his security detail. The crowd was hushed.

No one had attacked him. He was safe. A young woman from his table leaned over him as she helped clean the food off his face. Christ, he'd passed out and ended up face down in a plate of bigeye tuna. How much worse could it get? At least the press wasn't in attendance. They would have had a field day.

Two hours later, video clips were all over the internet and on the major news channels, proclaiming *"Breaking News."* His cardiologist at Drexel had called repeatedly until Walters finally answered. Yes, he would go to Drexel that week for his cardiac procedure. He'd figure out an excuse later.

MONDAY, MAY 9
7:15 PM
WEST MAIN STREET, DURHAM, NORTH CAROLINA

Mason didn't want to bump into Carrie while leaving the hospital. He knew Aaron Goldstein's unexpected cardiac arrest was hard for her, and, with all he had going on, he had decided to wait a few days before reconnecting. The ability to compartmentalize was one of his greatest skills. But when he saw her pained smile, his resolve went out the window.

"Tough day, huh?" she said.

"No kidding. Let's get something to eat."

Carrie nodded, her expression lacking any component of hope.

"You think Bullock's is something special? I'll take you to dinner at a place that serves real southern food: Dame's Chicken & Waffles. Nothing's as comforting as original comfort food," said Mason.

That earned a quick smile from Carrie, but there was little talk while they drove downtown and parked. Goldstein's death had cast an unspoken pall over them. Then, suddenly, as they were walking toward Dame's, Carrie grasped Mason's hand and pulled him to a stop.

"I haven't been able to get Mr. Goldstein out of my mind. I need a break and you do, too. Let's think about something different. Tell me about yourself." She gave him a playful elbow to the ribs.

"My favorite topic," he said as she rolled her eyes. "Okay— Mason Fischer, cardiologist, hospital badge #54369, at your service, ma'am." He saluted.

"I'm serious," Carrie said, delivering another of her perfectly-balanced, trademark shoves.

"Don't try any of those Kung Fu moves on me again."

"Shotokan," Carrie said. "They told me you were plenty smart, but you don't seem to be getting that one."

They? Mason wondered.

"Here I tell you all my secrets, about my father, what I remember of my mother, my dreams. And you…."

They neared a bench just off the sidewalk. Mason sat and held out his hand to Carrie.

"What do you want to know?"

"I don't even know where to start," she said. "Okay, how about this? You were such a big deal in Texas, so why'd you come to Drexel? Not that I'm complaining, mind you."

"Are you sure you want to know?" said Mason, suddenly looking quite serious.

She looked at him questioningly. "I don't know. Do I?"

Mason took a deep breath.

"It's not pretty."

"How bad can it be? Tell me everything." No doubt, he was exaggerating, Carrie thought.

"It's bad," Mason started. "A patient of mine died. I was accused of intentionally causing his death."

Mason was pleased by the shocked look on Carrie's face. He wasn't sure how far that story had spread. But Carrie hadn't known. If she had, she'd covered it extraordinarily well. He took her hand in his and continued. "I did nothing wrong. The chairman of obstetrics and gynecology concocted the entire accusation because of a woman. I was innocent and that was proven beyond a shadow of a doubt." *An exaggeration, but she'd never know.* "What hurts the most is that I know I could have done better."

Carrie stared at him.

"I was the attending physician for a slimy investment guy from Houston. He'd ruined more lives than you can imagine. Not Bernie Madoff, but not far from it. He had renal failure and multiple medical problems, including heart disease. I left early to get everything ready to fix dinner for a woman there, an OBGYN resident. Got the steaks, flowers, everything. We had only gone out a few times, but it felt like we really connected."

Mason assessed Carrie's reaction—a flickering wince, nothing more. He continued. "Halfway through dinner she said she liked me, but there was nothing more. The timing seemed strange, but it turned out she was in love with another man. Not just any man, but the head of her department, Richard Henderson—a worthless, womanizing turd. The whole time I was thinking about her she was having an affair with a married man. I don't know what was worse, finding that out, or wondering how I missed it. It didn't matter. I was crushed."

Carrie reached over and touched his hand.

"She left, and I finally snapped out of what seemed like a bad dream. I dragged myself back to the hospital to check on my patient. It felt like I was sleepwalking. I went over everything with the resident on call, an excellent guy, and then left, bought a six-pack, and drank it in my car. I hadn't felt so low in a long time. Finally, I wandered home and went to bed. Sometime in the night, the patient had a cardiac arrest and died. His kidneys had shut down, his blood chemistry was totally out of whack, especially his potassium. That was what killed him."

"Mason, that wasn't your fault. What more could you have done?" Carrie could feel the tears welling in her eyes. *Why had she pushed Mason to talk about something so painful?* That thought was quickly followed by another: *That's exactly what happened to Goldstein.*

Mason continued. "The head of cardiology agreed, said he wouldn't have been suspicious of the potassium levels based on the totality of the information we had at the time. But I know I shouldn't have missed it, and I'll never miss a case of hyperkalemia again."

He read Carrie's face again; it was filled with compassion. *Good.* "Somehow, Henderson found out. I saw him in the parking lot that night and he practically accosted me. I remember what he said, word for word: 'I know what you did, and I'm gonna make an example of you unless you get the hell out of Galveston. Got it?' Two weeks later the Dean called me in. Henderson claimed he'd received an anonymous tip noting that I was the one thing that three patients who died recently all had in common, accusing me of intentionally harming the patients. My relationship with his resident had never really started, he just wanted revenge."

Carrie gently caressed his forearm.

"In the end, it was best that I start clean somewhere else," Mason said. "Drexel seemed as good a place as any."

She leaned over and kissed him warmly on the lips.

"I'm sorry I asked. Sorry you had to relive that."

"It's okay. Maybe it's good to talk about it. Sometimes, it almost seems like it never happened."

16

MONDAY, MAY 9
7:20 PM
INTERSTATE 40 NEAR DURHAM, NORTH CAROLINA

Charles Richmond's phone vibrated. He glanced at the caller ID screen. It was so sophisticated that it could identify virtually any caller, including when the President rang him from Air Force One.

But this time, the ID was blank. It had to be Torrence calling from the Cellar.

"See my email?" asked Torrence.

Something was up. Torrence typically would be yelling into the phone. But no yelling, no demanding, no cursing.

"Click on the URL in my note. Streaming video of Walters at a fundraiser in D.C. tonight. Keeled over and ended up face down in a plate of fish."

"Remarkable."

"It looked like someone had finally punched his ticket. No such luck. A few seconds later, some young babe was cleaning off his face and he was laughing about it, probably grabbing her ass under the table."

"I can't believe he let cameras into a private event."

"He didn't," Torrence said with immense satisfaction. "We're keeping an eye on him. They made everyone check their cell phones to prevent secret recordings, but we outfitted one of the waiters with a microcam. She captured everything, and Benny shared it with the world."

"I thought you had ceased your efforts against Walters."

"This isn't personal; it's business."

"You sure about that?" asked Richmond. "There's almost no chance Walters can stop us now."

"That's the difference between you and me, Charles—I make sure to strangle chance in the crib. Even if Walters can't derail the adoption of Drexel's EHR, he will never stop asking questions. The prick has set himself up as a champion of privacy, so he has no choice."

But Richmond knew it was personal. As a matter of principle, Torrence despised DC insiders like Walters who believed their charisma and wit entitled them to power. Torrence had lived through enough genuine crises—not Senate filibusters—to know that words never solved real problems. Tough problems required tough solutions delivered by tough men. Men like him, not spineless windbags like Walters.

Torrence had a special, deadly score to settle with Walters. Years before, when Torrence was still at the NSA, Walters had subpoenaed a long-time NSA analyst and subjected him to unrelenting interrogation in front of the Senate Intelligence Committee. Every question led to five more. Late one Friday afternoon, after a week of brutal testimony, the analyst let slip the names of two NSA operatives working undercover in Pakistan.

Before the agency had a chance to extract the men, they were brutally murdered, their bodies dragged through the streets by a rope connected to a roaring Toyota SUV. The analyst killed himself that night. Three agents dead, all because Walters was trying to dig up dirt. The tragedy was covered up. Months later, Torrence placed a call to Walters, who went on the attack. "Your unaccountable, illegal, un-American black ops are the reason those men are dead. Live with that." Torrence had lived with those words every day since. Words he could never forgive or forget, only avenge.

Now, as he watched Benny's video, Richmond asked, "This is embarrassing, but is it useful?"

"Humiliation is always useful," Torrence said.

17

With Van der Graf on a remote connection, Benny and Saied had worked through the night to meet Torrence's latest demand. Their effort was rewarded. Another patient on Fischer's "most likely to die" met their exacting standards: Ben Craver, a wealthy and nasty old goat, whose first love was Marlboro Reds. His daily disparagement of his nurses, doctors, and even Derrick Mumsford made it clear he'd never understand why the millions he'd donated to Drexel wouldn't be enough to cure his terminal lung cancer. Fischer had performed the routine heart evaluation that, amazingly, showed that his heart was normal. That didn't really matter. Every day that Craver lived was a miracle. A few less wouldn't matter; given his whiny rudeness, it might even be a blessing.

When Torrence arrived that morning, the staid Saied was almost excited. "Van der Graf has outdone himself."

"Details," responded Torrence.

"Craver's medical record is surprisingly thin. He's never been admitted to the hospital before. If he hadn't chain-smoked all these years, he could live to one hundred."

"So we have nothing?" Torrence snapped.

"No, because Benny and I discovered a little nugget: Craver's estranged brother and one of his aunts both died during surgery, both from complications due to anesthesia, which is rare these days. We told Van der Graf, who went to work on Craver's genome stored in the Drexel database."

Saied paused and smiled before continuing. "Craver has a mutation in a protein I never heard of, the ryanodine receptor, that is completely harmless, except—you guessed it—when he's given anesthetics. Then, he suffers a very rare condition called malignant hyperthermia, which is fatal nearly one hundred percent of the time."

"How does that help us?" interrupted the highly agitated Torrence. "Craver's not having surgery, so the gas passers won't be putting him under."

"You're right, except Craver is scheduled for an MRI this evening. We'll hijack his infusion pump and get it to withhold his morphine for a few hours, then give him a blast right before the test. His breathing will be terrible, so he won't be able to lie still. He's got to be still for an MRI. They'll call anesthesia because he is high-risk, given his cigarettes and lung disease. They'll put him to sleep and provide breathing support. Craver will have one final moment of consciousness before he fades to black, permanently."

"But wouldn't any competent anesthesiologist check his family history first?"

"Craver doesn't know about his risk or why his aunt and brother died, and we scrubbed their medical records. If his lawyer is looking to sue over his sudden, tragic death, he'll find no ammunition there. We also plugged in that two of Craver's kids had surgery with no problem—information we'll delete the moment he's put under. The anesthesiologist could never figure it out with that many misdirections."

As he rubbed the St. Christopher's medal in his pocket, Torrence paraphrased the Book of Job, "The EHR giveth and it taketh away."

~

Six hours later, Ben Craver's labored breathing caused some mild concern in the MRI suite.

"Can you stay still?" the anesthesiologist asked patiently.

Craver didn't respond.

"Let's make this easier for you, Mr. Craver," he said, placing a face-fitting green-colored clear plastic mask over Craver's mouth and nose. With high levels of morphine bathing his brain cells, they'd decided to use a very low dose of an inhaled anesthetic, isoflurane.

It was safe, with a short half-life, and if worst came to worst, they could just use the self-inflating Ambu bag to provide positive pressure, forcing oxygen into Craver's lungs until the isoflurane was out of his system.

"Just breathe in a bit, sir. This will make you groggy."

Within moments, Craver's eyes sagged shut. He was asleep.

Suddenly, his eyes burst open. His heart raced and his face burned. He couldn't breathe and he couldn't move. His wrists were fixed to the hard, cold MRI table with soft, cloth restraints. All he could see was the cylinder that surrounded him. His panic surged and he struggled to free himself.

"You seeing that heart rate?" the radiology resident called out to the anesthesiology resident.

"Shit."

"He's starting to move. Maybe you need to give him more gas."

The resident increased the rate and Craver calmed.

But then the blood pressure alarm blared as the monitor beep, beep, beeped—185 over 110.

"Abort the test."

Behind the control room window, the radiologist punched in the command to back Craver out of the MRI machine. The table where Craver lay abruptly reversed directions. In twenty seconds, Craver was out. The anesthesiology resident rushed to him. Craver was unresponsive.

"Call my attending, stat, and get me some help. I'm going to have to intubate him. Get the crash cart."

A moment later, two nurses ran into the room, one pushing a big red cart with drawers.

"Sux."

"What?"

"I need succinylcholine, stat. He's waking up and thrashing around and not getting enough O2." With every passing moment, Craver was becoming more combative, fighting for air.

The anesthesiology resident plunged a syringe into the IV tubing. Craver felt the flow of the cool, clear liquid into his vein. His hands tingled, and within a moment, he was unable to move. The anesthesia resident jerked Craver's jaw down, opened his mouth, and thrust a hard, cold blade over his tongue.

"Suction, I've got to get some suction here."

CODED TO KILL

One of the nurses ran to the wall, plugging in a tube. The other stood by helplessly.

"You—get a blood gas, stat, with sodium and potassium," yelled the anesthesiology resident. "And get my attending, dammit. This is going in the wrong direction."

Within two minutes, the room was filled with interns, residents, nurses, and an anesthesiologist from the operating room.

"What did you do?"

"Nothing. Just gave him some isoflurane. It was working, then his heart rate shot up and his BP spiked. We aborted the MRI, gave him sux, and intubated him. Two minutes after that, he's wildly hypertensive, 225 over 150. I've got no idea what is going on."

"Feel his forehead. He's burning up," said the anesthesiologist. "He's got malignant hyperthermia. The isoflurane might have started it, but the succinylcholine really got him going. Get some dantrolene to reverse the symptoms, now."

"There's none on the crash cart."

"Get it from the OR. Run!"

As the anesthesiology resident rushed out the door, the nurse by the monitor yelled, "V-fib!"

The monitor screamed a continuous tone. "Forget the dantrolene," said the anesthesiologist. "Get over here and do CPR."

Tyler Jensen paused just outside MRI Room 1. Doctors and nurses were running in and out. Stat code calls were blasting over the speakers. Alarm, panic, no reassuring monitor beeps. Perfect.

~

Derrick Mumsford cursed and slammed his fist on his desk so hard that the wood seemed to answer, *thwump*, in rattling pain. "Darlene!" he shouted to his executive assistant. "Get Justine Peterman on the phone right now!"

Yesterday, it was Aaron Goldstein. Today, Craver, one of his most generous benefactors. Dead. In his hospital.

Darlene buzzed in. "Dr. Peterman is on line four."

"Peterman? Mumsford here. I just got my ass chewed out by Ben Craver, Jr. He's saying that we killed his old man. I know he wasn't your patient, but his doctors are under you. What do you know?"

"I'd seen him previously, not for his present problems, though," Peterman responded forcefully. "He died. The anesthesiologist said it was a complication as rare as hen's teeth. Malignant hyperthermia." Peterman thought, *Had they— she—missed something?*

"He'll be lawyered up yesterday. I sure as hell hope there is nothing incriminating in his medical record. You know he donated the money for our big auditorium renovation in honor of his father. Plus, he's given millions more. I'm not surprised his son is busting my chops."

Peterman remained silent.

"You there, Justine?"

"Yes. Just got a page. I'll have to call you back later."

There was no page. Peterman just needed some quiet to try once more to understand how two of her patients could have died unexpectedly in two days. That was a first. Was she slipping? Burned out? The stress and feelings of inadequacy were not new. It had been months, maybe years since she'd felt like herself. She'd followed the advice she'd given to so many other doctors who struggled: don't be afraid to seek help. She sought psychiatric help, far from Drexel, at the Massachusetts General Hospital. A prescription for an antidepressant, bupropion, helped. It settled her moods, but she still had trouble sleeping. That led to a prescription for Ambien. It knocked her out, but she didn't feel as sharp the next day, so she took it sparingly.

With the weight of Craver's unforeseen death now on her shoulders, she was feeling withdrawn, remarkably unable to do what she had done for decades. She was about to call her psychiatrist when a wave of relief rushed over her—an undefined moment of clarity. This was what she did best: figure out medical mysteries.

Snapping herself back to the immediate problem, she focused on Goldstein and Craver. She opened the EHR on her laptop and began reviewing their medical records, looking for what was there—and what wasn't.

CHAPTER 18

"You know what I thought when it hit me, boys?"

Elvin Walters was holding court at the Press Club, his Southern accent in high gear. The media had been speculating on his fainting spell and it was time to provide some answers—his answers. He wouldn't tell them that it wasn't his first episode or that his cardiologist at Drexel had told him he had "a potentially lethal arrhythmia" and that he was "lucky to be alive."

And he certainly wouldn't share his plans to have a cardiac defibrillator implanted before week's end.

Instead, Walters looked with practiced sincerity at the assembled press. "Figured someone working for one of those three letter agencies…" Walters paused to let the reporters fill in the blanks (NSA, CIA, FBI), "had finally decided to do me in. With tuna! Bless their heart. Of course, I'm joking. Write that down. We're all on the same side: America's side."

After laughing off his fainting episode, Walters moved to phase two of the damage control strategy his team had cooked up: sounding tough to dispel those images of weakness. "But even a family has its differences, and that's what the sunshine laws are all about. The federal government spends more than a trillion bucks a year on health care. What the hell are we getting for that? If the American people aren't getting full and fair value for their hard-earned money, then who's got their snout in the trough? And what else are they up to? It stinks. Now, somebody's got to clean up this mess by getting the facts out in the open. It looks like I'm the only one with the guts to do it. Let the sun shine, shine, shine."

With that, he was off. His accent went from folksy to country as he offered a word salad of innuendo about black budgets, privacy, and unnamed bad actors that made it seem like he was taking a principled stand.

"Seems to me that a lot of that money goes through the National Institute for Medical Safety to improve health care. Or is it Health and Human Services, or the CDC, or Medicare, or what? And this is what we have to show for it?"

He shook his head from side to side, miming a sad look. Then he burst back into hyperbole.

"The whole damned bunch of them are crooked. They say they're telling us the truth. Hell, those boys wouldn't know the truth if it bit 'em in the ass. The truth to them is whatever version of the story they think they can get away with. And it's just getting worse what with all the computerized databases. They've got unlimited computing power, a ready source of deviant computer geniuses, and no scruples at all. There ain't a fact they don't know about your life and health. They got you pegged by your social security number.

They know where you buy your booze and what that hooch is doing to your liver. Hell, they probably know the websites you're cruising while you're telling your editor that you're writing your story." He raised an eyebrow whimsically at the press corps. "Big Brother ain't just a character in a novel. He's being born before our eyes. And, like all births, it ain't pretty."

One of Walter's interns had planted a question about nationalized health care with their favorite reporter. Walters started off on a tear about health care costs. It was his usual spiel. He even referenced electronic health records. The next day's stories would barely mention his fainting spell as they described his demand for transparency.

~

Charles Richmond grabbed the remote and angrily shut off the plasma screen TV in his office. Walters may not have made much sense, but his brief mention of the EHR fed Richmond's creeping concerns: *Did Walters know how the Drexel EHR had come to be? Did he know things Richmond had even kept from Hugh Torrence? Torrence would kill him, literally. And that might be the easy way out compared with the scandal of exposure. What he and the Cellar gang had accomplished, and how it was funded, was an explosive secret. For now, it was buried. But as a long-serving senator, Walters had sources available to few. And he had an agenda.*

This was the first time that Walters had mentioned the National Institute for Medical Safety. It was just in passing, but maybe he was just warming up. The man was on a rampage. Richmond's connection to Drexel was no secret. The only secret was the money—how Richmond siphoned many millions from Drexel's share of the HITECH Act and funneled it to Torrence. Derrick Mumsford knew nothing of the Cellar, but he did approve the off-the-books transfer of funds to the National Institute, agreeing to account for the money by inflating the line items for other expenses. Mumsford wasn't happy about it. But he trusted Richmond, his college classmate who had helped land the Drexel job and told him the National Institute needed the funds to support the EHR but that a formal financial relationship between the two would be frowned on. *Now there was a conspiracy theory that Walters could talk about for months.* A conspiracy theory Walters could ride all the way to Pennsylvania Avenue while sending Richmond to a Supermax.

Just a few years earlier, Richmond and Torrence had been stuck in traffic, and the conversation naturally drifted towards how to rid the world of Walters. The senator was such a high-profile figure that they agreed there was no clean shot. His death would trigger a massive investigation. Given his life-long criticism of the intelligence community, they would come under intense scrutiny.

But that was before the emergence of the EHR, the invisible instrument of death. It was also before last week when, after a drink or two past his limit, Derrick Mumsford told him that Walters was getting health care at Drexel. He would continue to keep Torrence in the dark about that—but for how long? If Walters kept up his tirade, he would soon be agreeing with Torrence on how to deal with the old blowhard. An added bonus: his patron in Florida would be more than pleased if a chief rival to control the GOP went toes up.

Just then, Richmond's iPhone began to buzz. It was an email from Torrence—*a coincidence, or is he more insidious than I imagined?* It got worse. The note was a forwarded email from Benny, six words, all lowercase with minimal punctuation. What was it with these millennials?

jd-17 coming to drexel, big opportunity

He picked up his phone and dialed Torrence's mobile. Torrence picked up.

"Got my text, huh?"

"What do you have?"

"Took some time, but we know what's up with the John Doe identities."

"What does that mean?" Richmond said, feigning ignorance. He'd known they were working on patient identification. They'd get it figured out one day, and it sounded like today was that day.

"It's complicated, but so sweet. How soon can you get here?"

Richmond glanced at the clock on his desk. "No way this afternoon. My schedule is packed."

"You've got to hear it in person. How about tomorrow?"

"I don't know...."

"We play this thing right, the sky's the limit. You'll be glad you made the trip, trust me."

"Okay, I'll be there. Give me a hint, though. Anything."

"You'll be thanking me for the rest of your life. That's the hint."

CHAPTER

19

TUESDAY, MAY 10
5:35 PM
DURHAM, NORTH CAROLINA

The waiter lowered the shades, blocking the late afternoon
sun burning through the plate glass window. Cool air wafted
in from above. The wood paneling was genuine, the bourbon
smooth, and the bowl of deluxe mixed nuts in front of them
warm. Nothing was as simple as it seemed. For Mumsford, it
was the patient deaths; for Burgess, the ever-present concerns
about the security of Drexel's EHR. Tonight, as they settled
into the soft, deep burgundy leather chairs at their usual table
at the Drexel Club, it was about to get worse.

"The talk yesterday seemed to juice up interest,"
Mumsford said. "The CEO of Wells Fargo called this morning about preferred stock in DrexelMed. The fourth call I've
had from an investment banker in the last twelve hours."

Mumsford swirled the ten-year-old Pappy van Winkle
bourbon in his snifter, almost afraid to ask Burgess, "How's it
going on your end?"

"Well, two high-profile people died this week, as you know," replied Burgess. "But those tragedies don't have anything to do with the EHR. The way I understand it, they both were complicated patients. Craver was a one in a million, particularly given the guy had never had anesthesia at his age."

"Knock on wood," Mumsford responded, "there doesn't appear to be any liability for us, despite what the plaintiff buzzards will say."

"I know Carrie's had it tough, too," Burgess said. "Goldstein was one of her patients."

"She's such a compassionate kid, and it's even harder for her because of her concerns about patient safety."

"Maybe we should call it a day so you can spend some time with her," offered Burgess.

"I asked if she wanted to have dinner tonight, but she stiffed me. She has a date."

"Who's the lucky guy?" Burgess knew, of course.

"Mason Fischer. He's that cardiologist from Texas who joined us late last year. Carrie likes him. But he's almost a dozen years older than her, too old. A jock from Texas isn't exactly the type to be Carrie's soulmate. It won't last."

"Fischer," Burgess said. "He's the Zelig of medicine, here, there, everywhere."

"How's that?" Mumsford asked.

"His name came up at my Harvard reunion. One of my classmates, Dick Henderson, wanted to tell me about him."

"Fischer went to Harvard?"

"Nah, Henderson did. They both worked at the medical school in Galveston until Fischer left. Henderson said they practically ran him out on a rail after some patients died unexpectedly."

"You're shitting me."

"Maybe it was nothing. Henderson was hammered by the time we talked. Weaving and slurring all over the place. When I tried to pin him down further, he stopped talking. It was odd, as if he'd gone a little too far. He just said to keep an eye on him, that Fischer's a loose cannon."

"Do you believe him?"

"The guy's a drunk, but he's not insane. That said, there's nothing in Fischer's personnel file or other records to suggest any problems. I will say, though, he does seem particularly interested in the EHR."

Looking down at his glass, Burgess lifted an eye to gauge whether he'd gotten Mumsford's attention. Mumsford looked off into the distance.

Burgess continued. "I don't have to tell you the last thing we need is a crazy doctor running around mouthing off, especially about the EHR. We already have Peterman for that. Like all the docs, Fischer has his list of complaints."

Mumsford leaned in and squinted, swirling the last drops of bourbon around the glass. "Anything to them?"

Reading Mumsford perfectly, Burgess tried reassurance. "He's like all the rest. He talks in anecdotes. Yeah, every once in a while, the system slows down and it takes longer to enter an order. Three times, we've had to go offline during the day. Never more than ten minutes. There's the 2 AM maintenance we do most weeks. That's no different than it was with the old system."

"You're sure. No problems to worry about?"

Burgess gave it one more try. "At this point, absolutely everything is on track. With time, we'll get the maintenance down to short periods. It's just a matter of bandwidth. And we've kept it safe. Let me remind you, we've never had a single successful hack. In fact, the number of attempted intrusions is decreasing because the hacker community is beginning to realize it's impossible." Burgess's facts were correct; his explanation was wishful thinking. He'd never heard of a system hackers wouldn't go after—the harder the better. Until now. But, as usual, he wasn't inclined to interrogate his own luck.

Mumsford relaxed, visibly relieved.

"We've got to be right on this. Walters is coming in this week. Everything has to be perfect."

Burgess just nodded. But he was worried. Probably time to give Charles Richmond an update; the man seemed to have answers before you even asked the question.

~

The neurons firing in Mason's brain brought more confusion than clarity. Goldstein's death seemed highly improbable; to have lightning strike twice with Craver…. Something was wrong, but what?

He also couldn't get Carrie out of his mind. He had told himself that he needed her as an avenue to her father, Burgess, and their thinking about the EHR. That was still true. Now, he had other reasons for wanting to see her that he was afraid to admit to himself.

He shed his gloves and gown and paged her. "How about going out to dinner tonight?" She responded immediately to his text, with a terseness that felt like a one-two punch.

"Not likely," was her reply.

Did she have other plans? he wondered like a teenager. "Busy?"

"Nope."

He dialed her number.

"That was fast," she laughed.

"So?"

"Instead of going out, why don't you come over to my place?"

"Want to show me your etchings?" Mason joked. "How about if I pick up a couple of nice steaks for the grill?"

"A cardiologist eating steak?"

"It's all in how you grill them. Texas-style adds years to your life."

"Right. I'll make a salad to dilute the cholesterol. Better get here soon."

~

Mason knocked on Carrie's door an hour later, heard her steps, and stuck his eyeball up to the peephole.

"Very funny," said Carrie as she opened the door. Her denim work shirt was unbuttoned halfway down, and her eyes said the rest as she leaned up and kissed him.

"Come in here," she said, grabbing him by the hand, then leading him down the short hallway. She took his hands in hers and backed into the bedroom. "Dinner can wait."

Carrie pushed Mason back onto the bed and climbed on top.

The first time was a violent collision of bodies that left them both beaded with sweat and panting for breath. Somewhere in the fray, the rest of their clothes had magically disappeared and were wadded on the floor. The second time was slower, gentler, more tender. Afterward, they lay holding each other in bed until Mason summoned the strength to get up and light the charcoal and start the steaks.

"Tell me something personal, something that made you who you are," Carrie said, joining him on the patio.

Silence.

"Oh, come on. Something, anything, about your father or your mother."

"I already told you," Mason responded, a little too forcefully. "My mother died when I was three. I've seen lots of photos but don't remember her at all."

"Then your father. Tell me your fondest memory."

"Fondest?"

"Yes."

"Okay." Mason thought for a long minute.

"I grew up on a ranch, in Texas."

"I know that, you dummy."

"One day Pop told me he was going to take me noodling for catfish.

"Noodling? What's that?"

"It's kind of like fishing with a noodle, instead of a hook, and your arm is the noodle. You reach down the catfish's mouth into its gullet and yank it out. No mean feat."

"Lovely."

"There was a river that ran through our ranch, the Llano River. The riverbed is limestone and a lot of the water is from springs. There are shallow rapids over big rocks and lots of big deep pools. It's so clear that on a good day, you can see clearly enough to watch a bass catch a minnow in ten feet of water."

"The big reveal is you caught some fish?" asked Carrie.

"Patience. One day Pop mentioned a local guy, Judge Latham, who knew of a special place in the river near our house. There was a big rock with a small pool of deep water near it. Judge Latham told us that the huge catfish hung there. He positioned me and my pop so that the fish couldn't get past us into the main river. We stood there, with our hands and legs in the water. The judge waded in, up to his neck, just below the rock. I saw him reaching around with his hands. Then I felt a big bump against my legs, and then another. Pop did too. 'Stay steady, boys,' yelled the judge.

"All we could see was him poking his arm down underneath the rock, over and over again. Then he yelled 'Bingo,' and hauled up the biggest catfish I'd ever seen. Must have been fifty pounds. His right arm was stuck down the monster's mouth and he was hoisting it with his left arm underneath its belly. Damnedest thing I ever saw."

"So, your most touching childhood experience was somebody sticking his arm under a rock and pulling it out with his hand in a catfish's stomach?"

"It was life-changing."

Carrie rolled her eyes. She had asked him to confide in her and he'd told her a fishing story.

"Carrie," he said, pulling her close. "It really is meaningful."

She straightened herself. "Okay, bozo, let's hear you talk your way out of this one."

"I'll try," said Mason, smiling. "After the judge pulled off the catfish, he laid it on the water in front of us. The fish just lay there, working its gills, slowly moving its tail, almost like when a dog lies at your feet. But this was a huge catfish. The judge slowly worked his arm out of its mouth. Then with a whip of the big tail, the monster was gone. I was disappointed. I'd wanted to hold it up, get a photo, something to show what we'd done. Pop told me it wasn't about catching fish."

"Then what was it about?"

"Later that night, the three of us sat there on a sand bar in the middle of the river, grilling steaks and cooking foil-wrapped potatoes in a big campfire. Turned out the judge and my father were good friends. The judge started talking to me. I'll never forget that conversation.

'Mason, did you feel that fish bumping into your legs?' he'd started.

'Yes, sir,' I'd answered him. 'I kept him boxed in, just like you told me to.'

'He wasn't trying to get away, son. He was trying to run you off.'

'Why?' I'd asked.

'You were in his special place, son. He didn't want you there.'

'But then you caught him?'

'Did I catch him? Or did he catch me?' the judge responded.

"We kept on talking, but nothing more eye-opening. I was only about ten, and I never really got over why we didn't just keep that old catfish and get it mounted, or fry it up."

"Mason?" prompted Carrie. He was staring off at nothing.

"About ten years later was the last time I talked with my pop before he died. Maybe he knew the end was coming. We went back out to the sandbar and grilled steaks, just like we'd done twenty times before. He asked me if I remembered when we went noodling with the judge. I said, 'Of course.' Pop told me he knew I couldn't understand it then, but maybe I could now. He said 'Sometimes, son, we don't ever know whether we got what we were looking for, or it got us. Like that catfish. Did the judge catch the catfish, or did the catfish catch the judge? Think about that in your life, whenever you're feeling really good about yourself. Was that really your accomplishment, or was it somebody else's?'"

"Your dad was wise."

"Indeed. Coming over here tonight, I was thinking about how I came to Drexel and got involved with the EHR, trying to understand it. I've told you about the little stuff that worries me. Some days, I think that Bud Burgess believes I'm trying to tear down what he and your father have built."

"No. I know you're not."

"Let me finish, Carrie. Then there's you. I've never felt like this about anyone before."

It was a truth he had not wanted to recognize.

"Here I've been, feeling so good about myself that I found someone like you. But now I realize I am taking too much credit, attributing it all to my delightful personality and dashing good looks. The fact is, I didn't catch you. I was just in the right place at the right time, and we found each other."

Carrie didn't know what to say. As she listened, she tried to reconcile the playful but intensely private, maybe secretive, man she'd been seeing these past few months with the earnest person telling this heartfelt story. She wanted the story to dissolve the nagging doubts she had about what—about who— Mason was. And it just about did. However, she hadn't gotten through her mother's death, the challenges of being Derrick Mumsford's daughter, and the tribulations of medical school without developing a wary steeliness.

Mason continued, "When you were telling me about your family, I thought about mine. Maybe my dad was right. In the end, it doesn't matter at all whether I caught you, or you caught me. We got caught and that's all that matters."

She kissed him—a long, tender kiss. "I'd never have imagined a fish story would hook me like that," she quipped, eyes twinkling.

"Promise me this, okay?"

"With that story, anything."

"I don't know how things are going to work out, but whatever happens, don't ever doubt that I honestly care for you in ways that surprise even me."

Carrie looked at him, searchingly. Her mind repeated two words: *fish story*.

~

Around 1 AM, Bud Burgess plopped down in front of his high-octane computer with its twin oversized flat screens. He took a run or two at the EHR, nothing too innovative, just enough to keep the boys on their toes. But his heart wasn't in it tonight.

He toggled over to Google and started tracking Mason Fischer. Something about Fischer was bugging him. He'd read everything he could find on the Net and the usual databases. He decided this time he'd try images. A few dozen appeared on the screen. Most from Fischer's football days in high school and college, precious few were more recent. He called up Fischer's Drexel ID photo and squinted. Was it all the same guy? Hard to say. Pattern recognition was his life, and the patterns weren't identical. The nose had gotten sharper over time. *Normal aging? Perhaps. Plastic surgery? Unlikely.*

An injury on the field? Probably. He glanced at it and then away. Same thing when he looked back. No logical explanation; it just didn't seem to fit. Burgess had access to facial recognition software but put that on hold for the moment.

He scrolled down his list of dark websites, places with federal tax returns, billing records, credit card accounts, known addresses, and phone numbers. Back and forth he went, using Mason's social security number, birthdate, phone numbers, and known addresses. Gaps emerged, small but significant to his trained and somewhat paranoid mind. One time for six months, another time for nearly a year. Where had he been? What had he been doing? Fischer's military record didn't give a clue.

Burgess didn't know what to think. *Should he worry?* There was no answer. Fischer, after all, had breezed through all the steps required for hospital privileges. He came with the finest credentials and recommendations. The criminal background check, the check of state medical board records, the fingerprint analysis—all were clear. There was nothing there. The photos could have a logical explanation, as could the missing time and even Fischer's constant questions about the EHR. And then there was the dirt his Harvard classmate, Richard Henderson, had unloaded at the reunion.

Was Fischer's twisting and turning path through his career just the way life can happen? Or was a troubling pattern emerging?

History had proven time and time again that medicine's most notorious miscreants were sociopaths. Clever enough to get away with their crimes for long periods, but ultimately undone because they favored a particular form of death. Antoinette Scieri killed at least a dozen patients by poisoning them with the herbicide pyralion. Kristen Heather Gilbert was convicted of killing four patients by injecting their IV bags with epinephrine, triggering massive heart attacks. Niels Högel used the same approach, but a broader range of drugs—including ajmaline, sotalol, lidocaine, amiodarone, and calcium chloride—to murder perhaps ninety patients.

If Fischer were a psycho—responsible for deaths at Drexel and Galveston—then his pattern most closely resembled that of Richard Angelo, the famed "angel of death," who would give his patients a lethal injection and then heroically try to save them.

Of course, all of those killers were nurses except Dr. Michael Swango, who was now a permanent resident of the ADX Supermax Prison in Fremont, Colorado. Doctors don't show as much interest in killing their patients—or maybe they are too smart to get caught.

Still, Burgess thought, *patterns don't lie.*

There was definitely a pattern of events, and Fischer certainly played the role of the handsome, charismatic jock well. Well enough to snag Carrie Mumsford. That pairing might have been a lot more than a coincidence.

Patterns.

When Richmond arrived at the Plantation that morning, Torrence and the kid, Benny, were waiting for him.
Introductions were made. There was an awkward silence.

"You said you have some news to share, Hugh? Urgent
news that necessitated this trip?" Richmond said, "Something
that involves young Benny?"

Richmond's face gave away nothing. Not anger or impa-
tience. No anxious anticipation.

Torrence knew Richmond's game and was content to wait
him out. Not Benny. Before Torrence could answer, Benny
blurted, "John Doe 17."

Torrence shot him the death stare. The kid might be a
computer genius, but he had a lot to learn about controlling
and manipulating the thoughts and feelings of others.

"Benny has a rather unique skill set, although it doesn't include restraint. Benny, proceed. Charles, you judge whether your trip was worth this tidbit."

Richmond directed his attention to Benny dispassionately.

"Okay, you know about Drexel's John Doe system for deadbeats and charity cases?"

Richmond gave a small nod of acknowledgement.

"It's also used for hotshots who want to be anonymous. They have a different system now, and none of them has kept their old John Doe identity. Except for one, John Doe 17. Guess who he is."

Richmond stared at him blankly.

"Elvin freaking Walters. That's who. And he's gonna be in the hospital on Sunday."

Richmond appeared completely unfazed, even as his heart did flip-flops. *They couldn't be monitoring my communications with Burgess. Mumsford must have spilled the beans on his tapped phone or email. How else could Benny have figured that out?* "Elvin Walters?" he said. "Drexel? Interesting. Frankly, I'm surprised, Hugh. As a senior senator, Walters gets free medical care at Walter Reed. It doesn't get any better than that."

Torrence took over from Benny. "He's been going to Drexel for years for his heart. We have him on the hospital closed-circuit recordings. Facial recognition software confirms it. The EHR, times, dates, it's perfect. He may not be a bum like a lot of the other John Does, but he does have a bum ticker."

Torrence smiled smugly. "Worth the trip, old pal?"

Richmond narrowed his gaze. "It is. When are you going to release this to the press? They will not look kindly on lying about a serious medical condition."

"We have something better," Torrence said. "We're going to give the EHR a final test run before it goes national."

"I see," Richmond said. "Ten years. That's a very cold plate of revenge, Hugh."

As he spoke, Richmond's mind ran through the permutations—all of which involved the relative risks to himself. Knocking off Walters would silence a self-righteous bastard who was one of the EHR's main critics. It would remove a potential rival to Richmond's own dreams of occupying the Oval Office, and it would also please Torrence, which was good for Richmond. On the other hand, it could ruin all their plans.

"Walters dying in the hospital certainly raises the stakes," Richmond mused. "I don't want to tell you your business, but getting around his security will be challenging, and if you succeed, his death might bring unnecessary attention to the EHR, don't you think?"

"We're working on that," Torrence replied brusquely.

"On the other hand," Richmond continued, "if Walters is coming for some secret procedure for a medical condition he's hidden from the public, his family will not demand a full inquiry into his death. You and your team will determine how to do it. Post-mortem, I can suggest that it will be best for all if, say, he felt chest pains for an undiagnosed condition and rushed to the closest hospital, which was Drexel. Anyone who dies within twenty-four hours of hospital admission in North Carolina is required to have an autopsy. Drexel has the best pathology department around. They'll find he has severe heart disease. You must find a means that is absolutely untraceable—that is essential. Then, and only then, this might be the right play."

Torrence and Richmond smiled at one another.

Benny looked at them in awe. On the outside, Richmond and Torrence were different phenotypes, Richmond with his suave aristocratic presence, Torrence with his G-man gruffness.

Inside, they were the same. Cold, ruthless bastards. Totally focused on their own goals. Those traits had helped them grasp what they already possessed and would be key to seizing what they still desired. Benny just had to make sure he stayed out of their line of fire.

Right now, when their aspirations aligned, Torrence and Richmond were an indomitable team. If, one day, either saw an advantage in separation, it would be ugly. Richmond or Torrence? There could only be one king of their jungle.

Benny was getting quite an education.

21

WEDNESDAY, MAY 11
2:20 PM
DREXEL MEMORIAL HOSPITAL

It wasn't the fact that RT was alone in the empty hospital corridor that caught Mason's attention. Or that he was carrying a silver laptop with a long black antenna that flopped back and forth as he moved. Or even that the Bluetooth headset with a long antenna made him look like a Martian.

Instead, it was the odd manner in which RT was working his way down the hall. He'd take a few cautious steps. Then stop. Stand perfectly still, hunched over the laptop, listening. After fifteen or twenty seconds he'd rest the laptop on one of the small tables in the corridor and type for a few seconds.

Mason watched in silence.

When he couldn't stand it any longer, he spoke loudly in RT's direction.

"What are you doing?"

RT's head shot up with a startled look, and he fumbled the laptop, grabbing it before it fell to the floor.

"Damn, man. Don't go sneaking up on people."

"You look like you ought to be in the psych ward, wandering down the hall like that. All you need is a bathrobe."

"Sure, laugh. But this is serious shit that I'm up to."

Mason cocked his head quizzically.

He is one curious cat, RT thought. "You know how just about everything at the hospital is connected."

"The Internet of Things," Mason said.

"You got it. All that connection creates certain vulnerabilities. It's becoming a major concern for companies, hospitals, power vendors. The idea that someone could hack one machine and spread malware over their entire connected system is for real."

"Again, what are you doing?"

"I'm mapping where we have signals extending out to hallways or anywhere else a clever hacker could sit. Our wireless traffic is up two hundred percent from only three months ago. Most likely, it's just more people watching Netflix or Tik Tok on their phones."

"So just block them."

"Take away their constitutional right to watch movies on their lunch hour? Man, that would be ten times worse than that uprising last year when they closed the parking lot and people had to take shuttle buses. No, the problem is that some outsider could log into our wireless network."

"And then they'd be in the system!" Mason exclaimed. "That could explain it."

"Explain what?"

"I had a patient who died in the ER, Jesse Gutierrez. Someone put up the wrong X-ray and it got everyone looking in the wrong direction. And another one of my patients,

Aaron Goldstein. Everything pointed to his potassium being way out of whack, but his records showed no potassium had been ordered, and his level was normal."

A thought he didn't want crept into RT's mind: *Both men who died were Fischer's patients. The man has rotten luck, or...*

"Man, I don't know about potassium levels, but just getting into the system is a far cry from what you're talking about. The EHR is programmed to override bad orders, so that ought to stop 'em in their tracks. But between you, me, and the wall, I'm not so sure our system is as perfect as Burgess says. Almost anything you can imagine is possible with these connected devices. If someone was up to no good, they would have left a trail. I'll look into it."

"You do that. Trusting machines to do a human's work has caused more than a few catastrophes."

RT and Drexel's IT team spent the rest of the afternoon performing a precise forensic analysis of every digital signal sent and received by the devices involved in Gutierrez's and Goldstein's treatment. There was nothing unusual—no strange orders, malfunctions, or odd IP addresses. Worried that he might have missed something, RT had even called in Burgess, who ran through all the data and came to the same conclusion: Fischer was wrong. There was no evidence that the EHR had been compromised. But something prevented RT from completely trusting the facts, the evidence, the record they had assembled and analyzed. Fischer had seemed so sure that it gave him pause. After Burgess left, RT phoned his Uncle Alphonse. He'd know what to do.

~

Bud Burgess also had nagging doubts as he sat alone in his corner office, staring out at the lights of Durham. Despite his bravado with Derrick Mumsford, he was concerned—and the afternoon session with RT had done nothing to calm him. Something wasn't right, and, as was almost never the case, he had no idea what to do.

Before this week, he could confidently dismiss Carrie Mumsford's concerns about patient safety as bleeding-heart claptrap. But not now, not with two patients unexpectedly dead. Fischer was right about the problem—the wrong X-ray had shown up in the Gutierrez case. He'd attributed that to human error. Goldstein died of what looked like classic hyperkalemia, but the orders showed he hadn't been administered any potassium, and his level from the stat lab was normal. He could not come up with a logical explanation. Craver's death was a one-in-a-million genetic mutation. His analysis had given the EHR a clean bill of health, but he couldn't shake the suspicion that someone might be manipulating his creation.

His mind kept returning to the doctor who had treated two of the dead patients: Mason Fischer. He remembered the now ominous detail his drunken classmate Richard Henderson had told him at their Harvard reunion: a patient of Fischer's in Galveston had died with sky-high potassium.

Serial killers have their signature—was potassium Fischer's? What if the guy was not just noticing those EHR glitches, but engineering them? It was time to fill in Charles Richmond on his concerns.

~

Carrie paid for her nitro cold-brew coffee and headed to the corner table where Justine Peterman sat, sipping a piping-hot tall green tea.

"Hot tea on a hot day?" Carrie remarked.

"Maybe you missed that class where they showed it cools you down," Peterman replied with a smile. "Are you hanging in there?"

"Sort of," answered Carrie. "I really hate watching people die in the hospital who shouldn't. Isn't that what the preventable harm movement is all about?"

"First Aaron Goldstein, then Ben Craver. It makes no sense." Peterman nodded. "I've been praying on it."

"You're religious? I thought that was verboten in our line of work."

"I don't wait on miracles, but only a fool would believe that life is limited to what we can see, hear, and know. I'm part Choctaw. After med school, I worked for a few years on the reservation in Durant, Oklahoma. A truly magical place, but full of human suffering. The Choctaw were a proud people for centuries. Now, 150 years after being relocated to the reservation, they've been destroyed by the ills of the white man. Alcohol, drugs, obesity, diabetes…you name it. I was the only doctor for a hundred miles. I saw more than I wanted to, and probably less than I needed to. It took me a while to realize I couldn't save them all. At the end of the day, I told myself that if I'd helped someone, anyone, it was a good day. On a good day, it was only one or two of the thirty or more I saw, but it was gratifying. And I loved the people."

Carrie nodded. The steely reserve she'd developed to demonstrate her professionalism weakened as repressed emotions began to flow in the safety of Peterman's company.

"I'm telling you this because the Choctaw helped save me. They showed me that there are more things in heaven and earth than are dreamt of in our philosophy, or our medical books and machines. They helped me appreciate that people are mind and body *and* spirit. There's a difference between knowledge and wisdom. I think women can be more attuned to this than men. That makes life harder, especially in a high-stress, high-stakes field like the one we've chosen because we know and feel more deeply."

"Sometimes, I wish I could just take my dad's advice and shake it off."

"Then you'd stop being you, a brilliant, committed, and caring physician."

"You seem to understand it so well."

"Trust me, I have my demons like everyone else. The main thing is to keep the main thing the main thing." Justine chuckled. "I saw that on a bumper sticker. But there's a wisdom there. You can work twenty hours a day and there will still be people like poor Mr. Goldstein who have a tragic outcome. That happens outside the hospital every day. A drunk walks away from a horrific accident, while a wonderful mother looks away from the wheel for an instant and dies in a wreck. My point is that you can't fix everything, but you can save a few—maybe even yourself."

She paused.

"Even if we accept that there are forces, for good and ill, that are beyond our control, it doesn't mean we can ever stop trying to understand the world and fix what's broken." Carrie shook her head.

"Like the EHR?"

"Exactly. It's a great tool; it is full of knowledge, but it lacks wisdom. That's the Faustian bargain we're making when we remove that most human quality from medicine. And those bargains never turn out well as I fear Goldstein and Craver might attest. I'm going to delve into both of their records tonight. I'll let you know what I find."

CHAPTER

22

WEDNESDAY, MAY 11
9:15 PM
STONEBRIDGE ESTATES, DURHAM

"*What the hell is going on?*" Justine Peterman asked herself with mounting frustration as she scoured Ben Craver's medical record once again in her home office. She'd turned to Craver after failing to find anything untoward in Aaron Goldstein's file. She knew something was wrong and was hoping Craver's file might be more revealing. She still hadn't found anything that could explain Craver's reaction to the anesthesia; his family history, medical records, and even his genome suggested no vulnerability. Now, Peterman was asking a more fundamental question—*why did Craver need anesthesia at all, especially for a simple MRI?*

She looked at the notes: "patient uncomfortable," "can't stay still," "labored breathing."

As Peterman's cursor scrolled over these words, one of the geeks in the Cellar noticed and alerted Benny.

What's on the doctor's mind? Benny asked himself.

142

CODED TO KILL

Benny saw a Word document pop up on Peterman's home computer titled "Craver." It had a running commentary of her questions, numbered in order. The most recent, written just ninety seconds ago, asked: "5 mg IV push, repeat as necessary??? Who the hell wrote that order?" It listed a doctor, an anesthesia resident. This was a major medical error. With no stop parameters, an unwitting nurse or assistant could have given Craver fifteen milligrams, twenty milligrams, or more, over a short period of time. *But why was Craver so restless in the first place?* she wondered. There was no notation of a change in status otherwise. No pain, no acknowledged anxiety or dyspnea. Craver's morphine dose had been stable for days. But that didn't sync with the toxicology from the autopsy. Morphine levels were sub-therapeutic. That was impossible.

Little did Peterman know that Benny, with Van der Graf on the phone, was rapidly fixing inconsistencies in Craver's medical record. Peterman's long perusal of Craver's final hour was bad news, especially as Fischer had looked at the same section of the record earlier in the day. Benny would not tell Torrence this news, not until he knew more. But it was time to call Saied.

It got worse.

Peterman resumed typing what seemed to be a draft email.

Derrick:

As you know, security concerns exist with any EHR. Recent events have convinced me that the Drexel EHR is no different. I strongly believe that Ben Craver died because of a series of technical malfunctions, one being

143

a problem with his continuous morphine infusion. This would explain his restlessness, increased respiratory agitation, and rapid heart rate. The initial toxicology data confirm that was likely the case. But why didn't anyone check the infusion when Craver became agitated? I thought this was the very point of the Drexel EHR, to provide constant and comprehensive oversight of all aspects of care.

The only logical explanation for Craver's malignant hyperthermia was that he had a rare genetic predisposition, which raises another question: *why was this unknown?* Since all of our patients undergo complete genome sequencing, the abnormality certainly should have been found.

While I've complained about how much time doctors waste with the move to electronic health records, I've not complained about potential problems *caused* by the EHR, at least not publicly. But Craver's death, on the heels of Aaron Goldstein's inexplicable death just days ago, has changed my thinking. You can be sure that I will be bringing these concerns forward. You and I have always enjoyed a cordial relationship, but I simply cannot ignore my growing concerns.

Peterman saved the document but left Craver's record up on her screen. She needed a short break. She rose from her desk chair, but the energy she'd felt from her discovery dissipated almost instantly. Her body felt heavy. The same old doubts arose in her mind: *You're losing it. You're burned out and have lost perspective. You want to blame someone, anyone, but yourself.*

With Saied at his side, Benny called Torrence on the speakerphone. Torrence's response was predictable.

A half hour later, Tyler Jensen parked his car at a sprawling mall 1.2 miles from Peterman's home. It was a warm evening and the lot was full. Jensen wore blue jeans, a black leather jacket, and a plain baseball cap. A small backpack was slung across his left shoulder. He crossed the service road then entered the woods that bordered a golf course. Peterman's house, an imposing stone mansion surrounded by a protective barrier of trees and shrubs, was on the third hole. Benny had disabled the security system, though when investigators later combed through the records there was no indication that the alarm was ever off.

Peterman, who lived alone, was sitting in her Stickley recliner, listening to Mozart's "Requiem." *Perfect.* Jensen came up behind her and delivered a *vagus strike*, a rapid, three-finger punch, right over her vagal nerve. A little trick from his SEAL days. In moments, she was unconscious. He would have two minutes to complete his work.

He went to Peterman's computer. Craver's record was still up. Good. Especially because she was a woman, the powers that be would see this as her obsession, her despair.

This was where planning saved the day. On Torrence's order, two days before, Van der Graf had prepared a death package for Peterman—the booze, the drugs, the story. Just in case. This was Peterman's *in case.* Back in the Cellar, Benny entered the prescriptions directly via the EHR, backdated them to two weeks

earlier, and signed them with Peterman's name and unique identifying number. Self-prescribing—a nice touch.

Meanwhile, Jensen quickly returned to Peterman and
located the vein behind her knee that Van der Graf had recommended. A tiny needle entering the vein would never be
detected. He injected the mix of 100-proof alcohol, a slug of IV
potassium, and solubilized Ambien. The potassium would take
a few minutes to kill her, plenty of time for the Ambien and
alcohol to be in her system, and measurable if an autopsy were
performed. The potassium was transient and not measurable.

The mix was just right: more than enough to kill but
insignificant enough to be undetectable. He took the vial
of Ambien out of Peterman's medicine cabinet—dated two
weeks ago—and pocketed four pills. He put a half-empty bottle of potassium supplement from GNC next to the Ambien.
The coroner would conclude that she took over-the-counter
potassium because her level was slightly low. Benny had
entered four blood test results for potassium over the past
month, all lower than normal. The final step was to place a
near-empty fifth of Jack Daniel's in Peterman's hand, get her
fingerprints on it, then put the bottle next to her computer.

Jensen felt for Peterman's pulse five minutes after his
injection. Nothing. He waited another ten minutes. Peterman's
face was a husky gray. No pulse, no breath. Perfect.

Back at the Cellar, Benny had permanently scrubbed
Peterman's notes on Craver's case. They considered
making Peterman's death look like a suicide but decided that
would raise questions; a mistake would be a tragedy everyone
could just sweep away. Given Peterman's history of depression and the death of her patients, it wouldn't surprise anyone that she was self-medicating.

She was a great doctor who cared so much, maybe too much, for her patients, Derrick Mumsford and the rest would say. *We must honor her life, not focus on her death.* And there was the self-interest they would dare not express: *why draw more attention to Craver's case?*

Benny did send a text message from Peterman's phone to Mason Fischer: "amny thooghts on ptients g and c? Les talk."

Benny felt like Dr. Pavlov after he'd rung his bell as he watched Mason act almost as he had expected: Mason texted Peterman—nothing. He called—straight to voicemail.

Five minutes later, as Jensen walked back to his car, pausing twice to admire the full moon, Mason was driving to Peterman's. Something didn't feel right, so he'd left his cell phone at home, parked a few blocks away, and then donned a ski mask and gloves, which he could quickly remove if Peterman was home. He rang the bell, no answer. He jiggled the door, it was locked. Some lights were on and he heard music. He saw the back of Peterman's head in a chair. *Something is definitely wrong.*

He knew he should call the police, but seconds could mean life or death. Mason tested the perimeter of the house until he found an open crawl door into the basement. But when he opened the basement door at the top landing, the alarm system went off. He figured he had four minutes, tops. He rushed to Peterman, whose head was collapsed onto her shoulder. She wasn't breathing. Mason felt for a pulse. It wasn't there. He laid Peterman on the rug and administered CPR, to no avail. Two minutes had gone by.

Benny watched it all through the webcam attached to Peterman's computer. He was impressed. There was no way to ID Mason from the footage, which clearly showed someone trying to save Peterman. Still, there was plenty to work with.

Mason lifted Peterman's body and returned her to the chair. He knew his presence would be hard to explain so he gave his friend a hug and fled back to the basement. He heard the police sirens as he wiggled out of the crawl door and sprinted to his car.

Mason's phone rang as he was opening the door to his apartment. It was Derrick Mumsford, who had just spoken with the police. He relayed what he heard and said there didn't appear to be any signs of foul play. "Peterman's alarm system went off, but the house was locked tight so the police assume she tripped it, somehow. Looks like an accidental overdose. Tragic."

Mason said, "I understand."

Then Mumsford took him aback. "Did Peterman try to contact you tonight?" He relayed information Richmond had just provided him.

How does he know that? Mason wondered. "Yes, she texted me. I tried to call her back but got voicemail."

"The police will be interested in that," Mumsford replied.

"Of course."

Mason's mind was racing. He wasn't close enough to Peterman to know whether she might have killed herself, intentionally or not. Doctors are among the most likely group to take their own lives because of depression and burnout, some three hundred to four hundred a year, so it was possible. She was tough, but she had been unnerved by the deaths of Goldstein and Craver. Still, Mason wondered:

> *What had she known?*
> *What had she discovered?*
> *And how did Mumsford know about Peterman's text?*

~

By 4 AM, Mason still couldn't sleep. He put on his gear for a ten-mile run along the greenway. As he jogged through the darkness, he thought about Goldstein and Craver, Peterman's text message, Mumsford's phone call, all the mysteries he couldn't crack, all the people he couldn't save. He tried to focus, but his mind wandered back to the car, his mother's distraction, and the tree. *Why?* he thought for the millionth time. He felt nauseous. *Focus, Mason.* What tied it all together? There was only one common denominator—the EHR—and he knew its power all too well.

As he returned to the road back to his house, he saw headlights coming toward him. The car was swerving. When it got close, it almost seemed to head straight for him. He lunged into a yard as it whooshed by. The license on the black Camry was obscured by mud. Maybe a drunk driver. Or maybe not. Was his brain operating in a paranoid overdrive, or was this more than a coincidence?

23

The town car dropped Tyler Jensen at the safe house in Southern Virginia. He grabbed a motorcycle from the garage and took a series of back roads to the Plantation that was six miles away. He passed through the two screening devices, which were far more advanced than those at airports, before entering the dining room. Torrence rose from a royal blue wingback chair and extended his hand. "Thanks for coming," he said.

This politeness can't be good, Jensen thought. He responded: "You call, I come."

"First, nice work on that doctor."

"Thanks, but I'm guessing you didn't call me here to personally deliver an 'attaboy.'"

"The boys in the Cellar finally cracked the John Doe list."

"No shit."

"One of them is a person of interest. John Doe 17. And that's not all. He has a heart problem, and he's coming to Drexel on Sunday for a defibrillator implant to shock his heart back to normal if it goes haywire again. Same deal Cheney had."

"You're thinking of using the EHR to eliminate his problems permanently."

"There could be no better target than that bastard."

"Who?"

"Brace yourself: Elvin Walters."

"That's a big scalp," Jensen responded, almost salivating at the news. "What do you need me to do?"

"Just be ready."

"Four days from now? That's plenty of time."

"You won't be on the first option. This is going to be another Van der Graf and Benny show, remotely, from the Cellar. But it's got to be one hundred percent certain that Walters is dead. You are our no-fail backup, just in case. Keep a couple of passwords handy. Benny will get you the specifics on what to do if you have to step in. If you need to enter an order on-site, you won't have much time."

"Any special concerns?"

"Walters is gearing up his campaign for the presidency, so security will be tight. Nothing you can't handle, but you'll have to go around, not through them. We cannot have a war in the hospital. If you have to act, you'll have to get out of there fast—out of the country, probably, with a new identity. The usual."

Jensen understood the plan, but he would have much preferred staring Walters in the eye until he shit himself before breaking his neck. One of the agents who died because of Walter's witch hunt had been a fellow SEAL. Call him old-fashioned, but Jensen liked the personal touch. As the world became more connected, Walters might be his last chance to use his old-school skills.

Senator Elvin Walters...that would be legendary.

On the other hand, he'd still get credit for the hit in the dark circles that mattered, and using the EHR would make him attractive to overseas buyers in need of his skills.

He smiled wryly at Torrence. "I'll miss Tyler Jensen."

He had assumed so many identities that he and Torrence were among the chosen few who knew his ultimate secret: his given name.

They laughed.

Torrence felt a slight twinge of remorse. Not about killing Walters, but the possibility that Jensen might have to disappear, one way or another, and would no longer be available to him. The guy was arrogant but so very effective.

"One more thing," Torrence said. "We need to make sure the EHR is clean."

"Meaning...?"

"We've got to stay out of the business of using stolen password access. We cannot leave an electronic paper trail."

Jensen nodded. *If you only knew,* he thought. *I've been in and out nearly every day over the last month, and I've got far more stolen passwords.*

"Get up with Benny and give him every password you've used. He'll bleach any record you entered."

Fat chance of that, thought Jensen. "Will do," he said. "Shouldn't be a problem. No trail to follow."

"Unless someone accesses a record after you've made a change but before you change it back. You know that, right?"

"Theoretically," replied Jensen.

"I need a complete list of patients, too," Torrence said.

"It's short. Just five."

Torrence pulled a notecard from his pocket.

"I don't have the birthdates or medical record number," said Jensen. "Might be hard for Benny to pick the right ones."

"Just give me the list. Benny will take care of the rest. You can call him with information about the stolen passwords," said Torrence with his pen poised.

Fifty miles south, at Drexel Memorial Hospital, Mason Fischer was also writing down a list of his patients who had died unexpectedly. They were the same names Hugh Torrence was transcribing.

24

"Darlene, may I see Mr. Mumsford?"

"So serious today? Usually, you tell me to get the King. He just picked up the phone, but I don't think it will be long, Dr. Burgess."

"Tell him it's an emergency. I have to see him. Now."

Darlene lowered her eyebrows as she hit the intercom button. *Dr. Burgess could be so irritating.*

"Dr. Burgess is here to see you."

Mumsford started to reply, only to see Burgess marching in.

"Bud, what's wrong?"

"I had a long night. Thinking."

"About Peterman?"

"Such a sad waste. But no, another doctor."

"Who?"

"Mason Fischer."

Mumsford was silent.

"Outwardly, he appears to be a straight shooter. But he's made such a big deal of the EHR glitches, I'm wondering if his earnest concern is a smokescreen."

"For what?"

"Remember my conversation with Dick Henderson? Well, I did a little more digging. Turns out that Fischer was under a cloud when he left Galveston. There was an accusation that he was involved in patient deaths."

"What?"

"No one will go on the record and absolutely nothing was proven. But I found some information suggesting something bad enough went on that no one wants to talk about it."

Mumsford was stunned. "I almost deleted this anonymous email I received this morning, but you better have a look at it."

Burgess read the message: "The recent deaths share something in common—not what, but who."

Mumsford looked at Burgess. "This probably has nothing to do with it," he said, "but of all the people in the world, Fischer was the last one Peterman reached out to before he died. Peterman sent him a text about Goldstein and Craver."

"Jesus. Do you think Peterman found out Fischer was involved so he whacked her?"

"That's getting ahead of ourselves. The police tracked his phone; it was home the whole time, and Fischer says he was with it. Peterman's text was short, cryptic, full of typos. Maybe she was already fading."

"But still, there's always Fischer!" Mumsford said. "What a shit-show. Let me think. In the meantime, see if you can trace that email. Whoever sent it knows something we don't."

The bugs in Mumsford's office were working perfectly. Back in the Cellar, Benny smiled.

As he entered the grand lobby of Drexel Memorial Hospital, Mason paid little attention to the Italian marble floors and Brazilian mahogany walls. He could only hear the caffeine calling on the heels of a sleepless night.

After plopping down in the cafeteria with a large coffee, black, inspiration came to Mason in a flash—he knew what to do, and he needed RT.

RT answered his page immediately.

"I need your help," said Mason when they met down the hall from the IT offices, "big time."

RT shrugged. "No problem. And man, so sorry to hear about Dr. Peterman. I know you were friends. Burgess told me she just up and died in her sleep. Weird."

"Weird doesn't begin to cover it RT. Two patients Peterman and I treated, Aaron Goldstein and Ben Craver, died this week. Totally unexpected."

CODED TO KILL

"It sucks. The Grim Reaper seems to be stalking you."

"Let's go somewhere we can talk and use a terminal."

"Private, right? Away from the prying eyes of Bud Burgess?"

"I wouldn't put it quite like that, but yes."

"I feel ya. I know just the place."

In minutes RT and Mason entered the quiet and cool server room on the eighth floor. RT flipped on the lights.

"No one's going to walk in on us here, are they?" asked Mason.

"Look around. Just you and me, man. What's the big secret?"

"I've been thinking about Goldstein and Craver."

RT cocked his right eyebrow.

"We've been going about it all wrong, taking too narrow an approach by just looking at their records. Can you pull up every patient who's died in here in the last month?"

RT's fingers danced on the keyboard.

"Sixty-four people. Man, that's like two a day," RT said.

"Yeah, it's a lot, but I'll bet nearly all of them came here basically to die. End-stage cancer or heart disease. Some on hospice care. We need to focus on the unexpected deaths. Let me see if I know any of the names. Scroll down, slowly."

After a few minutes, Mason said, "Three were patients I took care of. Theresa Wilkerson died a few weeks ago, and Goldstein and Craver both died in the last few days. For the others, is there any way to figure out if they were expected to die?"

"Wait a minute. You asking me to look at those records?"

"Just to find out if there was a Do Not Resuscitate order or a living will or anything like that."

"What will a DNR tell you?"

"It could help us identify some of those who had a terminal disease."

"What's this 'us' crap? Ain't no us, Doc."

"Come on. Look it up. It's important."

"You're lighting matches to put out a fire. I'll give you a couple of minutes, then I'm out."

RT's fingers flew again. Now when he clicked on a patient, the physician's order sheet came up.

"We have to go through them one by one?"

"Yeah, only we sure aren't supposed to be doing this," said RT. "There's all kinds of hospital rules and the Federal Privacy Act. You know that."

"So just leave me here. I'll do it."

"Right, using my account? Bad shit goes down, someone comes looking and finds I've been poking around in private medical records without Burgess's approval? No, thank you."

"Okay, sign me in."

"You don't have administrative privileges."

"Print the damned list then. Give it to me, and I'll look at the records."

"You're crazy, man. Don't do it, Doc."

"Print the list," Mason demanded, his face drawn and stern, exhibiting a ferocity RT had never seen from him. "They're all dead anyway. HIPAA rules don't apply to dead people."

"Your funeral." RT hit print screen. The printer next to the terminal hummed. He grabbed the sheet of paper and thrust it at Mason.

"No one will ever know how I got this. Trust me."

"Got that right." RT closed the open files and continued typing commands into the computer until it shut down.

"What did you just do?" asked Mason.

"Making it so I was never here," replied RT as he stood and held the door open.

"I still need your help," Mason insisted.

RT pulled a three by five index card from his pocket, handed it to Mason and told him to write down a series of numbers and letters—*not in my handwriting.* "That's the IP address and logon information for a unit clerk I know named Jeanie."

"Jeanie is working the seven to four shift today. Probably eats lunch around noon. You should be able to remote access records for the names on that list through her account for about an hour. Maybe a little more. She likes a long break."

"How will I know she's back?"

"When she signs on, you'll get kicked out. Don't remote back in because then she'll get the boot. Jeanie will probably call the help desk if that happens. I've trained them well, so they figure pretty quickly that she got remoted. They'll also be able to identify what computer was used for the remote access but not who was on it. Problem is, they'll also look at the records that got accessed. That might point in your direction. Just get what you want and get out. And you never heard any of this crap from me."

With that, RT grabbed the door and was gone, left wondering if he had done the right thing. *Was he helping a do-gooder or a psychopath?* He thought the former, but had little proof.

RT had come through, thought Mason.

~

After what seemed like forever, noon finally rolled around. Jeanie must have been watching the clock as closely as Mason had been watching her because at precisely the moment the hands joined in prayer, she stood and announced to no one in particular that she was leaving for lunch and would be back at one.

As Jeanie stepped on the elevator, Mason took off up the stairs leading to the residents' conference room on the seventh floor. It was empty. A lone terminal sat in a metal cubicle in the corner. After following RT's instructions, he was looking at Jeanie's screen. He pulled out the printout of the sixty-four patients who'd died at Drexel in the last month. How was he going to get through it in an hour?

Almost immediately, he struck eighteen people from the list—they had either been pronounced dead upon arrival or died from the gunshot wounds, car crashes, or home accidents that had brought them to Drexel's emergency room. It took twenty minutes to eliminate another thirty patients. All were advanced terminal cases admitted for comfort care; each died within a few days of admission.

There was no easy pattern for the remaining sixteen. Mason glanced nervously at his watch as he pulled up record after record. With less than fifteen minutes to go, he noticed orders from the care management team on one of the records. With the ever-increasing pressure to get patients out of the hospital, the care management team was essential and worked magic. If a patient needed a hospital bed at home or round-the-clock home care, it was arranged the same day. It saved Drexel bundles of money and enabled patients with terminal diseases to spend their last few weeks at home, in hospice, or in assisted living. Seven of the patients on Mason's list received care management consultations. Although their deaths were premature, they were not unusual. A hospital the size of Drexel would do four or five care management consultations every day, nearly 150 per month. It was to be expected that some of these seriously ill people would die unexpectedly.

A quick check of the nine remaining names—which included Goldstein and Craver—showed no care management orders, meaning they weren't near discharge. None of them had end-of-life protocols. What else tied them together?

The clock read 12:59 PM. Mason folded his list of patients and stuffed it in his pocket. All but the nine were crossed out. He hastily signed off.

Jeanie returned promptly at one, announcing loudly to the near-empty nursing station, "Back from lunch." She plopped down at her computer, signed back on, and sighed.

Mason's screen went blank. He texted RT: "J's back. Locked out. Help!"

RT did not respond.

~

Benny was writing a new subroutine to decode identification numbers when the pop-up flashed on his screen at 12:14 PM. Had to be a mistake. Just twenty-four hours earlier, Torrence had asked him to write a program that would send an alert if any of five specific medical records was accessed. It provided the user's ID number, the computer used, and twenty minutes of all keystrokes made on either side of the inquiry. It would have taken most programmers a month to write it; he'd done it overnight.

He ran his hand through his spiky hair and massaged the ring in his ear. This was weird. One or two of the records, maybe. But all five? All at once? Strange shit. And now, with

John Doe 17 coming to the hospital, it was Torrence who was going to be jacked. Benny entered access codes and two commands that froze the information. His printer began spewing pages. *This is gonna suck*, he thought, turning to Saied.

~

Saied scanned Benny's printouts. Was it something or nothing? A hospital unit clerk had looked up records on the five patients in question. But she had also looked at fifty-nine others. They only had one thing in common: death. Other than that, there was no discernible pattern to her meanderings. It was probably nothing.

Maybe she was in charge of compiling a doomsday file.

The question was whether to alert Torrence about this right away or spend some more time trying to understand *the what* and *why*. The last thing Saied wanted to do was give Torrence an excuse to take out somebody else. He wasn't concerned about the woman's life; if she proved to be a threat, fine. But Torrence's knee-jerk penchant for eliminating any potential threat was becoming a significant liability. Soon, someone would notice that it was more dangerous to work at Drexel than to buy drugs in a dark Durham alley.

He'd hold back for now.

But Saied wondered...*one day he'd need to bounce this up a level, but to whom?* Richmond clearly had juice, even if everything about him was vague. Likely by design. Not far beneath his urbane surface, Richmond was a street fighter. Of that, he was sure.

As if reading his mind, Benny said, "Should we tell the boss, or maybe someone else?"

"See what else you can find, and we'll take it from there," he responded, acknowledging Benny's dangerous suggestion by ignoring it.

FRIDAY, MAY 13
1:03 AM
DUKE COURT APARTMENTS, DURHAM

Carrie awoke to the sound of Mason's soft breathing. She could see his chest rising and falling by the light of the moon, which streamed in through the blinds. She slid from underneath the covers, picked up her scrubs, and glanced at the bedside table. The red digital numbers on the clock next to the bed glowed 1:03 AM. Her second night with Mason had been even better than the first.

She was glad she'd awakened. Mason had come by late, at her request, hours after she spoke with her father. One thing led to another, and they'd missed dinner entirely. Not thinking of spending the night, Mason had parked on the street right in front of her apartment. His car had to be moved by 6 AM or it would get towed. Best to move it now, Carrie thought. She started to reach to nudge him, but thought better of it. Mason looked too peaceful to disturb. She found his clothes wadded on the floor, and searched the pockets. In his right front pants pocket, she found a pen and an assortment of change. Out of the left pocket, she pulled a ChapStick, a folded piece of paper, and his keys. She idly opened the paper and held it under the light from the hall. Below the Drexel ERH logo were a bunch of names in a column on the left with numbers to the right. She squinted. They were probably patient names. Most had a line through them. Others were circled and underlined.

Just as she was going to put it back in his pocket, she noticed Goldstein's name. Underlined and circled. Craver was also circled. Both were Mason's patients. They were also dead. There were other names she did not recognize.

Alarm bells went off in her mind, like when she knew a patient was tanking but didn't know why. *Mason? Harming patients?* She forced the thought out of her mind. A moment later it was back. *It can't be,* she told herself. In the morning, she'd ask him and he'd tell her. End of problem. She moved his car and went back to bed. But sleep was impossible.

~

The stream of sunlight that woke Mason five hours later brought a moment of confusion. During that fleeting moment between sleep and consciousness, he wondered, *Where am I?* Galveston? Castell, where he'd grown up? Drexel, or some other place where he'd lived in the shadows?

He stretched and opened his eyes. The sheets wrapped around him in a bundle. The comforter was on the floor. He was in Carrie's apartment, but she was already up. The digital clock on the bedside table now beamed 6:08 AM. It had been a while since he'd slept so soundly.

He knocked gently on the bathroom door. No answer. He went in. No steam, no standing water in the shower. He squeezed toothpaste on his finger and rubbed it over his teeth, took a handful of water, and swished it around his mouth while relieving himself. He spit, washed his hands, and then called out, "Carrie?"

"In here," she replied from the kitchen.

"You must have gotten up early."

"Lucky you. You flopped all over my side of the bed. It woke me up enough to realize that your car was going to get towed."

"You moved it?" He kissed the top of her head.

"You were sleeping like a baby."

"I was waking up every two hours crying?"

"You looked at peace, resting after a satisfying workout." She gave him a knowing smile.

Mason chuckled. "That I was."

"I've got a question," Carrie said.

"Fire away."

"What's with this list of patient names?" she said, pushing the paper toward him.

"Where'd you find that?" asked Mason. His tone held an accusatory edge.

"I was looking for your keys. It was in your pants pocket. I wouldn't have given it a second thought, but I saw Goldstein's name circled."

Mason's face reddened.

"What?"

"I was looking up a few things, trying to get a handle on what could have happened with him and a couple of others."

"Were all of these patients yours?"

"No," he admitted.

"You can't just browse medical records."

"Forget it, okay?"

"I'm not forgetting about it. You'd better think twice if you expect me to make conjugal visits to prison." There was that smile again, enough to make him feel she'd give him a pass for now.

"Okay," he said quickly. "Listen, I've got to run, and you'd better get going, too."

Mason reached for her. Carrie pushed him away—playfully—and gave him a peck on the cheek. "Get out of here, go."

After he left, her smile disappeared.

27

RT spotted Mason outside the CCU.

"We gotta talk, Doc." RT pointed to a door just off the corridor. "Don't send texts connecting you and me to this EHR stuff."

"Are they watching?" Mason whispered as he looked up and down the hall and around the corner in a show of mock concern.

"Not funny. In answer to your ill-advised text, I can tell you that Jeanie didn't suspect a thing. Now, you tell me: what's going on?"

Mason described his analysis of the patient records. RT was surprised—something that didn't happen very often. Mason's work on the list was smart, very smart. He'd gotten further than he or Burgess, or maybe even his Uncle Alphonse, could have. That was impressive. Maybe too impressive.

The last thing he needed was to get tangled up in whatever Mason was doing; RT would not look good in an orange jumpsuit. But whether Fischer was a sinner or a saint, the danger felt too great and the stakes too high to just walk away. Maybe the right thing to do was ask Burgess—or maybe that was the wrong play, as his Uncle Alphonse had told him last night. His uncle had also instructed him to turn off his phone, pager, and GPS and come to Greensboro where they could work on the case with Alphonse's team of computer experts. "Come," he'd said, "right after you help Dr. Fischer stay safe."

"If you're going to keep at this," RT told Mason, "you gotta take a lot more precautions. You got one of these?"

"A laptop? Yeah," Mason said.

"I need to install a remote access icon to make sure it's signed off right. It'll work automatically."

"I thought you said I should use a computer in the hospital."

"You can, but they can always trace it back to the terminal you used. Still not you, but close. Maybe they dust for prints; maybe they stake it out. Maybe, maybe, baby. With this, you're untraceable. Jeanie is in some HR training today until lunch, so you can take your sweet time."

"You're going to help me out?" Mason asked, retrieving the patient list from his pocket.

"No. Hell no! I'm just supporting a member of the staff."

Mason set the list beside his laptop. RT had already remoted into Jeanie's computer. The screen was identical to what he'd seen last night.

"Later, dude," said RT.

Mason began combing through his list in the EHR. The nine remaining patient names had this in common: an unexpected death. No advance planning for care management outside the hospital, no plans to transfer to a nursing home, nothing to indicate a terminal illness.

He began with the records of four patients whose deaths were odd but did not seem to involve the EHR. Jon Torme, thirty-seven, had a history of intravenous drug use. Tox screens tested positive for heroin. He had injected himself using an IV and developed a severe bacterial infection. Together with his compromised immune system, the infection was enough to do him in over several days. Gavin Malone, eighty-one, slipped and fell in the shower. He was on warfarin, a potent anticoagulant, and had succumbed to a bleed in his brain. Carol Conboy, sixty-three, was a life-long smoker with chronic lung disease who developed pneumonia in the hospital.

The fourth patient was Giselle Kayoun, a fifty-five-year-old who had her left hip replaced. Her chart noted a propensity to clotting. The appended autopsy identified a massive pulmonary embolism, a clot obstructing her left pulmonary artery, as the cause of death.

He scratched Torme, Malone, Conboy, and Kayoun off his list.

Goldstein and Craver were clearly questionable. Three other deaths had an eerie feel to them.

Olivia Santiago, a forty-two-year-old recently diagnosed with breast cancer, died of a cardiac arrhythmia. The first thought was she had chemotherapy-induced heart failure, but testing showed normal cardiac function. It shouted electrolyte imbalance, but the lab data were normal, like Goldstein's.

Ambler Moss, fifty-five. Clean living, admitted after an automobile accident. Massive internal injuries made his case touch and go, but he died of respiratory arrest, officially attributed to a "severe asthma attack." Although Moss's file in the Drexel EHR listed asthma, his older paper records, which Mason had tracked down, had never mentioned the condition.

Finally, there was Geoff Edgers, a sixty-eight-year-old runner, lean and fit but having a devil of a time with his right knee. The replacement surgery went well. On day two, off monitoring, he was found unconscious. Resuscitative efforts failed. A trace of insulin was found in his IV bag. That finding was dismissed as a lab error even though, Mason now suspected, everything else pointed to an insulin overdose in a man who was not diabetic. As with Craver and Goldstein, all three deaths were totally unexpected, difficult to explain, and inexplicable by their whistle-clean medical records.

And so, Mason had whittled his list of sixty-four patients down to five. Five people who should not have died at Drexel. Five people whose state-of-the-art medical records left something out. But what?

~

Benny's first thought was that he'd forgotten to reset the program. It was less than twenty-four hours since the last pop-up. An audible stream of profanity followed his second thought.

"What is it?" demanded Saied.

"We're screwed sideways and upside down," rattled Benny. "Maybe we should have told Torrence about that unit clerk. Check this out. When Jeanie Smith logged in before, our five hot medical records were in a list of sixty-four. Today, she looked briefly at nine records, including our five. Then

171

she honed in on just those five, spending more than ten minutes on each."

Saied reached for the emergency call-out hotline but reconsidered. "Get everything you can about Jeanie Smith, Benny. *Now!* We've got to get Torrence in the loop, but not before we know what we are dealing with."

Benny went at it with furious intensity. He found nothing useful. Her employee records consisted of years of average, unremarkable service.

Glancing back at the log, he spotted a tiny clue he'd missed. He shouted another slew of profanities. Small time gaps existed between when commands were sent and when they were received and processed. It told the story. Milliseconds, but significant. Someone was remoting into her computer.

There was more bad news: whoever it was had skill. Their tracks were covered.

When Benny told Saied, the unshakeable Saied was shaken.

CHAPTER

28

FRIDAY, MAY 13
10:47 AM
THE CELLAR

Benny had web-sleuthed all he could. The phone call to Torrence hung over his head, like the three-ton slab that fell inside Boston's Big Dig, waiting to crush him.

"Torrence."

"It's Benny, sir. From the Cellar."

"I know who you are. What is it?"

"Someone is looking at those five records."

"What?" said Torrence from the back of a limo working its way across D.C.

"I said—"

"I know what you said, dammit," Torrence interrupted. "This is a problem," he said, thinking out loud. Then, "Who? When? Tell me everything from the beginning."

Benny walked Torrence through the hijacking of Jeanie's account and the use of remote access. "Whoever's doing this is a pro. He's got some pretty sophisticated protection on his computer."

"You're assuming it's a him. Do we have any reason to know that?"

Benny did not reply, but thought, *what a dick*.

"We'll worry about *who* let this happen later," Torrence said in a menacing tone. "For now, find him—or her, or it."

"He must be working inside the hospital, remoting into the unit clerk's computer. That way, he can eyeball her to make sure she's gone before he enters."

"He cannot know that we're onto him."

"I said the guy was good, but he's not in my league. No, no trace," Benny said.

"How are we going to ID him?"

"I've got an idea; give me a couple of hours."

Torrence hung up and called Charles Richmond.

Miles away, Mason Fischer continued to puzzle through the last files, unaware of the forces, both sinister and clueless, about to pin those deaths on him.

~

Derrick Mumsford's cell phone swiveled as it vibrated on his polished desk.

"Mumsford," he said gruffly.

"Good morning, Rick. Charles here. I got some interesting news that's going to knock you for a loop," Richmond said. "But after you get up, you'll thank me. I think we have a lead on your EHR problems."

Mumsford nodded, forgetting to speak.

"You there?"

"Yes. What is it? Bud Burgess and I are making ourselves crazy over all of this."

"Someone has been repeatedly logging in to patient records."

"How do you know it's not that person's doctor or one of the staff?"

"I'll spare you the details for now, but trust me, I know. This guy is sharp, flying underneath the radar. We were impossibly lucky to notice him. I don't know exactly what he is doing, but it can't be good."

"Any idea who?"

"No. But I'm pretty sure it's one of your physicians." Richmond was guessing. Maybe Mumsford had suspicions of his own.

Tiny explosions erupted across Mumsford's cerebral cortex. *Who?* The answer was obvious. *Oh, Carrie.*

Richmond said nothing, waiting for Mumsford.

"There is a doctor we've wondered about. I hesitate to mention him; I surely don't want to implicate him in any way."

"You can tell me. I'll handle it, of course, with the utmost discretion. You'll be doing this person a favor if they're innocent."

Silence.

"Rick?"

"Fischer…" Mumsford finally said. "Mason Fischer."

Mumsford pushed a button on his intercom, signaling Darlene to come in.

"Rick, we'll check this out."

"You keep saying we? Who is *we?*"

"You know that I have access to small group of cyber sleuths. I told you that before. You don't know who they are and don't need to. *What* they are is an added level of security. I asked them to look into this irregularity, and they did."

Darlene entered. Mumsford placed his hand over the receiver. He pointed to the notepad in front of him where he had scribbled, "Get Burgess." He mouthed, "Right now." Then he said, "Charles, are you there?"

"Yes, Rick. Your concerns about Fischer are helpful. I've got to go," Richmond said. "Ciao."

~

Torrence's phone rang.

"Hugh, Charles. I believe I have pertinent information. Does the name Mason Fischer mean anything to you?"

Torrence took a deep breath. Time for his own dodge. "Not sure who that is. Remind me."

"He's a physician at Drexel. Tell your team to get Fischer's info. I'm guessing he's the man examining your five test cases." Torrence had stumbled. A rare error. Richmond had been there the day Saied reviewed the potential threats.

Torrence quickly realized his mistake. "Fischer. Of course. That SOB. I've had so much on my mind…. Where did you get his name?"

"Sources."

Richmond paused to let that sink in. Then he said, "Keep me in the loop, and I'll do the same for you."

Just like that, Richmond had shifted the balance ever so slightly in their relationship. Torrence, a man unaccustomed to taking orders, had just been one-upped by a politician. Richmond would pay.

~

Torrence's phone rang. It was Benny. "Boss, I know who our hacker is."

"Let me guess: Mason Fischer."

"Uh, yeah. How did you know?"

"Never mind about me. What's your evidence?"

"Two words: access cards. You gotta swipe your card to get into nearly all patient care units and conference rooms at Drexel. Yesterday, Fischer used his access card to enter the residents' conference room. No one else swiped in or out during the same time the patient records were being looked at. This morning, the card of one of Burgess's IT employees, Reginald Taylor, opened the door. You remember him—RT. Maybe Fischer had lifted Taylor's access card because video feeds show Taylor at his desk while the hacking was going on. Or, maybe they were working together. Given the highly sophisticated protective software on the laptop used to remote in, I'm guessing they're in cahoots. Whoever installed it knew what they were doing. But they weren't perfect. They failed to erase a shortcut to an email account on AOL. With a little extra work, it became clear that the email account belonged to Mason Fischer."

There was silence on the other end.

"Boss?"

"Yes."

"Looks like the guy we're setting up doesn't need to be set up," Benny concluded. "Which makes him a perfect set-up. Especially with John Doe 17 set to arrive."

Instead of giving hard-earned praise, Torrence snapped at Benny, "What about his email, phone, pager, and texts?"

"They're clean so far. But we have a surprise in store for him. If he signs in with the same laptop, I'll load it up with all kinds of sweet shit. Pimp his ride into a GPS beacon so we can track it anytime, set the battery on fire, wipe the hard drive clean, almost anything...."

Between the time it took to hang up the call and dial Richmond, Torrence muttered one word with deep hatred: "Fischer."

29

FRIDAY, MAY 13
10:47 AM
DREXEL MEMORIAL HOSPITAL

"Darlene, gotta see the big man," said Burgess, who was carrying a weathered brown briefcase.

"Go right in. He's not happy."

What else was new? they both thought simultaneously.

"Chief," he called out as he entered the office.

Mumsford spun his chair around from his terminal and glared at Burgess, his eyes narrowed and red.

"What's up?"

"We've got a problem. A big one."

It had been a long time since he'd seen Mumsford so ruffled. "Okay."

"I just got off the phone with Charles Richmond. Sources tell him someone inside the hospital is hacking the EHR."

"Bullshit! ...And where would he even get that information?"

"He's connected. He didn't tell, and I didn't ask. Do you really want to know?"

"Who?"

"I don't know. But I gave him a name."

"Fischer…" said Burgess, invoking the name with slithering sibilance.

"With everything we suspect already, it just seemed… Charles said he's on it and will be back soon," responded Mumsford.

"I can help," Burgess said, picking up his briefcase. "I've been doing my own digging. I wasn't going to share it yet, but with Richmond's intel, I hope I'm not too late."

Burgess opened his briefcase and pulled out five thick folders, which he stacked on the glass conference table. It took fifteen minutes to walk Mumsford through the information. In the end, there was no doubt Fischer had been searching the EHR, carefully analyzing patient records. Most of them weren't his—the ones who were, were dead.

"No question, Fischer is not just a doctor," Burgess said. "This is the work of a sophisticated hacker—who might be a murderer. Maybe he's another Swango?"

"Swango? The doctor who killed patients?"

"He had a medical degree but was no doctor. Started when he was an intern, injecting patients with potassium— same way Goldstein died. The sicko got away with it for fifteen years. Once he started raising suspicion at one hospital, he'd lie on his application to the next and start killing people there."

"Fischer went through the credentials committee, right?"

"The credentials committee. Ha. They are supposed to be investigators, but they just rubber-stamp the information put in front of them. Remember Dr. Shoesmith, the top-notch surgeon who'd hidden three prior malpractice suits?"

"Of course."

"Well, that information was easy to find, once we went looking. Fischer is far more sophisticated. He's probably hacked into a slew of databases—schools, the social security administration, medical licensing, you name it—to plant false information. More than enough to throw off the committee."

Mumsford just shook his head.

Burgess opened another folder. "These are photos of Mason Fischer the football player, Mason Fischer the medical student, and our Mason Fischer. There are similarities, but they don't look like the same guy to me."

Mumsford squinted at the photos. All different times and photo conditions. "Maybe...."

But Burgess was not to be stopped. "There's more. I checked on his work records I could access—his Army years are a black box. They're all just like it says on his CV, except when I looked at his Medicare billing, I found three periods over the last six years, each lasting three to four months, when he saw no patients. Meaning, he might not have been there at all. During those same periods he almost never used his bank or credit card—there was just enough activity to fool someone doing a routine background check, someone who isn't suspicious."

"Maybe he just took some time off."

"Maybe, maybe not. I've been thinking about this nonstop," Burgess continued, his pace quickening. "Maybe during the missing months, he was in a psych hospital. He's supposed to disclose any medical or psychiatric illness on his application for hospital privileges. But those records are protected, so it's hard to catch someone covering it up. Maybe he has deep problems. Or, maybe our guy isn't the real Fischer.

Maybe the whole damned thing is concocted. He's got the computer skills to build a past that looks so real you can't sort it out without talking to his best friend."

In normal times, Mumsford might have taken a step back and told Burgess that was an awful lot of maybes. But Carrie was involved. "What have we gotten ourselves into? And Carrie—did he cozy up to her to get to me, or you?"

"Who knows? Tell you what, though, I wouldn't want him anywhere near my daughter," Burgess said. "If it's any consolation, these guys tend to be rigid in their patterns, and his seems to be killing patients, not residents."

"That gives me zero comfort."

"I can't pin it on him yet, and maybe, just maybe, he is the victim of horrendous coincidences. But I promise you, I will know soon enough. In the meantime, we have to put him under wraps. I'd bet my house that when we stop him, our EHR problems will end too." Burgess stopped speaking and pulled his iPhone from the holder on his belt. He scrolled and scowled.

"What now?" asked Mumsford.

"One of my best guys, Reginald Taylor. They can't find him anywhere. Hasn't answered any pages in the last hour. RT is a good kid, and reliable. He's also friendly with Fischer. This can't be good."

"You think he's part of this too?"

"RT? No way. But if Fischer is a psychopath, he might figure RT is too close. Maybe he had the same thought about Peterman. With RT missing, who knows?"

Burgess typed a quick message to his crew: "call police, report RT missing."

Mumsford walked to his office door, opening it partially. "Darlene, please find Dr. Mason Fischer and tell him I need to speak with him. Immediately." Mumsford let a moment pass for emphasis. "Buzz me when he arrives. After he's in my office, call security. If you hear anything suspicious, send them in right away. Don't think about it, just do it."

"Dr. Fischer?"

"Yes."

Mumsford closed his door and turned back to Burgess. "Maybe we'd better shut down the EHR."

"Have you lost your mind?" snapped Burgess. "I know this is disturbing, but let's not turn it into a disaster. The hospital would drag to a stop. The doctors would go batshit. They hated the EHR at first, but now they'll scream if they don't have it. I guarantee you."

"I don't know."

"The EHR is secure, especially if Fischer is out of the picture. I'll investigate this personally. If we can't figure out something else, we can shut it down. But it won't come to that. Don't forget the billions of dollars out there dependent on our system going national."

"Oh golly, Bud," Mumsford said sarcastically. "I forgot all about that. Are you, the ultimate purist, all of a sudden interested in cashing in?"

"It's a patient safety issue. You want to do the right thing. Think of all the medical errors that could occur if you shut it down without warning."

Mumsford swiveled his chair back to face his computer. "I'll wait, but not long."

~

The intercom sounded. "Dr. Fischer is here to see you," Darlene's quivering voice announced.

"Thank you," responded Mumsford, taking a deep breath.

Mumsford opened the door. "Mason," he said with a forced smile. "Come in."

Mason stiffened when he saw Burgess.

"I have just received some very disturbing information," Mumsford said. "We have evidence that you've been accessing the EHR inappropriately. You've been looking at patient medical records for which you have no responsibility, repeatedly."

Burgess fidgeted and drummed his fingers. When he could contain himself no more, he burst out, "Well? What do you have to say for yourself?"

Mason offered no reply.

"You're accessing the records remotely, using another person's password and terminal. Sophisticated stuff. Every time you brought a concern to me about the EHR, you gave me this dumb shit act, like you're a novice. You tell me you're worried about network security. Now, we catch you looking like a top-notch hacker. Explain yourself."

Mason cleared his throat, but before he could speak, Burgess continued.

"You'd better start talking, or your days at Drexel are over. And that's just the start. Criminal charges, losing your medical license...."

Mumsford reached over and placed a hand on Burgess's forearm, holding it firmly. Burgess got the message but continued to glare.

Mason collected his thoughts. What could he say that would make any difference? He certainly couldn't tell them the truth, or, at least, his version of the truth. He decided to try and earn their sympathy and trust by using his relationship with Carrie.

Burgess's fidgeting accelerated. Mumsford appeared calm, but below the surface, his heart was pounding. Why hadn't he taken a damned Xanax? He found himself glancing nervously at the door, desperately hoping security was waiting.

Finally, Mason spoke.

"When I heard that I'd been hired at Drexel, it was one of the happiest days of my life. I came here full of energy and enthusiasm. For the first few months, working here was exhilarating. Then, slowly but surely, I started seeing problems with the EHR. Most were nothing more than a nuisance. Then I was in the ER when the wrong CT scan showed up for a car accident victim. A few days later, orders appeared out of nowhere on two of my patients. Orders I didn't write. I brought the problem to IT. But Dr. Burgess didn't have a good explanation either."

"That's beside the point," Burgess shot back. "Even if that's true, and I'm not saying it is, it doesn't give you a license to start canvassing medical records for patients you have nothing to do with. And the remote access, explain that."

"For months, something seemed off. Initially, no harm resulted, so I figured it was just the kinks in the new system. I've seen it over and over with cardiac cath lab equipment. The problems get fixed, and life goes on. Then, Carrie got swept into all of this. One of her patients, Aaron Goldstein, died inexplicably; his lab results were impossible to figure out. You know about her concerns regarding patient safety, so

I looked through his record. He was a patient of mine, too, so that was perfectly legal. But nothing. No reason for his death and absolutely no errors by Carrie. You've got to understand." Mason looked at Mumsford. "Carrie was so distraught. Until then, there was no way I would get involved. With Carrie, I had to do something. Has it ever occurred to you that someone here might be harming patients on purpose?"

Mumsford and Burgess glanced at each other with the same thought: *Yes, it had occurred to them. Not just someone, but him.*

Mumsford was confused; Fischer was making some sense. Burgess became angrier.

"Goddamn it, Fischer," Burgess said, his voice building toward a shout. "You're so predictable. Don't give us any more of your bull crap."

Outside the door, the pair of armed officers exchanged concerned glances. One tried to look through the crack in the door but could see nothing. Then the shouting stopped. They edged forward.

"You could have come to me," said Mumsford. "Or pushed Burgess harder. I'm not anxious to fire people who are just trying to do their job, but I have to know what they are up to."

Mason paused to choose his words carefully.

"What if there's someone out there, maybe more than one person, who's putting in phony orders, dangerous orders, and changing lab results somehow? Maybe that person has targeted certain patients, maybe not. I rejected the idea at first. Who would do that? Then I thought it would be so easy with the EHR."

Burgess and Mumsford shot each other another look— *was Fischer edging into a confession?* Mumsford wrestled with the urge to call security and the desire to hear what else Fischer would say.

"So," Mason continued, "I thought of a way to look at it. I used remote access to get a list of patients who died last month. There were sixty-four deaths in the hospital. Not unusual for a hospital of this size that cares for many sick patients."

"So?" Burgess said.

"Most of the patient deaths could be expected from their medical histories; many were already in hospice care. But there were five patients whose deaths were totally unexpected. Goldstein was one. Craver, another."

Mason paused and spoke directly to Derrick Mumsford. "Despite all his complaining, Mr. Craver was not in bad shape. He was just getting older and not dealing with it so well. I wondered if I could find anything different among these patients. Perhaps there was a little something off in their medical records—a lack of consistency between nursing notes and lab results or the doctors' orders. Without looking for this specifically, I'd have never noticed. Once I even saw the record change right in front of my eyes. Maybe this was a new database glitch. Maybe not."

"Goldstein was your patient, so was Craver," Burgess said. "You tell a good tale, but I learned long ago that the most obvious answer is usually the right one. It's you!"

"It's not me," said Mason firmly with a steady voice.

"Do you just happen to be a doctor and an IT wiz? Or did you have help?" asked Mumsford.

Mason was silent.

"I'm guessing there's a lot we don't know about you, Fischer," Burgess said. "Are you even who you say you are? What are you hiding?"

Mason remained silent.

"What did you do to RT?" Burgess asked. "He's missing."

The RT comment shook him. Mason had no idea where RT was.

"Don't you see?" Mason said. "Someone used the EHR to kill patients. I can't say exactly how, or who, or why. But I know the system is vulnerable in a way that even Dr. Burgess can't figure out. Meaning whoever it is has skills and tools beyond ours."

"Goddamn it, Fischer, cough up the truth!" Burgess yelled. He jumped up, knocking into the table. A glass pitcher fell onto the floor and shattered.

That was enough. The two security men burst through the door.

"What…?" Fischer was stunned.

Mumsford kept his composure. Burgess threw his hands into the air.

"This man is dangerous," Mumsford said. "Get him out of this hospital."

The security guards started toward Burgess.

"Not him," Mumsford said. "Him," he said, pointing to Fischer. "Take Dr. Fischer to his office and give him five minutes to collect his personal effects. Escort him from campus. Revoke his access to the hospital and the hospital information system, including email and the EHR."

Mumsford stood. "You've raised some questions, and we'll get to the bottom of them. As of now, you're on administrative leave. I don't know if criminal charges will result or not. I'd advise you not to leave Durham. I'm sorry it has come to this, but I have no choice."

~

Once the security team left, Mumsford and Burgess huddled in Mumsford's office.

"You know what pisses me off the most?" Burgess asked. "This guy is manipulative as hell. Claiming that the only reason he started looking at records was to protect Carrie. Does he think we're that gullible?"

"What's our next move?" Mumsford said.

"First, we need to get hard evidence on the bastard. I'm going to call in the entire team. We'll work on it all night if we have to."

"In the meantime, we should touch base with Richmond."

"Why?"

"I'd rather he hears it from me than from someone else, and you know he will."

Mumsford placed the call himself. "Charles, I'm here with Bud Burgess. I've got you on speaker."

After telling Richmond about their suspicions regarding Fischer, he said, "We're going to have to shut down the EHR while we make sure he hasn't done more damage."

"No," interrupted Burgess. "We don't have to go that far. I told you I'm on it."

"Little disagreement, boys?" said Richmond.

"How can we justify keeping the EHR up and running?" Mumsford said. "We've got a data trail that shows Fischer logging into the system with impunity. What if he's not the only one? If he can do it, someone else could."

Little do you know, thought Richmond. He said, "Shut it down now and you will do irreparable damage to your patients and America's health care system. And let's be honest, your hospital will have a hard time functioning without it. If the talking heads get ahold of this like they did the NSA's cybersecurity programs, the concept of electronic health records will be set back years. At best."

"Are you advising me not to shut it down?"

"I'm suggesting you think about it overnight. One more day won't make a difference. It does seem likely, after all, that we've found our man. We'll talk tomorrow. I've got another call coming in. Keep in touch."

With that, Richmond hung up. He had to call Torrence. He was about to hit speed dial but hesitated. Torrence would go wild. This required some serious thought.

~

Derrick Mumsford had to have one more conversation—the hardest one of the day. He paged Carrie. When she arrived, he told her almost everything.

"Honey, I'm so sorry," he said, moving to hug her.

She stepped back. "Daddy," she said, in a tone that seemed flat, not because she was without emotion, but because her swirl of contradictory feelings seemed to cancel each other out. "I can't believe it. Mason? A criminal?"

She hadn't called him Daddy in a long, long time. He'd hit a hurt spot in her soul. Maybe he'd overplayed the criminal part, but he had to make sure she didn't just suspect Fischer. He needed her to fear Fischer. That was the only way to keep her safe.

Carrie's mind raced. Her medical training urged her to challenge her father's diagnosis by running more tests on the evidence and considering other possible causes of the symptoms. But to do so, she would have to share her doubts and concerns: *Was everything about Mason an act? Was the patient list a smoking gun? And his troubles in Texas. Did he just have the world's worst luck? Or was her father right? Should she tell him what she knew? To whom was she loyal? No, no, that wasn't it. What was right? What was fair? What, what, what?* Her head felt like it might explode.

"I know this is hard for you," he said.

"I've been through worse," she said pointedly. She made her decision. As she hugged him, she said, "Thank you for telling me. I know you're doing your job. It will take me time to process all of this, and I can't really focus on it until I finish my patient duties. Maybe we can get together for dinner?"

FRIDAY, MAY 13
5:05 PM
GREENSBORO, NORTH CAROLINA

The afternoon at Alphonse's headquarters in Greensboro had been illuminating. RT's first concern was whether the EHR was secure. Was there a hole in the security program that he and Burgess had missed? Alphonse brought in his partner, whom RT had met once before. The tall, strong, slender man named Jet produced a long list of possibilities.

"Let me start by saying hats off. Y'all have written some mighty fine code at Drexel that will stop all but the most special talents and visionaries in our chosen field." He smiled at RT. "But maybe some of those visionaries are up to some monkey business in your EHR. NSA, CIA, Russians, Chinese—could be any of those usual suspects; the only one we can eliminate is the DOD."

"Why not them?"

"Because they're the ones who hired us. If your little system goes national, it will have major implications for national security. They want to make sure everything's copacetic."

RT paused. What had he gotten himself into? He figured the best way to get some answers was with a simple question: "What about Fischer?"

"You want to take that one, or should I, Alphonse?" asked Jet.

"All yours."

"I'll keep it short and sweet. The dude is okay. We're Lebron taking the last shot, sure of that. He's not your problem. Help him any way you can."

RT had mixed feelings as he started his car to drive back to Durham. He no longer trusted the EHR, but maybe he could trust Fischer. Nothing in the conversation with Alphonse pointed in the direction of his friend being a serial killer.

He was about to turn his phone back on when Alphonse came running out of the house. RT rolled down the window.

"You know they have an all-points bulletin out on you? Says you're missing. Tells anyone who's seen you to call the Durham Police."

"What?"

"You done anything I should know about?"

"Not me. I need to check in and clear this up."

"Not so fast, son. Don't know who wants to find you, or why. They might already be trying to track you. Keep that off," Alphonse said, gesturing at RT's cell.

"Serious?"

"Like a heart attack."

"Use this," he said, handing him a burner.

"What about Fischer?"

"You figuring he might be getting some heat?"

"If I am, he's got to be in the pits of hell."

~

Mason caught sight of the shadow moving outside his apartment. He tensed.

As he arose from his kitchen table, the doorknob jiggled, followed by a pounding knock.

"Who is it?" Mason said loudly, from across the room.

"RT. Let me in."

He opened the door. RT stood there in baggy pants, a Chance the Rapper tee shirt, New York Yankees cap crooked on his head, and untied Nikes. Mason had only seen him as the young up-and-comer he appeared to be in the hospital.

"Deep cover?" asked Mason.

"I might get killed wearing my work threads in your sketchy 'hood,' man."

RT expected a smile. Mason wasn't in a smiling mood.

"You didn't just happen by. What's up?" Mason asked.

He betrayed nothing, waiting to see what RT knew—or, at least, what RT would say he knew.

"There's some serious shit going down."

"You heard," said Mason.

"Heard what?" asked RT.

"Mumsford placed me on administrative leave for searching the EHR. Your name only came up when Burgess said you were missing."

"Do I look missing to you?"

Mason had to be sure RT wasn't playing a double or even triple game. "Burgess called you, right?"

"Nope."

"You're not here because of him?"

"Nah, and I should be offended. Snitches get stitches, yo."

Mason saw RT look at his open laptop where the Drexel EHR logo was scrolling across the top of the login screen.

"They kicked me out so quickly they forgot to ask for the laptop."

"Thought they cut off your access."

"Are you forgetting the remote access program you installed?"

"Right. What else is there to check? Thought you narrowed the list down to a few patients already."

"I thought if someone could figure out that I had remoted into the records, maybe I could figure out who they are. Which strikes me now as crazy since I wouldn't even know where to begin."

Mason practically held his breath, hoping RT would take the bait and prove his trust. RT rolled his eyes and shrugged.

"Let's see what you have. Close up your laptop; mine's faster."

RT logged in to the EHR. "Okay, I found a nurse who's logged out, probably on break. Don't know for how long, so we gotta move. Give me a medical record number for one of those patients."

Mason unfolded the printout and looked down the list. "Aaron Goldstein, medical record number 013-76895-A."

A few keystrokes later, RT looked up. "Something just doesn't feel right here. If somebody's been messing with this record, he ain't no ordinary cruiser. He's got some fancy shit going on."

"Can you break it down?"

RT licked his lips. "What do you think?" He hit a few more keys and watched the screen scroll down. "We're way beyond the everyday crap now," he said as much to himself as to Mason.

~

In the Cellar, the pop-up notice seized Benny's attention. Some SOB was back in one of the restricted records. It was a different laptop, but the same deal, remoting in through the nurse's terminal. The dumbass had logged into Aaron Goldstein's record again.

Okay, buddy, I own you now.

Saied had instructed him clearly. If it happens again, download a fire hose of shit on his computer. It would look innocuous at first, but it would waste his computer and fire continuous GPS signals. Torrence would send in the troops. The guy was toast.

He entered the code and hit send. As the data dump began, he put on his headset and speed-dialed Torrence.

~

RT hit the keyboard with another burst of energy. "Yeah, oh yeah, homie…. Play with me, man…. What the f…?" In seconds, following another flood of keystrokes, he slammed the laptop shut, leaped from the sofa with laptop in hand, and sprinted to the front door.

"Time to leave. Now!"

"What for?"

RT was already through the front door. "We'd better be out of here unless you want to get pinned." He tossed the keys to his Honda Accord to Mason. "You drive and haul ass. To the bridge."

~

Benny was losing it. What should have been his finest hour, a triumphant phone call with Torrence, was a dress-down.

"You just don't get it," Torrence snapped.

"What? The dude is hosed. He won't be logging into the EHR anytime soon, not after my little goodies smack the crap out of him."

"This isn't fun and games, kid. Connect the dots. Fischer is the one person in position to figure out our game. From what we hear, he already knows that someone is entering orders into the EHR and covering their tracks."

"It would be impossible to trace any of that back to us. I thought the plan all along was to have the psycho-doc take the fall if things went south."

"Yes, yes," Torrence replied impatiently. "But the plan never called for Fischer being the one to raise the alarms—at least not until it was too late. Fischer has to be dealt with. Now and permanently, while he's still the prime suspect. If he were to somehow get a line on Jensen, we're screwed. He could shut us down. Our chance to deal with Walters will be gone forever."

Benny briefly considered giving his thoughts to Torrence but quickly dismissed that notion. The hit team might head for him.

"Please, God, tell me you put the GPS tracking software on Fischer's computer."

Benny smiled and nodded, then remembering he was on the phone, replied, "Yes, boss."

Torrence quickly ended the conversation. "Work to do."

Within minutes, Saied, Benny and the other boys in the Cellar watched a red tracking light on their screens flashing a location they knew to be Fischer's apartment. If Fischer were in the mountains of Tora Bora, they could mobilize a predator drone in seconds, and in five minutes, there'd be nothing left but settling dust. Fischer's presence in Durham would take more finesse. The flashing red light began to move slowly at first and then faster. Fischer was on the run.

~

"What's going on, RT?"

"Damned if I know. I had to shut down in a mega-rush. What kinda shit you dragged me into? You've got Feds on your tail. All kinds of government security and chasers, all that crap wound up like a snake, just waiting to hit me. Don't you know anything? Those guys have GPS locators, all kinds of nastiness. Didn't you see *Enemy of the State*?"

"I've got no idea what you're talking about."

"You got some heavy-duty folks hacking back at you. Now it's on my laptop."

"Can you figure out who?"

"I'll try again, but don't let up on that damned gas. This is going to take somethin' extra special."

Their silence was only interrupted by flurries of hammered keystrokes. When they got to the bridge, RT shouted, "Stop the car!"

Mason slowed down.

"Stop. Now!"

The tires squealed.

RT jumped out and threw his laptop onto the ground as hard he could. Once, twice, three times, until it was in six or seven pieces. He laid them next to each other.

He yelled, "Run 'em over!"

Mason complied.

RT grabbed the pieces and started throwing them, one at a time, into the lake forty feet below. As the sound of the last splash reverberated, he jumped back into the car.

"Go! Fast!"

It was five minutes before RT spoke.

"You're buyin' me a new laptop."

"What was all that about?"

"Like I said, some bad boy out there dumped a hellstorm of software onto my computer. I ain't figured out how he did that. Must have been logged into the EHR at the same time you were. Had to lose the laptop. Good thing there's a lot of trees here. Might have nuked us back there."

"Little dramatic, aren't you?"

"I've never seen anything like that, and I don't ever want to again."

"Now that the laptop is drowned, how are we going to figure out who it was?"

RT held up a USB-port external drive. "Got him right here. Gonna take a little work, but we can track him down. His program has loaded my laptop with so many cookies and crap, he could find me anywhere. But he can't track one of these babies. Now, I just gotta find somewhere secure to work it."

"I can't go back to Drexel, and now I can't go back to my apartment," said Mason.

"We're going to Greensboro."

~

"Lost signal," whispered a Cellar geek.

"Problem?" asked Saied.

"He's on to us."

"Not likely."

"I think so. He transitioned from stationary, to walking speed, to normal auto speed, to traveling over eighty miles an hour down a country road. Then, nothing."

"Shutting down the computer doesn't interfere with transmission, does it?"

"No," said Benny.

"Maybe he dropped it."

"Don't think so," the geek answered. "The satellite images are going to be on the screen right and center in thirty seconds."

They all watched as the images went through several waves of refinement. What had been a blur became clear. Two men ran to a Honda in the parking lot. One had to be Fischer. The other was a slender man dressed in baggy clothes.

"Motherfucker," said Benny. "That has to be RT. It's starting to make sense now."

The car shot out of the parking lot and raced towards the lake. They watched RT jump out and smash the computer.

"Can we follow the car?" Saied asked.

"Lost it. We programmed the satellite to follow the GPS signal."

"How about their cell phones?"

"Fischer's is off, and let me see…so is Taylor's. Shit."

"Zoom in on those plates," Saied instructed. "Then cross-check with the DMV. I am sure it belongs to Taylor. See if he's received any tickets that might tell us where he goes.

Meanwhile, Benny, tap into the electronic toll collection systems within a fifty-mile radius and find those plates. With a little luck, they'll get back on some main roads, where their plates'll be read every three minutes. That should get us close."

"Technology is your friend," Benny quipped.

CHAPTER

31

FRIDAY, MAY 13
7:54 PM
GREENSBORO, NORTH CAROLINA

"Just to recap," RT said, "Mumsford and Burgess think you're a psycho-killer, and the deadly spooks who are using the EHR to waste patients are tracking you with space-age spyware."

"And my father always wanted me to be a doctor," Mason responded.

"What about your babe?"

"What do you think? Her old man's the guy who just fired me."

"You gotta get some new cards, man. Lucky for you, my uncle is aces."

"I have no doubt."

"He's the one who taught me about computers."

"I know," said Mason, so quietly and cryptically it went right past RT.

202

"He'll know what to do. The man's a genius. There's another guy he works with who's got some badness too. Guy named Jet."

"Like that name?" Mason asked as a smile crossed his face. "It's always brought me luck, in a roundabout way."

A big yellow moon was hanging in the sky by the time they reached Greensboro. RT directed Mason to turn off Interstate 40 onto East Lee Street, then right on Denver Drive into a neighborhood of small clapboard and brick homes that had seen better days. Most had peeling paint; a few had broken windows. Several lots were empty, except for the stray dogs.

"Nice neighborhood your uncle lives in," said Mason.

"Turn up here," RT said, "at the next corner."

After parking the car, they walked several blocks on foot to a ramshackle red brick house behind a high chain-link fence and foot-high weeds that passed as a yard.

"We're here," said RT.

"This is the palace of the poohbah who's going to save my bacon?" Mason's little smile was back.

"Give it a chance."

RT pushed through the front door. They entered a small living room. Mason saw a broken sofa and desk chair were the only pieces of furniture. Empty fast-food restaurant bags were wadded up on the floor along with empty beer cans and some clothes. A perfect picture of disarray—but clean. And the air smelled sweet and fragrant. *Nice.*

RT walked to the back of the room and pushed open the door that led down a narrow hallway to a newer addition. At the end of the hall was another door with a keypad. RT entered several numbers and waited. He looked up at a pinhole security camera and flashed his smile. The pad emitted a high-pitched beep, and Mason heard the door unlock.

The room's contrast with all before it made it feel like Oz. It was at least as large as Derrick Mumsford's executive suite and designed with as much care. Indirect lighting from a series of polished brass-encased lights along all four walls produced the relaxed mood of a high-end hotel. A wave of cool air wafted down from the ceiling. A large cherry wood desk sat in the center. Behind it, a wall of flat-screen computer monitors glowed.

Between the desk and the monitors sat a tall, slender black man with a shaved head and taut muscles.

He swiveled and faced them. "RT, my young brother," he boomed, his voice deep and compelling. "Alphonse said you were on your way."

"Jet, what's happening? Uncle Alphonse around?" asked RT.

"He's in the other room. This the cat you've been telling us about?"

"This is Mason Fischer."

A smile crossed Jet's face. He looked at Mason, who was also grinning broadly and walking forward. RT was confused.

"Mason Fischer, the Great White Hope," Jet said.

"Jefferson Jenkins. The Jet," replied Mason, as the two men hugged. "I was beginning to wonder if I'd see you before they hauled me off."

"Well, what's done is done, and now you're here. Better kick it up a notch now. You getting caught ain't gonna look so good on your resume. We need you, but it looks like you need us even more."

A determined look crossed Mason's face.

"Got your game face on now, huh?" Jet said. "Protecting the field against all Hail Marys."

RT finally found his voice. "Jefferson Jenkins—that's your name, Jet? I've seen that somewhere," murmured RT. *Where was it?* Then it hit him—the *Sports Illustrated* article. Jefferson Jenkins was the Oklahoma receiver Mason had paralyzed, temporarily, it turned out, with a ferocious tackle. "You know each other!" RT said as both a question and a statement of fact.

"Sure as hell. The dude put me in a wheelchair. They said I'd never walk again, but here I am, a dancing machine," Jet said, making an elegant spin.

"Why didn't you let me in on this before?" said RT.

"No need. And it might have led to something being said or done to tip folks off."

"Thanks for the vote of confidence."

"I think it's important that you know about the quality of the man you're dealing with."

"It can wait, Jet," Mason said.

"No, it can't. You know your man here was a stud defensive back for the Texas Longhorns? And I was an even better wideout, bound for the pros. But then. Man, I should have hung onto that TD pass too. Fischer pancaked me, the ball came loose. Otherwise, the Sooners would have whupped up on those Longhorns like we like to do. I was carted off the field, so of course, we lost that game. 'Bout a month after I was in rehab, Oklahoma cut me off. I didn't know it because the treatments didn't stop."

"Nothing to be gained from ancient history," said Mason.

Jet ignored him. "After my injury, I figured Fischer was just another dumbass redneck, the kind they like to recruit at UT. Then, about the time I thought I'd have to leave rehab, they tell me someone's been paying the bills anonymously. Couple of the boys there were handy with a computer. Didn't take much to figure out it was him."

"Mason?" asked RT.

Jet nodded. Mason did not respond.

"At first, I just figured you were some rich boy, son of a plantation owner, all choked up with guilt at hurting the poor black boy."

Jet looked over at Mason. His voice deepened and slowed. "Found out he didn't have no money at all. He'd taken out a loan on his old man's ranch. It might have touched me. But to tell you straight, I didn't much care. I was too satisfied feeling sorry for myself."

Mason sat silently.

"Turns out my injury eventually led to a double conversion, praise the Lord. Our friend here realized that football might be a dangerous outlet for his aggression and not the best use of his talents. The boy's got a bit of a savior complex," he said, smiling at Mason, "and he became a doctor and so much more. Somewhere along the way, I found God, or He found me. Alphonse took me in. He and his ladies. They saved me, kind of like I saved Mason. The big man says we're all brothers. Black and white. Rich and poor. But some of us, we're destined to be more than brothers—we're meant to be teammates."

RT looked puzzled.

"We reconnected through Dr. Birck what, ten years ago?"

"About."

"A little problem NASA was having. Seemed the big time then, but this stuff at Drexel is off the charts. Literally! We had our suspicions, but nothing more. We needed a doctor on the inside. Voila."

Jet turned his attention back to Mason. "Teaming up with Fischer, that was destiny. Now we've got to make sure it isn't doomsday."

CHAPTER
32

After a brief huddle, the Greensboro crew had their marching orders.

First, RT had to convince Burgess to join them. As innovative and skilled as Jet and Alphonse were, Burgess went far beyond either of them in his knowledge of the EHR and Drexel's IT operation. If anyone could put the pieces together fast, it was Burgess.

Second, Mason had to convince Carrie to help. Her presence would go a long way toward convincing Burgess to hear them out. Mason knew that after all that had happened, their relationship wouldn't be enough. RT gave him more leverage when he said he'd learned that Derrick Mumsford was seriously considering shutting down the EHR. That was the worst thing that could happen from the group's standpoint. It would ruin any chance to unmask the real culprit. Mason would use this, telling Carrie that a shutdown would threaten patient safety and that they needed her to convince her father to keep it up to save lives. Saying Burgess was coming to Greensboro would also help.

~

"Hey, boss."

"RT?" After so many pages and phone calls, Burgess had about given up on RT. He'd pretty much decided that Mason had to be Drexel's Michael Swango, and RT must have been a casualty.

"Are you okay? Where the hell have you been? What number are you calling from? This one isn't yours."

"I'm fine."

"Thank goodness. We sent out an APB on you. We're in the midst of a major meltdown. I need your ass here right away."

"I know you think Mason Fischer is behind our problems, but I've got some information you don't. I can't come back to Drexel. I need you here, where I am."

"Here where?" said Burgess while thinking, *Is he in with Fischer? Were the two of them working together? That would explain a lot.*

"I'm in Greensboro, with my uncle. The dude I've told you about. No one knows more about networks except, of course, you."

Burgess felt his mind spinning. "Are you serious? I can't leave. Not now."

"You're thinking about shutting down the system, right?"

"Doesn't take a genius to guess that."

"Don't. We've got a better idea."

Now Burgess was really suspicious. *We?* He didn't reply.

"Nothing to say, boss? That's a first."

RT knew he was out on a limb. It might backfire, but it might just get Burgess's attention.

"Fischer is not our problem. Shutting down the system ain't the answer either. You've got to catch the dude who's doing this, figure out how he's working the system, or we'll never be secure. Not today, tomorrow, next month, or next year."

"Why shouldn't I think you're full of crap and in cahoots with Fischer?"

"Nothing, except you know me. I'm not playin' you, man. This isn't something we can run through a computer. This is about trust. If you trust me, come. If not, okay—but we probably can't solve this without you."

"Text me the address. No promises."

"No text, I'll tell you. You can get here in half an hour if you move it. If you don't show, I'll understand. If you do come, turn off your phone because you're probably being tracked. If you don't have a burner, stop at the mall and pick one up."

"I've got one," Burgess responded.

"Well, I'll be dipped," RT replied and hung up.

Burgess was speechless. If it had been anyone other than RT, he would have called Richmond and then the police. But he had a father's pride in RT and all he had accomplished under his tutelage. He doubted RT's story, but he couldn't believe he would betray him. Burgess made his choice. "Garry," he commanded his senior technician, "take over. I'll be offline for a while, but still send me updates every fifteen minutes. I shouldn't be gone more than a few hours."

"Gotcha."

"Everything's fine, but," he said, heading out the door, "if I'm not back in a day, call the cops."

~

Mason made it from Greensboro to Carrie's apartment in forty minutes—he would have arrived sooner, but he took back roads as he got close to avoid possible surveillance. When he arrived, Carrie was walking to her car. She was going to her father's house to spend the night.

"Carrie!" he called out.

Her expression was a mixture of surprise, relief, and hope before the fear set in. Mason was the last person she'd expected to see.

"Mason?"

"Carrie, can I just talk to you for a few minutes? Please?"

"Talk," she responded tersely.

"I don't know what you've heard."

"Everything."

"It's true I illegally looked at some patient medical records. You told me not to this morning, but I did it anyway. I thought if I had proof, Burgess and your father would take the EHR problems seriously. Man, was I wrong."

"Why are you here?"

"I need your help." His eyes were sincere and pleading. Carrie felt herself wanting to believe him.

"How could I possibly help you?"

"Your father is thinking about shutting down the EHR. If he does, people might die. You might be the only person who can get him to at least hear what we know and give us some time."

"Us? Do you mean you and me?"

"I mean you and me, but some others too. It's a long story, but we have some high-powered help, starting with RT."

"Go on."

Mason hesitated. There was no way to describe what was going on without sounding crazy. But there was also no other choice.

"RT and his uncle, who runs a network security company in Greensboro, have figured out way more than Burgess about problems with the EHR. They were asking questions that Burgess refused to. They think they can identify and possibly apprehend the real intruders, a highly sophisticated, well-financed group using the EHR as a lethal weapon. It's almost certainly the reason for Goldstein and Craver's deaths. And there are others. No patient is safe. They're also targeting people who might know of their plans. Remember Gutierrez, the guy from Physical Plant who died in the ER after a misdiagnosed aortic dissection? I don't think his crash or his incorrect scans were an accident.

"RT and his uncle need help. That's where you and I come in. They've got a plan. RT has already talked Burgess into coming to Greensboro to look it over. They think something even worse is going to happen in the next twenty-four hours."

"You're creeping me out, Mason. You've been fired, and you might be heading to jail. My father says you're not who you say you are. Then you show up at my apartment and start spouting a conspiracy theory. What am I supposed to think?" She glanced at her car door, which was open, wondering if she should leap in and lock the doors.

"Carrie, I wish there was something I could do to convince you. If you don't want to do it for me, do it for your father. If this blows up, he'll get blamed. I could explain it to you in the car on the way to Greensboro."

"Mason, I care about you. Maybe more. Or at least I thought I did. But with all that's going on, there is no way I'm getting in a car with you."

Mason got it. Their days together were probably over, no matter what happened. At this point, though, her ability to influence her father was mission-critical. He had to keep trying.

"How about if you follow me to Greensboro? If something doesn't seem right, call the police or head the other way."

Pause.

"Look, I know it sounds crazy," Mason said. "But Burgess should be there by the time we get close."

"Bud Burgess?"

Her thirty-second pause felt like forever to Mason.

"Okay. I'll follow, but I'm not promising anything."

She could see the relief in his eyes, as well as the sadness.

"We'd better get going."

Carrie jumped in and started the engine, her mind racing. If her instincts had been so wrong, what were they worth? Before hitting the gas, she sent a text to her father saying she would be late; maybe they could have dinner tomorrow. She also called her answering machine and left a short message saying where she was going and why. Just in case.

~

"The Honda's back on 40 again, heading east," a geek shouted. "We picked him up at two checkpoints, probably returning to Durham."

"Tell the team at Fischer's home to be ready. Have cars stationed at 15-501 and 147 to pursue if he exits there."

"Gotcha."

At almost the same instant, a notice popped up on Benny's computer regarding John Doe 17. The defibrillator implantation had been moved up from Sunday to Saturday morning. There was no notation of any sort. His first thought was that John Doe 17 had been admitted to the hospital early, but a frantic search through the hospital database showed nothing. He went to the web. The senator's schedule said he had a fundraiser that evening in Chapel Hill, where he would be spending the night, just eleven miles from Drexel.

There was hardly time to get Jensen in place.

Benny called Saied to discuss details to present to Torrence. Defibrillator implantation was no longer a big deal. It was outpatient surgery. Walters would arrive at six in the morning, have the procedure, be observed, and either go home the same evening or, at the latest, the next morning. Their window of opportunity was razor-thin. Walters would enter the hospital in less than twelve hours. There would be no sleep.

A geek shouted, "The Honda's back on 40, heading west toward Greensboro."

WTF, Benny thought. "Showtime," Saied declared.

33

RT was waiting for Burgess as he pulled into a gas station a mile from the Morningside house. "Nice neighborhood," he said to RT.

"Nice dinner badge, boss," said RT, pointing at the red stain in the middle of his tie. "You eat a whole pizza in the car on the way over?"

"Cut the crap. I took a real risk leaving the hospital. I'm here because you told a good story. It better be damned good."

"Even better."

"Park under that light," RT said, gesturing to his right. "I know what you're thinking, but my cousin owns the station. Your car is safe."

"You have a lot of cousins," Burgess said.

Five minutes later, they were at the house. After brief introductions, Alphonse and Jet asked Burgess what he knew about the five deaths.

"I know they died under suspicious circumstances. I know Fischer treated several of them. I know he went to elaborate steps to access their medical records. I know that is against the law and could be the least serious of his crimes."

"I know what Fischer did," replied Jet, "but you have it backwards. He was examining the records after the patients had died."

"They always return to the scene of the crime," Burgess snapped.

"In the movies, maybe. Let me ask you a question: why Fischer?"

"Would you like me to start with his illegal hacking or the suspicious deaths of his patients?"

"I mean, how did he come to your attention?"

"Because I pay attention," Burgess said, "and a reliable source outside of Drexel also confirmed Fischer's culpability."

"Who?"

"I can't say."

"Charles Richmond?"

Burgess froze.

"Yes," Jet said, slapping his big hand on the desk. "The limo, the note, of course."

Neither Burgess nor RT had any idea what Jet was talking about.

"What?" they said simultaneously.

"Richmond is smack dab in the middle of this. We're not quite sure what his role is. What we do know will chill you to the bones—good chance he's calling the shots. Just don't have time to dwell on that right now. What we need from you is help in figuring out how they're operating. Fischer found five patients who, sure enough, got dead somehow. Is there any way to see whether someone entered bad orders or phony lab results and then erased them like they never happened?"

"Fischer has already all but told us how he did it," Burgess responded.

"Doc, if you were certain of that, you wouldn't be here," Jet responded. "Believe me, it ain't Fischer, but if it is, you can help prove it by eliminating all the other possibilities. Also need you to do one more thing. If we're going to save your system and some lives, I need you to believe that what we're saying might be true. You need to try to see what we're seeing, and maybe you will. If not, fair enough."

Burgess was silent.

"If it makes any difference, Carrie Mumsford is on her way here."

"Carrie…huh?" Burgess replied.

Then he thought, *so you can kill us both.*

~

Burgess's warm greeting of Carrie ended the moment he saw Mason Fischer behind her. He glared at Carrie.

"You didn't tell me he was tagging along."

"Hear him out," she said firmly.

"Talk."

Mason let his temper get the better of him as he began. "If you're half as smart as they say, you know I only logged into those records after the patients died. I wasn't trying to do anything but find out what happened."

Burgess just stared at him.

"Do you have any idea how I got into this mess?" asked Mason.

"You made up that cockamamie story about being worried about Carrie."

"That's true. But it's only half of it."

"Go on."

"I know you know more about Galveston than what's listed in my official record," Mason said.

"I do, and it's damned concerning."

"Well, it's all a cover, a lie," Mason said as he glanced over at Carrie. "I'm sorry I couldn't tell you everything. Alphonse, Jet, and I have teamed up before. And about a year ago, we were contacted by a man who was becoming very concerned about the Drexel EHR. Alphonse and Jet worked from the outside, and I left Galveston to work on the inside. That's why I was asking so many questions about the EHR."

"Coming over here," Burgess said, "I thought you might be insane, now I'm sure of it!"

"Then so is everyone else. Look around you," Mason continued. "Think this setup is just a way that Alphonse keeps some of the ladies from church employed and off the streets? The bottom line is if I hadn't looked into the patient records, Goldstein and Craver would have just been two more patient deaths, filed away as routine, unfortunate outcomes. Everything would be chugging along according to someone's plan, and we wouldn't be here today."

Jet, who'd been listening as he and RT worked furiously in the corner, interrupted. "Enough with the past. We got work to do."

Mason switched gears, explaining how he winnowed his list of sixty-four strange deaths down to five inexplicable ones.

"I've reviewed Goldstein and Craver's records thoroughly," Burgess said, "and nothing in the EHR suggests foul play."

"That's the point," Mason said.

"We're looking for something that doesn't exist?"

"Something we just can't see," Mason continued. "Look at Goldstein. His EKG, his clinical picture with the ventricular tachycardia, and his response to treatment all indicated that he got a big slug of potassium."

"Only his labs were fine, his record clean," Carrie interjected.

Burgess's mind raced.

Glancing at Jet and then back to Burgess, Mason said, "Our working assumption has been that hackers took advantage of the connected devices to hijack the system and the records—to control the action and the history. But despite all our efforts, we've found no evidence to prove any of that, much less who might be behind it. All we've done is watch people die and put a target on our backs. We're here because you're our last hope."

"I suppose I should be honored," Burgess said, "but I've looked at this ten ways from Sunday and have nothing for you. If the EHR says Goldstein didn't receive potassium, he didn't."

"What if someone gave the order and then erased it?" Carrie asked.

"Then we're back where we started, trying to find something that doesn't exist."

A silence fell over the room.

"Hold on, boss," RT suddenly exclaimed. "What about the legacy system?"

"Yes, of course," Burgess said, looking at RT with fatherly pride. "Access the database."

"What are you talking about?" Mason asked.

"Pharmacists don't mix IV solution bags at Drexel. Robots do. They are programmed to do exactly what is ordered. If someone hijacked the system, he could direct them to put potassium into any IV solution and then, theoretically at least, delete the order. But, there's a redundancy. When we originally set up the EHR, the pharmacy refused to give up their old legacy system for tracking orders. They insisted on being able to double-check the EHR-generated doctor's orders to make sure there weren't any screw-ups. It was a pain in the butt, but not worth the fight. They double-checked for a few months. Of course, there were no errors. So then, they went to spot-checking and finally stopped altogether. But the old system is still running. If the robot dumped potassium into Goldstein's IV solution, it would be recorded there. You better hope your evil cabal missed that."

After a moment, RT swiveled in his chair. "Got it."

Burgess scrolled through several screens before stopping and staring incredulously. "My God—there it is, big as life. Potassium, four hundred milliequivalents, added to Goldstein's IV bag without labeling instructions. That's ten times the max we allow. Four hundred is lethal! There was no doctor's order at all. It went directly to the robot, and the bag went straight to the cath lab."

Burgess toggled back to the EHR, scrolling through the doctors' orders, nurses' orders, and the notes. "There is no record that the potassium was ever in the bag. Nothing. What are we dealing with?"

CHAPTER

34

The Cellar was a study in controlled chaos. A group of geeks hacked into highway cams and plate readers to find the elusive Accord. Saied and Benny were on the line with Van der Graf discussing the end of Elvin Walters. Repeating Goldstein's potassium overdose would be too much of a coincidence. Walters had no known drug allergies or hidden genetic booby traps, so the Craver approach wouldn't work either.

Van der Graf ran through the entire list of medications that Walters would be administered during his procedure— an intravenous sedative, narcotics for pain, a slow infusion of a saline solution to keep his IV open. Nothing popped out as an obvious tool of death.

"This is fun," Van der Graf said. "I love a challenge."

"Why not just wait until he has the defibrillator implanted and modify the programming?" Saied said.

Van der Graf laughed under his breath. "Ah, the Holy Grail, turning the life-saving device into a time bomb whose tick can be tocked at any moment. Unfortunately, the manufacturers got wise when it became public knowledge that Dick Cheney had one. The man did not lack enemies. They added more safety features than you can count. It might work, but it might not, and I don't think that's an option—yet. One more item for your to-do list, Benny."

"Okay," Saied said. "How about one of the cancer drugs that causes heart damage? Walters's heart is already abnormal."

Van der Graf pondered for a long moment. "Adriamycin is the drug that comes to mind. In a large enough dose, it will kill anyone, at worst, over a week or two, particularly if the person has heart disease. Let me look into this. You'll be around?"

"Anytime is my middle name," Saied said.

Van der Graf was back on the line in twenty minutes.

"Adriamycin won't work. It's called the 'red devil.' Love that name because, well, it's red. If we hang a candy apple IV bag, even the janitor will know something's up. But you got me on the right track. It led me to Cytoxan, which is colorless. The trade-off is that Cytoxan is bad news for the old ticker, but it's not an absolute guarantee. It needs a little help from some other cardiotoxic drugs. I know you can instruct the pharmacy robot to add one substance without detection. How about an infusion with multiple drugs?"

"Only one way to find out," said Benny. "What's the recipe?"

Van der Graf carefully spelled the name of each drug. "Take your time," he said. "You'd be amazed at how many patients die every day because the doctor's order is unclear. In this case, a small mistake, and ours might live."

"What's this mix gonna do besides the obvious?"

"It's a nice cocktail," said Van der Graf. "Some morphine so he's feeling no pain, three drugs that are a no-no for someone with a sick heart: a psych drug, haloperidol, plus a pinch and a dash of two heart drugs, quinidine and sotalol. Give them together, you get twenty times the potency, triggering the same response as high potassium. Funny thing about the saintly haloperidol. It caused so many deadly cardiac arrhythmias when given intravenously that it's no longer recommended. If the EHR is doing its job, it should throw up a few roadblocks, but you can override them. Right?" he said.

He waited, listening to Benny typing on the other end until it finally stopped. The anticipation was thrilling.

"Done," Benny finally said. "Two warnings on the haloperidol, but it accepted my override. Locked and loaded for when Torrence tells me to pull the trigger."

"You're sure it's enough?" asked Saied.

"Ever the perfectionist," Van der Graf replied. "It is, but just in case, I built in an insurance policy: the Cytoxan. It's a cancer drug. We'll give him ten times the maximum monthly dose in half an hour. He'll feel awful for a few hours before he ends up on a ventilator, unable to communicate. Dead in a week. Ten days max. Even if they think of looking for something like this, the drug doesn't hang around in the body long. Once the damage is done, it's done. Beautiful."

"Okay, then," Saied said. "Thanks."

"Always a pleasure."

After clearing the plan with Torrence, Saied turned to Benny. "The system maintenance is still scheduled for tomorrow, correct?"

"They do it the second Saturday of the month between 2 AM and 4 AM. I looked at it right down to the tech responsible for turning the system off and back on. Definitely scheduled for tomorrow. It's a good thing. It gives us a double layer of protection. While the system's down, we send the order for Van der Graf's cocktail straight to the pharmacy med robot. It will be a pending order. No one will see it. When the system comes back up, we'll confirm it when Walters arrives, and presto—sayonara, senator."

With that plan in place, Saied turned to another problem. "Find the damned Accord. We need a real-time position, now!"

~

Charles Richmond dialed Derrick Mumsford's cell.

"I can't talk now," Mumsford said. "My daughter's missing. Fischer is the prime suspect. He may have already done something to one of Burgess's IT men."

"I can get some resources on that too," said Richmond.

Richmond and the help he kept offering raised another red flag for Derrick Mumsford. Richmond's access to the cyber sleuths, his ability to make a problem go away, and now an offer to bring in a hotshot investigative team—*what was that all about?*

"Rick," Richmond continued. "I appreciate whatever you can do, but rest assured I have top-notch security on it. And don't worry about the IT issues. We're making good progress.

I'm calling to let you know that and will keep you updated through the night. No need to shut it down."

Richmond's continued push *not* to shut down the EHR set off more alarm bells. In a few short hours, Elvin Walters would be at Drexel. Richmond knew all about that too.

"Do you know how I can find Bud Burgess?" Richmond asked. "He's not answering his phone. Did he tell you where he might be?"

"What, him too? No."

Richmond considered ordering Mumsford to keep the EHR up, but that would raise questions he didn't want to answer. He spoke slowly and sincerely.

"Derrick, you've got a major problem. It's my problem too. No one is more invested in the success of your EHR than I am. The reputation of the National Institute for Medical Safety depends on it. I won't let you down. Keep Fischer locked out of the EHR, and the system is protected. The important thing now is not the EHR, but Carrie's safety. That's what matters."

35

The Greensboro team was paralyzed. If someone else had control of the EHR, they'd be tracking their every move. The one source for answers, the EHR, was off-limits.

Mason sat, deep in thought. There had to be a way.

Carrie placed her hand on his shoulder. Maybe he wasn't all that her father had said.

"You never told me you were involved in this, providing medical information to these guys on the EHR."

"I couldn't."

"What about me?"

Mason looked straight ahead.

"Was I just a cog in your plan? A way to get to my father?"

"At first, yes, but then no, despite myself," he said, wanting to say much more. "Please know we need you. I need you… more than ever."

LaToya, the lead of Jet's team of church ladies, popped her head into the room.

"RT," she called, holding up the plug-in USB memory. "Whoever downloaded these programs on your laptop was a pro. Took us two hours to unwind it. It's government all the way. Not DOD. We know all their tricks. Can't say for sure, but I'm guessing NSA or CIA. Probably NSA. They are using the best of the best."

Jet paid close attention. This was escalating into very dangerous territory.

"Here's what I'm figuring," he said. "Richmond must have been the outside person who tipped off Mumsford and Burgess. That right?"

Burgess nodded.

"About the same time," Jet continued, "Alphonse and I got word that Richmond was coming and going from a place 'bout forty-five minutes from here in Virginia. We'd picked up on some kind of high-level web traffic. Had to be some hidden facility. It's the middle of nowhere, and you can't build something like that overnight. But there were no permits filed or orders we could track for material or men. Google maps and satellite images showed nothing."

"I didn't understand at the time, but my friend, Longorio," Mason said, "tried to tell me something before he died. It was all garbled, 'gov op vir sell'. Maybe he was saying government operation, Virginia."

Alphonse took over. "Interesting. Starting to see some connections. One, LaToya tells us the malware on RT's computer could have been NSA. Two, the kind of facility hidden somewhere in southern Virginia sounds a lot like the compound the NSA builds under the radar in developing countries. They hire locals with construction skills, get the work done, and bury the evidence."

"Longorio," Mason said.

"Which bring us to three. All this killing on American soil, that's more than even the NSA could get away with. Could be something way off the books; maybe a current or former spook has gone rogue. But even they would need an insider. Which bring us to Charles Richmond."

"Keep going," said Mason.

"No one except Mr. Burgess here has been more involved in the creation of the Drexel system; no one knows more about it. Seems like a match made in hell. Richmond is the only person who can provide the access they need, and someone with NSA level skills is the only one sophisticated enough to work without a trace."

"That pharmacy order is very disturbing," Burgess said. "But it's a libelous leap to then say that a man as accomplished and respected as Charles Richmond is working with an arm of the United States government to murder innocent Americans—"

"It is a leap, agreed," Alphonse replied. "But the evidence we have points that way, and it's all we have. What I'll ask you to do right now, Mr. Burgess, is to appreciate your creation. Since Adam and Eve were in the Garden, knowledge has been power. Medical records document our most private physical and mental selves; they are also a history of our sins. The Drexel EHR is a blackmailer's dream. Your creation is also the ultimate killing machine. Every murder is the perfect crime; it has no perpetrator and no apparent weapon. If your EHR goes national, the potential is unlimited. Honestly, it's hard to imagine that powerful forces wouldn't try to seize that for themselves. The five cases Mason identified could be test runs for something truly frightening. I don't know this Charles Richmond, but my Bible teaches me how easily worldly desires can tempt people. 'The spirit is willing, but the flesh is weak.'"

Burgess seemed drained of emotion; his face had gone white. "I understand what you're saying," Burgess finally responded, "but it's still all conjecture. Short of catching them in the act..."

"So far, these murders seem random," Mason said.

"Except that several of them were your patients," Burgess couldn't help but add.

"So should we start monitoring all of Mason's patients?" Carrie asked. "Unless, of course, some high-level person is coming to Drexel that the NSA wants to rub out."

"Jesus and Mary," Burgess said. "There is a VIP coming on Sunday for a secret procedure. A man we call John Doe 17 who has no love lost with the NSA."

"Who is he?" Jet asked.

"I took an oath not to reveal patient's names or protected health information."

Mason, smiling wryly, spoke up. "Dr. Burgess, none of us is going to turn you in for a HIPAA violation."

"Shut up, Fischer. You're not off the hook."

"This VIP would explain what's been going on in the last twenty-four hours," Mason said. "If this guy is their target, they need access to the EHR. If Richmond is working with them, he knows that you and Mumsford are thinking about shutting it down."

"Richmond has been very clear that he doesn't want that to happen," Burgess heard himself saying.

"Of course," Mason said. "Shutting it down would scuttle their plans for John Doe 17, and it might raise questions about the Drexel EHR, just when it's about to become the national standard, giving them control of patients across the nation. It fits for Richmond and fits for his telling Carrie's dad that I'm the problem, not the system."

"If Fischer's even close to being right, this may be our last real chance to stop them," said Jet. "They'll probably go silent for a year or two until the Drexel EHR is adopted widely. Then, one day a death in Durham is followed by one in Seattle, then Austin, then New York. No one would pick that up. If we want to figure out who this is, it's now or never."

"I can almost believe this," Burgess said. "But there are too many *what-ifs*. Richmond, shadowy hackers, some government agency or an agency look-alike, murder—there are a lot of stray pieces in this puzzle."

The room fell silent, but for the hum of computer fans.

Mason finally spoke. "Let's put aside what we don't know and assume our theory is correct," Mason said. "They may be willing to take extra chances to bump off a VIP. We can use that to our advantage. To do that, we've got to keep the EHR up."

"Carrie," Mason said. "If anyone can sway your dad's opinion at this point, it's you."

"It's not just Derrick's decision," Burgess said. "Richmond also has a say."

"Richmond, again, the man keeps coming back from the dead, like a zombie," Jet said.

~

Despite innumerable cups of coffee and two hits of Adderall, Benny was fading. His phone rang. The sound of Torrence's voice provided the jolt of cold fear he needed to focus. "Benny, talk to me."

"We think we know how Fischer figured out he was being surveilled. He's got help; that black kid from Drexel IT, RT."

"I told you something was going on with him. Go back to his file. Find the connection," Torrence ordered.

"On it. We found the car they were driving—RT's Accord. We tracked them to the Lee Street exit in Greensboro. Then the CCTV feeds stop. We're assembling the chopper team now and organizing a street-level search. Saied pointed out there's no reason to believe they know anything about us. The malware I put on his computer is untraceable."

"Find him. Now."

"We will," Benny said.

"What about Walters?" Torrence asked. "How's he getting to Drexel? When is he arriving?"

"Has to be early morning. We've got imaging and sound at every entrance to the hospital, including a loading dock in the basement parking lot. He'll try to slip in, but we'll know."

36

"I got it, baby!" Jet shouted. "We cut off access to the EHR."

"We just spent an hour deciding not to shut down the EHR," snapped an exasperated Burgess.

"I didn't say shut down the EHR. I said cut off *access*. Follow me now."

Mason alone smiled. He understood he'd be the human bait.

"We've been tracking Richmond's phone calls," said Jet. "He's got all kinds of security, so even we can't identify whom he's calling or who's calling him. That in itself is pretty suspicious for a guy who is essentially running a think tank. He also seems to call phones that have at least as much security as he does. Doubly suspicious. But, with a slick little piece of programming, courtesy of LaToya, we can track the general location of those calls. Of particular interest are the three times he's called some cat using burner phones in and around Durham. Once on I-40, near Southpoint Mall, a few miles from Drexel. Another time from the Drexel employee parking garage, and once from the ER. What if he's calling his man on the ground? Maybe someone working in the hospital?"

Mason held his hands up like he was under arrest.

"Very funny," said Carrie.

"I said you have to follow me," Jet continued. "RT, what do you do for routine maintenance? You've got to limit access somehow, right? If for no other reason than to run your diagnostics."

"Of course," said Burgess. "The second Saturday of every month we limit access."

"Gonna start in an hour or so," said RT. "We sent out notices earlier this week."

"That won't do us much good if their target is coming Sunday," Mason said.

"Can we delay it by a day?" Jet asked.

"Too risky," said Burgess. "It would raise all kinds of red flags."

"It might," said Jet. "But John Doe 17 is a big fish, right? If he's their target and they're as cutthroat as we think, they might want to see this as a hiccup instead of a red flag."

"That's a lot of ifs," said Carrie.

"That's about all we got," replied Jet.

"Wait, wait," said RT. "How about this? We get everything back up on schedule except remote physician ordering. Say that function is still being worked on. We've had to do that a couple of times before. Remember?"

"How could I forget?" Burgess said. "The complaints were through the roof. Doctors had to come to the hospital in the middle of the night when they couldn't write orders from home."

"We send out the usual note saying the EHR will be back up, but remote access will be down awhile longer. We can tell our IT guys to get to the bottom of some phishing scam that might have dropped malware into the system."

"Is that a real concern?" Mason asked. "We have to presume that every move we make will be checked."

"Yep, we have phishing intrusions all the time. Every day," responded RT. "We've shut down remote access three times before because of them. That's in the record."

"How does that help us?" Burgess asked.

Alphonse cut in. "I get it, but we're relying on a damn lot of luck. If those calls to burner phones in and around Durham are really to the same person, and if that person does dirty work for Richmond, and if Richmond tells the dude to go to the hospital to enter medical orders that will kill Walters, we could—maybe—figure out who that dude is and follow him back to momma."

"More 'ifs,'" Burgess said.

"RT, you could intercept those orders, right?" Alphonse said.

"These people know what they're doing," RT responded.

"So do you," said Carrie.

"We'd be with you," said Alphonse. "We can see exactly when he places the order. Maybe we catch him in the act or when he's making his getaway. He can lead us to the head of the snake."

"We can't keep doctors' orders cut off forever. How do we know Sunday is the day?" Mason said. "And how sure are we that John Doe 17 is the target?"

"He is. I'm sure of it," said Burgess.

"If we're all putting our necks on the line, I want us to be sure," pressed Mason.

Burgess bent over the computer and started typing. RT watched over Burgess's shoulder as he checked admissions.

"Son of a bitch! He's not listed for Sunday. It got moved up—it's today, Saturday. Probably his security detail. Somehow the SOB got Secret Service protection, and they're always moving things around to catch people off guard."

"Secret Service? Who the hell is this guy?"

"I'm breaking five oaths and ten laws telling you this, but John Doe 17 is Senator Elvin Walters, the famous enemy of the CIA, the NSA, and EHRs. If all your conspiracy theories are right, he's a prime target. If you didn't see the news last week, he passed out at a fundraiser. He's kept his heart problems hidden for years by getting bogus clean physicals from Walter Reed while being cared for at Drexel. He had his first heart attack twenty years ago. Now he has dangerous heart rhythms. He's getting a cardiac defibrillator implanted. In eight hours."

"What a hypocrite," said Carrie.

"It's the human condition," said Burgess.

"Just to be clear," Carrie said, "we're going to let a trained assassin get close enough to kill a United States senator, so maybe we can figure out whom he's working for? You're hoping that RT can intercept the order, but what if he doesn't? That's a lot of hoping when a man's life is on the line. Why don't we just tell the Secret Service that Walters could be at risk?"

Mason shook his head. "This might be the last chance anyone has to take this group down. If the EHR goes national, there could be hundreds or thousands of Walters. It's a risk we have to take."

"I wonder how Walters would feel about being the human sacrifice," said Carrie.

"Don't kid yourself," said Mason. "We're all risking our lives. If the people behind this are as powerful and connected as we suspect, they will eventually figure out who we are and what we tried to do. If we don't stop them, they will stop us."

"RT," Burgess said, "like it or not, you're Walters's protection. You're faster than I am."

"And better..." said RT, grinning. "But I'm using your sign-in."

"First things first," Mason said. "Burgess, can you text your team something cryptic about the ongoing problem you've been discussing regarding phishing? Tell them to keep it quiet."

Burgess sent the note. "I don't know about you, but I could sure use a little shut-eye. Need to be sharp tomorrow."

"We got couches and new carpeting," said Alphonse. "Help yourselves. We've got a few hours."

~

At precisely 2 AM, a notice popped up on Benny's screen in the Cellar.

SYSTEM MAINTENANCE

"Reminder: The scheduled downtime for the Drexel EHR system maintenance is now taking place. The system will have limited operability until 4 AM. If you encounter any issues, please contact the IT help desk at IThelp@drexel.net or dial extension 1327."

Benny paused when he saw an additional advisory.

Attention to those submitting Physician Orders:

Access for Remote Physician Ordering through the DEHR will remain disabled until 12:00 PM today. We apologize for the inconvenience. This update will assure high-speed connectivity with Physician Ordering at all times, preventing a re-occurrence of service slow-downs. Residents working in the hospital may enter orders during this installation. Attending Staff Physicians outside the hospital this morning should coordinate with the resident covering their service until the Physician Order System is restored. We will notify all attending physicians by email and text when the Remote Physician Ordering System is available.

Benny had already sent the order for Van der Graf's cocktail to the pharmacy robot. It was labeled as 5 percent Dextrose in a saline solution. Benign. But the actual drug cocktail was venom. He could always cancel the order if Torrence had any misgivings.

He told Saied, and together they called Torrence about the system shut-down.

"Assessment?" Torrence asked.

"The maintenance is routine. It is done on a schedule made months in advance. The unusual aspect is shutting down remote physician orders. But it's not extraordinary," Saied answered. "They've done it three times before."

"What the hell does that mean?"

"It means it's probably nothing. We picked up a text message from Burgess to his staff that seemed to suggest some concerns about a phishing attack from Malaysian hackers looking to plant malware on the EHR."

"I thought we were on top of that?"

Benny jumped in. "Drexel gets ten thousand cyber-attacks a day. We've stopped all the real threats. Maybe that's why Burgess is freakin' out about some little one that got through."

"We could identify the specific threat," said Saied, "but it will take us past Walters's check-in time."

"Okay. Stay on top of it. Patch in Jensen."

Torrence spoke in full-on drill sergeant mode.

"Listen up, Jensen. Change in plans. The hospital has cut off remote access to perform some routine maintenance. We checked. It's for real. That means Benny can't confirm the pharmacy orders. You'll have to do it from inside the hospital. Do you have a resident's password?"

Jensen did not answer.

"I asked," Torrence started slowly, "do you have a goddamned *resident's password*?"

Jensen took an audible breath. "Yes. What's so special about using a resident's password?"

"For the next six hours, a resident can only enter an order under an attending doctor's name," Torrence said. "Until the system is back up, we can't erase the orders. To cover our tracks, we're pinning this on Fischer. You're going to be a resident entering an order for Fischer."

"Wasn't he fired?"

"Yes, but Benny says we can use Fischer's laptop IP address to restore his privileges."

"Nice."

"Glad you approve. Next step, Saied will brief you on the details, including the doctor's order. It's not complicated. No errors. And do not, I repeat, *do not* go anywhere near the cardiac procedures area. Use a terminal somewhere else in the hospital. This is a direct order. Received?"

"Roger that."

Saied repeated the instructions twice. Jensen was to arrive at the hospital in a suit with his National Health Care access card. He would bring a set of scrubs, along with a series of hospital ID badges, including one that read, "Mason Fischer, MD."

"Nice touch," said Jensen.

"We'll let you know when Walters arrives and the precise moment to enter the order. Hole up in a bathroom stall until Benny can tell you whether more direct action is required."

"Sounds good," Jensen said. "And if there's a complication? What's Plan B?"

Betraying every promise he had just made to Richmond to abort the mission if the EHR approach failed, Torrence said, "Up close and personal."

Torrence could imagine Jensen licking his chops.

Saied jumped in. "Assuming the matter is not resolved during the procedure, you will receive clearance to use your radiology department ID badge. An X-ray is routinely taken with a portable machine at the bedside within fifteen minutes of completing the defibrillator implantation to ensure everything is properly placed and documented. You will have five minutes to take a portable X-ray machine to the procedure area if we call. You remember your X-ray training as a medic?"

"Point and shoot. It's what I do," answered Jensen.

"As you prep Walters for the X-ray, palm one of the injectors with Van der Graf's wonder drug, RSM-223. The slightest pat on the back and he's injected. He won't feel a thing. Take the X-ray and then move out. You'll have fifteen minutes until the drug activates. Walters won't feel a thing until about a minute before he's dead. Do you have the RSM-223 on you?"

"Looking right at it," Jensen said, removing the small hard-shell case from a non-descript canvas computer bag. Inside, four thin vials were nestled in foam slots. Each was no more than half an inch at maximal diameter and similar to the new single-use self-injection devices used by diabetics.

"Plan B will be enacted *only* on my command," Torrence said. "Under no circumstances are you to engage the target's security. If there is the slightest hint of detection, abort. Understood?"

"Completely," Jensen said as he recalled Peterman and the pleasures of wet work.

After ending the call, Torrence watched Saied roll his eyes. Torrence agreed there was no telling what that crazy bastard would do. The indispensable Jensen might have to be disposed of later.

Torrence's propensity to kill off his problems was no secret to Jensen. He knew if he disobeyed orders, Torrence would send a regiment after him. But he'd be long gone, sipping a glass of champagne in the first-class section of the Lufthansa flight from Charlotte to Berlin, sitting in a seat assigned to the man he would become: Mark DiStephano.

The problems with the EHR combined with Elvin Walters's imminent visit made Derrick Mumsford feel like Indiana Jones in a musty cave surrounded by poisonous vipers. A move in any direction could lead to disaster.

But his biggest worry right now was Carrie. He'd tried every which way to reach her. Nothing. Then, at about 1 AM, she called his cell. Told him not to worry—she was fine. She was with friends in Greensboro and would be back in the morning. He thought it was beyond strange that she asked him out of the blue if he was planning to shut down the EHR and thought he'd heard a sigh of relief when he said, "No." When he asked about Fischer, she was mute. She said he should get some sleep and hung up.

Carrie's call did not ease his mind. After a few restless hours, he decided to go to work. He turned on the shower and stepped in. The steam cleared his mind for a moment.

The relief didn't last. By the time he stepped into his car, he was anxious once again.

Cornwallis, the two-lane road that went from his ten-acre estate towards Drexel, was usually quiet in the pre-dawn darkness. There wasn't another car on the road.

Not yet, anyway.

In downtown Durham, Theotis Green had two minutes to ponder the skinny white guy who'd been waving the snubnosed .38 Special at him from across the street. The cracker had told him to look out for a dealer named Samuels. Said there was fifty bucks in it.

The first shot came as a total surprise. *What the...?* The second left a quarter-sized hole in his left ventricle. As a red neon sign for the strip joint named Heartbreakers pulsated above, Green's lifeblood pumped out onto the pavement. Inside the club, a breathless bartender rattled on to the 911 operator.

"That's right. A doped up white dude. Shot my man and hauled ass. Jumped in a car another white dude was driving. My man's bleeding bad and he ain't moving. Need an ambulance here fast, man. Corner of Dunbar and Lincoln."

"Did you see the car?"

"Yeah. Silver Mustang, looked old but souped-up. It was loud."

"Which way's it heading?"

"Towards 147, I think. Not sure."

In less than five minutes, police cruisers converged on the scene. A black Bell OH-Kiowa helicopter briefly appeared, headed west. A quick glance told the cops it wasn't one of theirs. Probably a military scout copter on maneuvers.

The Mustang made Highway 147 in less than five minutes. It was the only car on the road. Now sitting in the passenger seat, the shooter saw a bright light just before he heard the approaching whir.

"Shit!" he shouted to his companion. "Got to get off this road. Cops." He pointed overhead. The driver braked and barreled down the exit onto the 15-501 Bypass heading south. In no time, the chopper buzzed overhead again.

"What the hell?" the passenger exclaimed. The driver swerved off the bypass onto Cameron Boulevard, his head stuck out the window and looking back at the helicopter while heading down the exit ramp at seventy miles an hour. By the time he turned around and realized there was a red light at the end of the ramp, it was too late. As his skidding tires screeched, he torqued the wheel to the left but still slammed into the passenger side of a Mercedes 500 SEL, launching himself and his companion through the windshield.

By the time the ambulance reached the scene, the two men were dead, their heads battered and their necks broken from the collision. They lay splayed at crazy angles beyond the Mercedes. The second EMT rushed to the Mercedes. The back half of the big sedan was crushed by the Mustang. The windshield was broken, and the driver, Derrick Mumsford, slumped motionlessly behind the wheel, a deflated airbag draped over his right shoulder.

The helicopter was long gone, on its way to Greensboro.

~

"I got it," one of the geeks exclaimed while turning to Benny. "But the Chief is not going to be happy."

"What, dude?"

"Look at this."

It was a faded picture from a decades-old copy of an African-American newspaper published in Durham, *The Carolina Times*, recording the baptism of Reginald Taylor. The man holding the baby was identified as Alphonse Witherspoon.

Benny looked up from the photo then back at the geek. "What's the emergency?"

"Witherspoon is a crackerjack DOD contractor who specializes in medical espionage. His last known whereabouts: Greensboro, North Carolina."

"Whoa. This is some deep shit. Are they after us, or are they running their own game?"

"Don't know."

"Any link to Fischer?

"None."

"Except," Saied jumped in, "for his connection to Dr. Thomas Birck, who ran medical ops for the DOD."

"Damn."

"I'll call Torrence. In the meantime, we can be almost certain that Greensboro is their destination. Tell the vans to focus on a five-mile radius near the Lee Street exit. Chopper's there. This is real."

~

That's weird, Jet thought, as he heard a helicopter pass overhead for the third time in the last fifteen minutes. As the clock struck 4 AM, he announced to the room, "Game time!" Thanks to years of being "on call" and going from deep sleep to action, Mason and Carrie were able to snap into full alert mode from their "beds"—she on the Lazy Boy recliner, Mason spread out on the carpet. The few short hours had gone fast, but they were enough.

"Gonna need to be sharp. Get some coffee," Jet continued.

Mason noticed Burgess and Jet hunched over a computer.

"What's up?" he asked.

"Might be onto something interesting," replied Jet. "Maybe the break we were hoping for. Your pal Burgess here shakes me when I was at X or Y and just about to catch some Z's. Says he remembered something about the time he was going to call that fella from National Health Care…."

Burgess interrupted, "J. Frederick Seiberling. He used to be married to my sister's friend. He and Mumsford are golf buddies. Once he figured out that his wife was best friends with my sister, he cozied up to us. He was like a mosquito that I couldn't swat away, but sometimes he did say something useful."

He continued, "National Health Care contracts out some of its quality assurance work. There are three or four lackeys who cover Drexel. One of them, a guy named Tyler Jensen, got noticed at Mumsford's level when NHC wanted special ID access in the hospital for him. Mumsford kept saying no until he finally got sick of it. So, Jensen got a badge, which gave him access to most of the hospital. It says National Health Care."

RT spoke up. "We've all seen him around. Big guy, ripped. National Health Care ID badge. Most of the time, he's in a suit, but a few times I've seen him in scrubs, which, now that I think about it, is weird."

Mason squinted at the Drexel ID photo Jet had pulled up. "I've seen this guy! Just a day or two ago, he was outside the critical care area, right after Goldstein arrested. I saw him in the emergency room too. He was there the day Cabreja died. He was in scrubs both times."

"Who's Cabreja?" asked Carrie.

"You know him as Jesse Gutierrez."

"Let me guess: long story. Anyway, more creepiness. I know Jensen, too." Carrie continued. "I've talked to him in the hall a few times about safety concerns and the EHR."

"You never told me that."

"It didn't seem important."

"What did he say?" asked Jet.

"Nothing, really, just that he worked for National Health Care on patient safety. He asked all kinds of questions about ways I thought we might improve safety. He said he trusted Burgess and my dad to do the right thing. He seemed like a good guy, really listened, totally sincere. Of course, my batting average on that front has not been so great lately."

"We got lots more than feelings to go on here," said RT. "We tried to track him down through the web. One dead end after another. He's in one place, then gone without a trace. Credit cards, leases, bank records, cell logs—there's more than enough to convince the average HR person he's legit, but the information trail is thin, sketchy."

Mason could feel Burgess's eyes on him. They were the same gaps Burgess had found in his official record. He knew the explanation in his case and wondered if it was the same for Jensen.

"That's not the strangest part," RT continued. "There are no pictures of this guy—anywhere. That moves him to suspicious in my mind. How do you live a life and not have at least a photo out there? That's some impressive shit. And then," RT paused to savor the moment, "there's the cherry on the sundae. I located the computer he was using. Guess what the security looked like?"

"I'm guessing it wasn't standard issue," responded Mason.

"Like the crap that got downloaded on my laptop last night. I didn't get a chance to look at either one for too long, but the architecture and the logic were identical. I'm betting Jensen is our man."

"You're sure about the security software?"

"You forget?" asked RT. "I kept everything on my USB drive." He held up the tiny plug-in drive.

Jet cut him off before he had time to say more. "Sometimes, you get lucky. Sometimes not. We'll find out. We're leaving in fifteen minutes. I'll man the van. Got room for everyone, including LaToya, to run the computers. We'll be on it before the sun shines."

He heard the chopper again. "Take everything we need, copy all the info we have to the cloud, then wipe the drives. Don't know when, or if, we'll be back."

~

The physician-in-charge of the Drexel ER was handed a note. The man brought by EMS, unconscious and the only survivor of a high-speed automobile accident, was Derrick Mumsford. There was no clue as to why he was out driving so early. The preliminary toxicology screens had come back negative. A full-body CT showed no evidence of major damage to his brain, spinal cord, or other vital organs. He was responsive and conversant, but very confused. He'd taken quite a whack. His only relative was his daughter, Carrie. They all knew her, but she hadn't answered the phone at her apartment or her pager.

***

"One more twist, boss," Benny said to Torrence. "Derrick Mumsford was in a car accident, he's in the Drexel ER."

"Status?"

"He's messed up, but he'll live."

"This could be good—should draw some attention away from Walters. Give Jensen a heads-up."

"One more piece of good news, boss. We got an address for this Alphonse dude in Greensboro."

Torrence smiled as he rubbed his St. Christopher's medal.

38

The mid-spring sun was just below the horizon. Purple and blue streaks lit the scattered clouds that hovered over Drexel Memorial Hospital. Mason, Carrie, and Burgess nodded to RT, Jet and LaToya before jumping out of the paneled white van, now emblazoned with a blue and white AT&T logo. They scattered quickly, each entering through a separate entrance.

Meanwhile, two cars pulled in front of a one-story red brick house in Greensboro. A black chopper hovered overhead.

A call was placed to Saied. "Confirm target. High-tech center in low-tech neighborhood. Empty."

"Take the equipment, torch the place. Wait for further instructions."

"Roger that."

Saied called Torrence. He thought he'd explode at the news and then abort the mission. Instead, Torrence calmly said, "It's a go. We'll never have a better chance to get that bastard. Even if Fischer is a skilled asset with help, what are the odds that they know who our target is and that we're striking in an hour? Even if they figure all that out, they can never prove it was us."

~

Tyler Jensen, now in dark blue scrubs and new white sneakers, sat in the hospital cafeteria with a cup of black decaf. The news about Derrick Mumsford was intriguing. The smug bastard might be a very useful diversion and the perfect end to a truly historic day. As he waited for the signal that Walters had arrived, he thought through his carefully planned exit one last time. By noon, he'd be gone from Durham. Gone from Hugh Torrence's grasp. On his own. But the hours before then were harder to predict, as his mind wrestled with his dark desires. He kept telling himself, *Just enter the orders, it's safe, it's what Torrence wants.* That thought was quickly replaced by another: *It's not what you want.* He wanted to feel the kill. Walters, and maybe Mumsford, too. To show Torrence that no one owned Tyler Jensen.

For today's performance, Jensen altered his appearance. He wore black, heavy-framed glasses with clear glass. With his perfect twenty-fifteen vision, there was no need for any correction. His hair was streaked with gray, and he slouched when sitting and walking. These minor changes would likely confuse anyone accustomed to his erect military bearing, his hard-edged glare, and his neatly slicked-back dark hair. He'd attach the hospital ID proclaiming him to be a radiology technician only when he got closer to his target.

~

Jet and LaToya sat in front of the monitors in the van.

The partial EHR shutdown that prevented remote access didn't affect their ability to monitor everything else in the hospital. Just as Benny had done in the Cellar, LaToya quickly tapped into every security camera at Drexel. No one could come or go without their notice. By the time they'd decided to come to the hospital, it was too late to put a communications system in place. A hand-held two-way transmitter and a text-message-equipped cell phone were the best they could come up with for RT, Carrie, Mason, and Burgess. If their signal was lost, they'd have to deal with it. If anyone was listening…well, there was nothing they could do about that.

~

In the Cellar, another geek tapped Benny on the shoulder and pointed to the screen with the live-feed satellite images. Benny, Saied and Torrence stared intently as two Chevy Suburbans, all black and all new, left I-85, working their way along the back streets of Durham towards Drexel.

"Don't you wish you could call in one of those Predator Drones and nuke them right now?" asked Benny.

Saied nodded his head.

Torrence smiled. *That would be beautiful.* But it lacked the subtlety required here. The plan they'd crafted was the best option. Of that, he was sure.

~

Finally, the call came that Tyler Jensen had patiently waited for.

251

"John Doe 17 is arriving outside the cardiac procedures area."

"Got it," replied Jensen.

"No visual. Remote only."

Jensen rolled his eyes. What Torrence didn't know
couldn't hurt him. They wanted Walters dead, and dead he'd
be. That these guys, sitting in a nuclear weapon-proof vault
in the middle of nowhere, thought they could bark orders at
him was a joke. They were all the same. The same need for
control, with no idea what it was like in the field. This time
it was Durham, but it was the same in Panama, and in Libya
before that. There were orders, and there was the practicality
of onsite ops. He'd do it his way like he always had. No one
complained then, and they wouldn't now, as long as it got the
results they wanted.

"Clear?"

"Like an azure sky, sir."

~

Burgess grabbed his phone and watched the message scroll
across the screen. It was from Jet. *VIP just arrived in a cara-
van of unmarked Suburbans.*

Jet watched three powerful-looking men in dark suits and
white shirts pile out, surrounding an older man. "They look
so nice in their Sunday best. Must be heading to church next,"
said LaToya. She gave a knowing glance to RT, who sat beside
her, monitoring the EHR for any unusual activity. Walters
was their priority, but what if someone else was the target?

Inside the hospital, Mason checked as many terminals as
he could on the off chance he might spot Jensen or anyone

else who didn't seem right. Burgess did the same. Carrie monitored the lobby.

Burgess walked past the hall to the cardiac procedures area. Two unforgiving military types with earphones stared him down.

The senator had arrived, concluded Burgess, and so the clock started ticking on Walters's window of vulnerability. The seasoned staff would work swiftly: half an hour to prep him for the procedure and another forty-five minutes to complete it. If all went well, Walters would be in his private recovery room around 8 AM and out of the hospital by noon. If Walters was scheduled for assassination, it would happen before then. It would have to be done remotely. No one was getting past those agents.

A new scenario crossed Burgess's mind. *What if the interloper wasn't using a hospital terminal, but a laptop with access to Drexel's Wi-Fi?* He could be anywhere in the building. The most logical place was the cafeteria, just one of the horde of doctors, nurses, and family members sitting at tables, texting or surfing the web. It was worth a look, and he was dying for a cup of coffee.

Entering the cafeteria, he saw the profile of a man in blue scrubs sitting by himself in the corner and talking on a cell. Burgess took a quick step back and squinted for a better look. He had looked at the photo and had also seen Jensen in the flesh a time or two. The profile was similar, but the slouch and gray hair were all wrong.

CHAPTER

39

"It's go time," Torrence said. "John Doe 17 is in the cardiac procedures area."

"Did Benny get access to doctor's orders in the EHR?" Jensen asked.

"Still down. It's up to you. Access the system from a hospital computer, just like we discussed."

Like always, Jensen thought. "And there's always Plan B," he said, fingering the injection set in his pocket, preloaded with the custom-made paralytic drug.

"Negative. You know the drill," replied Torrence. It was clearly an order of the highest degree, but almost certainly for naught.

Jensen had already laid the groundwork to turn B into A; ten minutes before, he'd found the radiology tech assigned to the cardiac procedures area, broken his neck, and stuffed him in a dirty laundry hamper.

"I want to know every step of the way. Got that?"

"Roger that."

Jensen had visualized the entire sequence repeatedly: place the hard, cold X-ray cassette behind Walters. Set up the shot, remove the plate, inject him in the back where the cassette had been. The tiny needles of the injection set caused so little sensation that an average person would never know they'd been pricked. The medicinal chemist who made the drug was clever. Tiny particles of drug were encapsulated in a dissolvable coating that kept it inactive for about fifteen minutes. *Enough time to vanish.* There was also an antidote in a matching vial in case Jensen accidently injected himself.

Walters would never know what killed him. Nor would the doctors or his security team. And the cherry on the top was Mumsford. That bastard had to die too.

He'd call Torrence on his way out of Durham, let him know all had gone as planned. Then, poof. Since things seemed to be going all Wild West these days, it was as good a time as ever to make the break. He had more money than he'd ever need and a pocketful of new identities. Still, he knew the score. One day, someone might show up looking for him, but he'd be ready. In fact, he was almost looking forward to it.

He took a deep breath, palmed the quarter-sized killing device in his right pocket and strode briskly out of the cafeteria. The cardiac procedures area was less than a hundred yards down the corridor. He'd assess the situation and head to the closet where he had stashed the portable X-ray machine. But first, a quick date in the emergency room. Derrick Mumsford was waiting.

Jensen's recon run validated Torrence's preference for a remote approach. Walters's security was in force. Two men by the elevator, two in the hallway outside Walters's room and undoubtedly more scattered through the hospital. He'd dealt with agents from the CIA, the FBI, the British SIS/M16, the Mossad, you name it. The U.S. Secret Service, like all of the others, had subtle telltale identifiers. The way they positioned themselves, the walk, the talk, the look. Undercover, they could be hard to spot. But on routine duty, a Secret Service officer might as well hold up a sign.

Both were within an inch of six feet, standing stiffly as they scanned the corridor without moving their heads. They were wiry but muscular. Both had short, neatly trimmed dark hair and were dressed in identical generic black suits, white shirts, and thin black ties. They blocked the entrance to the cardiac procedures area with a wide, threatening stance. They wore earpieces and carried service revolvers inside their jackets.

Time to think. After fiddling with the keys, Jensen shrugged, turned around, and ambled down the hall back towards the cafeteria where he would play the part of a harmless X-ray technologist to perfection.

~

Jensen's phone rang.

"Status?"

"Technical problems. My access is blocked. Cannot work remotely. Should we go to Plan B?"

As he said each word, Jensen thought, *I couldn't have scripted this any better.*

"That makes no sense," Torrence responded. "I'll call back in five."

Torrence was desperate to follow through on his plan, but this was becoming too dangerous. Hospital cameras had picked up Fischer running through the hospital. Nowhere near Walters, so maybe he hadn't figured it all out, but not without purpose. Benny said the EHR appeared to be working normally. He called Richmond.

They quickly agreed something was off. Torrence called Jensen's iPhone to deliver the order: abort.

There was no answer. Richmond remained on the line.

This was beyond unacceptable. He and Richmond sorted through the possibilities. All led to the same conclusion. Jensen was no longer following orders. He was out of pocket and on the loose. That made Jensen a very dangerous man. A man who could bring them all down. He had to be brought back under their control. Immediately. Torrence instructed Saied to activate the extraction team that was standing by.

"Chopper's already in the air," Saied responded.

Torrence radioed them: "We'll maintain recon for you so you can pinpoint this guy. We do not believe he can be captured alive. He is armed and lethal. Instruct your men to use silencers. We'd prefer taking him from the ground, but if you have to, do it from the air. Call me when you're in the area. Out."

~

Derrick Mumsford was beyond confused when he saw the hulking figure in blue scrubs hovering over him. The badge read *Dr. Mason Fischer.*

"Mr. Mumsford, it's Mason Fischer. How are you feeling?"

"Uh," was all he could say. He noticed the man fiddling with his intravenous line. "What are you doing?" He tried to concentrate but was unable to focus.

"You thought you could ruin my career and take your sweet ass daughter away from me without consequences?"

Mumsford felt his eyelids drooping. The pain medications had nearly worn off, but now the effects were back, full throttle. He tried to speak, but nothing came out. He tried to reach the nurse's call button, but the man picked it up and moved it out of reach. He was falling asleep. The site where his IV flowed began to burn intensely. His tongue tried, but no words came out.

"Don't worry; I'll make sure it's painless. There was some pain-relieving Fentanyl in your IV along with some potassium. It can sting. Never can tell when an accident victim will need some extra potassium."

Mumsford tried to shake his head, but nothing happened. His arms were dead. His mouth was dry. He couldn't keep his eyes open. "Maybe they'll save you, or maybe they won't," Jensen told him, "but they'll all come rushing, and with all the traceable shit in your system, they'll believe you were the target."

Tyler Jensen smiled, even if Derrick Mumsford could no longer keep his face in focus. His idea to knock off Mumsford was brilliant, if he did say so himself. The perfect diversion from the main event—Elvin Walters.

~

Mason's search of the emergency room turned up no one who looked like Jensen. As he turned to leave, a piercing, high-pitched alarm stopped him in his tracks. The overhead telemetry monitor in the hall displaying the ECG tracings for all monitored patients was flashing red for one of the rooms. A closer looked showed the abnormal rhythm was in Trauma Room 5. Nothing was normal about that patient's ECG. The rate was fast, nearly 150 beats per minute, and the complexes were bizarrely widened.

"Who's in Room 5? Something is seriously wrong in there."

"Room 5?" Jamie's voice elevated an octave. "That's Derrick Mumsford."

The alarm became incessant and louder.

"Derrick Mumsford? He's arresting. Get the crash cart and a nurse. Print the EKG tracings for each of the last ten minutes."

Mason started CPR. In moments the room was full of doctors and nurses.

"VF," shouted Mason over the din. "Charge the defibrillator to 360 joules. Now!"

He applied the paddles to Mumsford's chest and shouted, "Clear!"

Mumsford's body jerked as the electrical jolt slapped his heart. Mason eyed the monitor as voices filled the room.

"Normal sinus rhythm," said one.

"I'm feeling a pulse," said another. "Weak, but present."

Mason turned to a nurse: "Look at the width of the QRS complex. Give me a list of medications he's received, stat. Give me those telemetry strips from the last ten minutes. Change out that IV bag immediately and save the one he's connected to now."

All hell broke loose again. Monitors screamed as a crowd pressed into the room.

"Ventricular fibrillation. No spontaneous respirations," said a nervous anesthesiology resident. "Do you want me to bag or intubate?"

"Bag for now," replied Mason. "Charge the defibrillator."

"Meds," called out a nurse, thrusting a piece of paper in front of Mason.

"EKG strips," said the technician, placing them in front of Mason.

He glanced at the strips quickly as a nurse yelled, "VF, charging the defibrillator."

The square-shaped defibrillator hummed while charging. Mason placed the paddles on Mumsford's chest and shocked him.

"Pulse?" he asked.

"Yes," replied the nurse at the bedside.

"Spontaneous respirations?" asked Mason.

"None," replied the anesthesiology resident.

"Continue bagging."

Got to focus, he said to himself. The EKG strips showed a rapid progression from normal complexes to the bizarre complexes he was seeing now. The attending nurse said Mumsford had been in pain, but awake and talkative ten minutes before. Now, he was moribund. It was déjà vu all over again, a replay of what happened to Goldstein; the same people had to be behind it. If this was hyperkalemia, induced by an IV full of potassium, hopefully Mumsford had not experienced decreased blood pressures for enough time to result in cerebral hypoxia and brain damage.

"VF," called the nurse for the third time. "Charging."

"I'm going to defibrillate him again, but in the meantime, listen up. We're going to treat this like hyperkalemia. Load up on everything, stat. An amp of calcium gluconate, twenty-five units of insulin, an amp of D50, an amp of bicarb."

He shocked Mumsford again as the nurses paused their infusions.

"Get those drugs in," he shouted.

"Pulse is back, and stronger," called out the nurse at the bedside.

Mason studied the monitor. The abnormally wide QRS complexes were narrowing.

"BP is 160 over 84," the nurse added.

"Still no respiratory movement," said the anesthesiology resident.

"Okay, let's go with an amp of Narcan to reverse the narcotics," said Mason.

"He didn't get any narcotics," replied the head nurse.

"Don't trust the record; just look at him," Mason replied. "Give the Narcan. If he didn't get narcotics, it won't hurt him."

"Narcan in," said a nurse.

Two minutes later, Mumsford's condition was better. *But for how long?* Mason asked himself. The most recent stat labs were pending. *If Mumsford had been given a slug of potassium, just like Goldstein, the labs might be normal again. If this was different and Mumsford was beyond saving.... At the very least, it was going to look bad.* His focus on Mumsford wavered as he wondered what the hell was going on. *If they couldn't prove someone was hijacking the EHR, then all the deaths combined with his backstory in Galveston could mean serious trouble.* A jubilant shout from the anesthesiology resident interrupted Mason's thoughts.

"Spontaneous breathing. He's opening his eyes."

Mumsford moaned in pain, grasping the red disks that had horse-kicked his chest.

Summoning every ounce of energy, he whispered, "Fischer."

"Yes," the nurse said, "he saved your life."

"Murderer."

The word jolted Mason. In the flurry to save Mumsford, he'd almost forgotten *Walters*.

As he headed toward the door, Mason told Mike Wiegand, the attending ER physician, "It looks like he got a slug of potassium and enough Fentanyl to knock him out. Can't know for sure, but he responded to the drugs we gave him. Draw blood and walk it to the lab yourself. Call the police and have them take possession of the IV bag. There's another emergency upstairs. Gotta go."

"What's going on?" Wiegand shouted as Mason sprinted away.

~

As Mason was saving Mumsford's life, Jensen had sprinted up the stairs to the cardiac procedure floor. *One down, one to go.* He didn't stop to think how far he had come: a young man who had pledged to serve and protect his country and constitution was now primed to commit an act that could only be called treason. He was no longer a patriot, just a killer. This would be his crowning achievement. He stepped out of the stairwell, just outside the cardiac procedures area, and loitered.

His timing had been perfect. In short order, a stretcher accompanied by a secret service agent was wheeled out of a procedure room to the room where Walters would recover—presumably. He slowly walked down the hall, retrieved the

X-ray machine from where he'd stashed it, and approached the cardiac procedures area, assuming his slacker slouch.

"Gentlemen, the doc wants a quick set of pictures to make sure he's as great as he thinks he is," Jensen said. "Got a portable X-ray machine here so we won't have to move him. I assume you'll want to come in with me—you do your job while I do mine." He laughed.

The agents scanned his badge. Both looked Jensen up and down, then straight in the eye.

"He's good," the first one said.

"About five minutes…ten max," Jensen assured them.

Jensen rolled the portable machine into Walters's room.

"How're we doing today?" drawled Jensen with a smooth Eastern Carolina inflection.

"No complaints," replied the slightly groggy politician.

"That's a good way to live your life," Jensen said. "Just going to take a few pictures and I'll be out of here faster than a one-legged man in a butt-kicking competition." Walters had used that very phrase in his most recent speech on YouTube. Walters smiled, pleased that the tech recognized him. Jensen smiled back and nodded. All part of his meticulous preparation.

As Jensen set up, his phone vibrated. *Fucking Torrence. Doesn't he get that I'm working?*

"The little woman," he said to the agents. "Can't make a move without me."

After finishing the X-rays, Jensen reached into his side pocket and pulled out the injector. He looked Walters in the eye and smiled. As he helped Walters sit forward to remove the X-ray plate, he deftly placed the injector with the deadly toxin in the hand he used to support him. Walters didn't feel a thing.

"It's been an honor," Jensen said, with a nod of acknowledgment to Walters. "Goodbye."

As he calmly left the room, the wheels spun in Jensen's mind, each calibrated to the ticks of the fifteen-minute clock in his head.

He'd already placed the contents of his safety deposit box—money, IDs, passports, and firepower—into a duffel bag he'd left in the trunk of his backup car, a green Ford Taurus parked on the third floor of the parking garage. He'd be a couple of miles away from Drexel when the proverbial shit hit the fan. And it would. He almost felt sorry for the Drexel people. *Letting a sitting senator die right there at Drexel. How could they?*

But that wasn't his problem. He'd be in his car in less than ten minutes, in the international terminal in Charlotte in two hours, and in the air in three. His planning would save his ass as always. Jensen was not the sentimental type, but as he left Drexel Memorial for the last time, he looked around and took in his surroundings.

He saw doctors and nurses walking with their breakfast from the cafeteria line to the hard plastic-topped tables with institutional chairs and standard-order salt and pepper shakers. Some held steaming coffee in white paper cups wrapped in nice little sleeves, just like at Starbucks. Others carried brown plastic trays loaded with fruit or cereal or scrambled eggs. Some were fresh in clean clothes. Others wore the stress of a long night on-call.

So long, suckers.

Eyes ahead. Twenty feet to the cafeteria exit. A brisk walk down the corridor. Out the front entrance.

What he hadn't counted on was Carrie Mumsford, who sat on a polished oak bench between the cafeteria and the hospital's stunning main lobby, inlaid with the Brazilian mahogany and black Italian marble paid for by Ben Craver. She figured Jensen would have to leave the hospital at some point. It seemed the best place to spot him. She still couldn't believe he was a monster. He struck her as anything but.

Then again, she hadn't suspected anything about Mason, either. Whatever Mason was, he wasn't who he'd said. All those years, she had prided herself on her innate ability to see right through facades, to know who people really were and what made them tick. If she ever really had it—*Who are you kidding? Of course, you didn't*—it clearly was out of whack now.

Carrie's mind was so filled with self-recrimination she almost didn't see the man in blue scrubs walking across the lobby. He was a dead ringer for Jensen—if Jensen had graying hair and wore glasses. Maybe it wasn't him. What did she know?

But then she saw his gait as he picked up speed. That quality—serene, powerful, purposeful—defined Jensen for her. It had to be him. *Trust yourself, Carrie.*

She rose to follow.

~

In the van parked near the hospital's entrance, Jet, LaToya, and RT were stunned. A few minutes ago, everything had been under control. Now there was an explosion of activity. There was trouble in the emergency room involving Derrick Mumsford.

Jet's phone buzzed. It was a text message from Carrie. Jensen was on the move, heading out of the hospital.

"Should we tell her about her father?" LaToya asked while calling up the cameras in Drexel's lobby. She pointed as Tyler Jensen, wearing scrubs, strode briskly across the lobby with Carrie following closely.

"Lord, forgive me, but no, not now," Jet said. "RT, page Mason again. We can't let this guy get away."

Mason's phone buzzed as he was taking the stairs three at a time in route to the cardiac procedures area.

It was a text from Jet: *jensen leaving hospital through north lobby carrie following. Move!!!*

~

Jensen felt a presence behind him in the lobby. He slowed slightly and caught the reflection off the glass of the front door. A blond woman, 5'7", 125 pounds, in a white lab coat and sneakers, approximately fifteen yards behind. She slowed as he did.

He picked up his pace as he went into the daylight outside. So did she. Her brisk, determined stride gave her away. Those bastards. Having a backup was standard, but Torrence should have told him. She must have been there all along... just waiting in case he failed to deliver. At this point, though, it was more likely that her orders were to terminate him. She could hide a lot of firepower under that white coat. They knew he was unarmed; he couldn't risk the metal detectors. He watched her reach into her pocket. Knife? Taser? Gun? He'd have to do her the hard way.

Reflexively his hand slid into his pocket. Joy and warmth overcame him. He touched both backup injectors. Now there was an equalizer. He'd let the woman get close, act unsuspecting, and hit her. If she admitted who'd sent her, he'd promise to give her the antidote. Then, he'd savor that look in her eye when she realized he was lying.

Jensen exited the hospital. A chopper whirred overhead. *Another will make three*, he thought. *Not a bad day's work.*

~

Jet maneuvered the van towards the Drexel entrance just as Jensen cleared the automatic glass doors and turned towards the parking lot. Because of the concrete curb and parking spaces, he couldn't get within a hundred yards.

Carrie hurried through the glass doors before realizing that Jensen had slowed. She paused and brushed her hair from her face, pretending she was waiting for a ride.

Fidgeting in his seat, Jet watched through the darkened windows of the van. "LaToya, I can't let this happen; I've got to do something."

"Don't, baby. You know what the doctors said. You get hit or twisted, that's it. No rehab the second time. You'll be paralyzed for life. Give it a minute. Text Carrie and tell her to back off."

"You do it. I'll try to distract Jensen," said RT. He slid open the door and jumped out. LaToya pointed at the monitor on her left. "Fischer's still a ways away but closing fast."

Mason now saw Carrie, who seemed to be following a man in scrubs: *Jensen.*

Carrie's heart nearly stopped when the man pivoted on his heel and charged her. He seemed to ooze violence; his eyes burned with anger. In the van, Jet tensed. RT yelled as he ran towards Carrie, but the distance from the van to her seemed like a mile. She couldn't hear him through the thunder of her heartbeat.

Jensen recognized the blond woman.

"Dr. Mumsford," he said. "Are you following me? Did he send you?"

"We know what you're doing," Carrie said. She tripped on the curb and nearly fell. "Damn," she muttered.

"That's okay, sweetheart. Everything will be fine."

Jet's mutterings in the van were more profane. "This ain't good."

"Oh, God," said LaToya.

Jensen palmed one of the injectors.

"Dr. Mumsford," he said with a laugh, "do you have fifteen minutes?"

As Jensen closed in, Carrie assumed a martial arts stance. Jensen's smiled. "Frisky. Normally, I'd like that. But I'm in a rush. Do yourself a favor and just take your medicine. If you resist, I can make this so painful you'll beg me to shoot you."

Carrie powerfully struck Jensen's right wrist with her left foot. His hand reflexively squeezed the injector.

"Bitch!" he shouted.

As he moved to strike Carrie, Jensen caught the slightest flicker of movement in his periphery. Low and leading with his shoulder, Mason laid a ferocious hit on Tyler Jensen, knocking him headfirst into the concrete sidewalk, unconscious.

"That's All-American," Jet cried. "Glad he's on my team this time."

"Oh my God," said Carrie. "Mason." She looked at Jensen. "What just happened?"

"Basically, you saved the day," Mason said. "That karate came in handy."

"It's Shotokan, you idiot!"

Hospital security and RT converged on them at different angles. Mason picked up the injector that had dropped from Jensen's hand. "I don't know what this is, but I'm guessing this isn't something insurance reps usually carry."

"Just before you tackled him, he said something threatening. He asked me if I had fifteen minutes and something about taking my medicine."

Still on the ground and barely conscious, Jensen reached for his pocket. Mason gave him a quick kick to the gut and patted him down. He gently removed what looked like a small box used by fly fishermen to protect their favorite trout fly. Inside, two discs rested in protective Styrofoam: one green, one red. Another red disc lay on the sidewalk.

Holy smokes, Mason thought. He'd never seen the macabre toxin delivery systems used by covert operatives, but he'd attended a lecture at Fort Bragg on injection devices for covert killers. He searched his memory. Toxins could be preloaded into one of the vials. Cyanide, anthrax, Ebola, or some custom-synthesized neurochemical. That one of the vials was green had to be important. *What was it? An antidote?* The essential component of a toxin separated so an accidental injection would not put the operative at risk. The green vial would save a life. The red would end a life. Alarmingly, there appeared to be one red disc unaccounted for.

"Did Jensen get to Walters?" Mason shouted to RT.

"Yeah, but he only took an X-ray," RT yelled as he ran toward him. "His vitals are normal."

"How long ago?" he yelled at RT. "How long ago did he leave Walters?"

"About ten minutes. Why?"

~

As Mason sprinted back to the hospital, RT and hospital security puzzled over Jensen. Then they had another mystery on their hands. The chop from a nearby helicopter, presumed to be a medical Life Flight, got louder and louder. It landed in an empty section of the parking lot thirty yards away. Five men burst out. They were not nurses.

Each man wore green pants and matching bulletproof vests emblazoned with FBI, metal helmets, and goggles. They all carried MP 10 submachine guns.

"He's ours!" they shouted.

"You can have him," the security guard answered, backing away.

Discretion is the better part of valor, RT thought.

Watching from the van, LaToya said, "If those boys are from the FBI, I'm Miss America," as the agents loaded Jensen into the helicopter, which quickly lifted up and away, vanishing into the clouds.

~

Mason missed the drama outside as he rushed back into the hospital, across the lobby to the stairs and the second floor. He was never so happy to see Burgess, who stood in the hall near Walters's room.

"I know this is going to sound crazy, but Walters is going to die if I don't give him this shot *now*," Mason said.

"What?"

"I've got an antidote for what Jensen gave him." He held the green vial in the palm of his hand.

"What?"

"You're going to have to trust me."

This is it, Burgess thought. He walked with Mason toward the room. *Maybe I save Elvin Walters's life, or maybe I allow a psychopath to finish his murder.* For all of Burgess's accomplishments, this was the one moment in his life when everything was on the line. He approached the Secret Service.

"Gentlemen, we have a very dangerous situation on our hands." The agents clutched their guns as they spied Mason. "Dr. Fischer has determined that the patient is in mortal danger. You must let him in, or Senator Walters will die."

The agents met gazes, seeming to confer silently.

"Right now," Burgess said with steely authority. "This is a hospital, and we are doctors."

The agents stepped aside.

"You're a hard-ass," Mason said.

"You better be right," Burgess whispered.

Mason stood next to the sedated Walters and pressed the green injector to Walters's left arm.

"Now what?" Burgess asked.

"Wait and pray."

In a few minutes, Mason felt reasonably sure that the antidote had worked.

Two hours later, Elvin Walters powered his hospital bed into a sitting position and dug into the vegan lunch. He nearly spit it out. *Do-gooder doctors,* Walters thought. With his shiny new defibrillator in place and oblivious to his brush with death, he decided it would certainly be steak for dinner.

CHAPTER

40

Tyler Jensen awoke with intense pain in his forehead and the clatter of helicopter rotors in his ears. He saw a pilot and five men with guns—probably friendlies sent by Torrence. They were the least of his problems. Drawing on all his training and survival instincts, he reached into his front pants pocket. It was empty. *In-fucking-credible.* He quickly searched his other pockets and everything around him. One of the medics raised an eyebrow at him curiously.

"Gotta go back to the hospital," he shouted to the closest man. "Gotta go now, or I'm gone."

The medic laughed. "Sure, we'll take you right back."

"I'm serious," Jensen said, grabbing the man's leg with his last bit of strength.

"Brother's in shock," said another. "He's been through a lot. Let's help him out," he said, pulling out a syringe filled with concentrated pentobarbital. "This should help you sleep."

He was right. Tyler Jensen never awoke.

~

In five minutes, there was no trace of the events that occurred. Standing alone in front of Drexel Memorial, Carrie Mumsford was shell-shocked. She couldn't find Mason. She phoned Jet, who cut her off, saying he had to roll. She stood, shaken and mystified, trying to absorb what had just happened.

After a few long moments, Burgess appeared and slid his arm around her shoulders. He spoke softly and calmly, offering reassurance. RT joined them as they walked toward the hospital. She turned back to see cars moving along the road in front of the hospital.

An AT&T van moved slowly past a black panel truck. Jet had left ten minutes ago. It couldn't be him, could it? The two vehicles pulled next to each other. Doors opened. A man with sandy hair jumped from one van into the other. Or did he? With the distance and the rain, she couldn't be sure. It seemed to have been Mason, if it happened at all.

"Isn't that Mason?" she said, pointing for RT to see.

The van drove off. The panel truck continued its slow troll through the parking lot.

"Where? I don't see anybody," said RT. "Sorry."

Burgess turned back towards her with compassion in his eyes. "Carrie, we've been through hell in the last twenty-four hours. Sometimes we see what we want to see. Let's get down to the ER. Your father had an accident."

"Emergency room. Oh God, no."

"He's fine. We just found out. He needs you."

Twenty minutes later, a Channel Six crew arrived, chasing a tip about an FBI helicopter swooping in military-style to make a quick landing in a parking lot at Drexel. They spoke of men dressed in black piling out and then back in as the chopper took off. The entire episode lasted less than three minutes. There was no one to answer their questions. Security knew nothing. The reporter and camera operator followed an old lady to her car, peppering her with questions to no avail. The valet parking attendants knew even less. A half hour later, the reporters left. It might as well have been a UFO sighting.

~

As he watched the shit storm unfold, Torrence knew what he had to do.

"Shut it down," he instructed his Cellar crew. "Upload everything to the server in Tajikistan. Then wipe 'em clean. Nothing can remain here. Ten minutes. Then we exit. Saied and Benny, come with me."

Trudging up the steps to the Plantation dining room, Benny was clueless. What Torrence wanted, he did not know. Saied showed no expression. Torrence waved the two of them ahead. "Meet me on the veranda." He punched in a few numbers on the keypad near the top step. A steel door slid silently from the left wall to the right and locked. The thick concrete walls of the Cellar stairwell were now blocked. There was no other exit. The geeks would never know.

Once Torrence entered the main house, he closed the aged wood door. No trace of the Cellar was evident. Soon, there would be no Cellar at all.

Torrence sank into one of the comfortable wicker chairs. "Have a seat," he said, motioning to Benny and Saied.

Saied took a deep breath and exhaled slowly. "Are you activating Andromeda?"

Benny's head shot up. Andromeda was the disaster plan. Step one locked the remainder of the geeks in the Cellar. Step two infused fentanyl gas through the ventilation system to knock them out; they would never know what hit them. Step three disbursed a massive dose of VX nerve gas through the ceiling sprinklers. Fifteen minutes and it would be over. All the geeks had been at their posts. With Benny gone, there'd be eleven bodies. The bodies would be removed and incinerated.

Saied shook his head. "It was a great team."

Torrence nodded. "It had to be done. You, Benny, and I will live to fight another day."

~

The chopper landed in a small clearing twenty miles from the Cellar. Torrence was surprised, but not displeased, to learn that Jensen was dead.

"What happened?" he shouted to one of the men over the whirring din.

"Gave him some pentobarbital to ease the ride. No respiration, no pulse."

The man paused and debated whether to report Jensen's demand to return to the hospital. "For the record, he seemed at peace, sir."

"Got it," said Torrence, bowing his head. "Make sure to say prayers when you cremate our brother's body in the name of the Father, the Son, and the Holy Spirit."

"Roger that."

Torrence watched the helicopter take off, then saluted as it ascended and crossed a nearby lake. He took out a small remote detonator from his pocket. His instinct told him to push the button. Blow it up. But that was messy, and he might need these warriors later. He slid his finger off the remote and placed it back in his pocket.

~

When Torrence returned to the Plantation, an ice bucket, a small beaker of spring water, and a bottle of his favorite whiskey—twenty-one-year-old Suntory Hibiki—sat on the table next to the white porch rocker. His phone rang. It was Richmond.

"Is it done?"

"It's done. Some good men died today. Jensen will be hard to replace."

"Everyone can be replaced," Richmond said. "You know that, Hugh."

"I pulled two from the Cellar, Saied and Benny. Saied is unique. Never worked with anyone so smart," Torrence said warmly. "And no one knows more about the Drexel EHR than Benny."

"Agreed. How long?" Richmond asked.

"The gas should have dissipated by now. I'll remove the bodies myself."

"That can wait," Richmond said. "Have a drink."

"Believe I've earned it," Torrence said. He poured himself three fingers and added a teaspoonful of water.

As he settled into the rocker, Torrence relaxed for the first time in months. Closing his eyes, he listened to Richmond, whose tone was both assertive and soothing.

"We learned a great deal over the past few years, owing entirely to your work," Richmond began. "Our friends are not unhappy. I want you to know that."

Torrence smiled and sipped.

"We've built the EHR, established its immense capabilities, and confirmed that we can control it. Burgess and his team at Drexel may tinker with the higher-level software, but our modifications and entry points are buried in the backbone software. Someone would have to go through millions of lines of code to find the worms. At the right time, the Drexel EHR will be most useful."

Torrence nodded. "Agreed."

"Still, we have some serious unfinished business. Who were the interlopers, and how did they learn so much about us? This Mason Fischer, undoubtedly not his real name, must be working with a sophisticated group. If I didn't know better, I'd think DOD. It stinks of them. I'd say NSA, but we know he isn't NSA. I'll have to do some digging to get to the bottom of it."

"Thomas Birck," muttered Torrence, losing his train of thought. He tried to remember what he was going to say.

"Birck?" said Richmond. "He's dead, isn't he? Why bring him up?"

Ordinarily, Richmond's tone would set Torrence off. But a soft swell of fuzzy relaxation embraced him.

"Ol' Tommy Bith," he finally answered.

"It's okay, Hugh. Before you go, I need to explain one more thing. I know you'll understand."

"Ahm, not go anwhere," Torrence mumbled.

"We've known all along it might come down to you or Walters. I placed almost all my chips on you at some risk to myself. I was happy to do it. But that wager didn't pan out. Now I've got to place a new bet. I'm sure you understand why."

Torrence slurred a response that sounded like, "You forking slum of a beast."

"Now that we've put the fear of God into Walters, even my friend in Palm Beach accepts he must be cultivated as an ally rather than an adversary."

The glass slipped from Torrence's hand, crashing on the porch.

"Of course, Walters will want certain assurances going forward that the threats against him are being contained."

The phone fell from Torrence's grip so that he did not hear Richmond's final words to him.

"It's the business we chose."

Moments later, two secure cell phones buzzed at once. Both answered to the same voice.

"Mr. Rasinko, Mr. Saied. It's over. Call sanitation. Spare the buildings for now."

"Yes, sir," answered Saied.

"I will be in touch at the appropriate time," said Richmond. "Instructions, along with everything you'll need, are in your vehicles." The line went dead.

Benny and Saied exchanged knowing glances. Saied walked over to Torrence and removed the St. Christopher's medal from his pocket. "He won't be needing this anymore."

"You sentimental bastard," Benny joked as they departed.

They walked to the front entrance, but the guards were gone. Two identical Toyota Camrys were parked outside. Each had a manila folder on its passenger seat. Saied and Benny slid into the drivers' seats and then looked at each other through their windows, pausing to see who would have the courage to turn his key first.

41

The days that followed were filled with empty action. For all the drama, Walters was fine. Blood tests revealed nothing unusual, neither the poison Mason had insisted was there, nor the antidote he had administered to save Walters's life. The FBI lab would later report that it had found nothing untoward in the injector discs Jensen had used—Van der Graf had concocted a synthetic death potion undetectable by all known reagents.

The Bureau's search for Tyler Jensen was fruitless. The man, whoever he really was, had vanished. Bud Burgess and Carrie Mumsford were convinced he had attempted to kill Walters. But the senator insisted that his treatment at Drexel be kept secret—"patient confidentiality," he thundered—and the lack of any hard evidence concerning a crime sealed the deal. Despite their suspicions, the Bureau agents chose the path of least resistance, deciding that they didn't have enough solid information to continue their investigation. Tyler Jensen would remain an open missing person case handled by the local police.

The FBI was also unable to explain the helicopter landing at Drexel. The men were certainly not their agents, the security footage provided few clues, and the cold trail led only to dead ends.

Two senior FBI agents interviewed Charles Richmond for more than three hours in his National Institute for Medical Safety office. He could not have seemed more helpful. The agents peppered Richmond with questions about limo trips to Virginia ("the back of a limousine is the only place I can be alone and clear my head") and his phone calls to, among others, Hugh Torrence ("an old friend who shares my interest in vintage stemware; would you like to see my collection?"). He called "a number I have for Hugh" in front of the agents. "Strange," he said, "it went straight to voice mail. But," he added with a laugh, "I don't have to tell you that he is a man of mystery." When asked if he suspected anyone of sabotaging the EHR, Richmond became indignant. "That project is my baby," he said. "No one is more invested than I am. If I even had a sniff of foul play, you would have been on speed call." Ultimately, they called it a day. If Richmond knew more, which they steadfastly believed he did, it was going to take more resources and authority than the two agents had to pry it from this renowned and revered man of science. They bounced it up to the director, who read their report and filed it, permanently, in the ultra-secure micro-cut shredder he kept by his desk.

Alone again, Richmond pulled out a single-use phone.

He heard no voice when his call was answered.

"All's clear," Richmond said.

"Now, we wait," was the response.

~

Derrick Mumsford was back at his desk in a week. In a closed-door meeting, Burgess convinced him that his would-be assassin was Jensen, not Fischer. The two men acknowledged that Jensen was involved in five patient deaths, but they also decided to believe that each had been so sick, their end was inevitable and imminent. Jensen hadn't killed them so much as given them a shove. The EHR indicated nothing to the contrary, and they agreed to keep this to themselves. Why open that can of worms?

When the two dissected the situation, they arrived at the reassuring conclusion that their prized EHR was unscathed, at least publicly. The skill of the stealth hackers now turned out to be a blessing; they had left no trace, a digital equivalent of RSM-223. They agreed it was long past time to delete the pharmacy's legacy order tracking system.

This convenient narrative prepared them to tackle the billion-dollar question of whether to proceed with the EHR. Burgess and Mumsford concluded that the EHR could live up to its potential, with some refinement. Yes, problems had been unearthed in the eleventh hour. But they resulted from an extraordinary and almost certainly one-time assault from a group whose leader, Tyler Jensen, was irreparably compromised. Now that he was on the radar of both Drexel and law enforcement, he was no longer a threat.

"They showed you their cards, right?" Mumsford queried.

"Yes," Burgess responded.

"And you can trump them all."

"Sure, yes, of course."

As the triumph of his life's work grew closer, it was easy for Burgess to convince himself to stay quiet about the events of the last few weeks. Besides, what would be the point? And who would believe him anyway? He also drew comfort from Mumsford's rhetorical questions that seemed to offer a clear path to the high road: "How many lives would be lost if we delayed the EHR to look into five deaths that were bound to happen anyway? How many reputations might be unfairly ruined?"

Mumsford and Burgess were further emboldened when Senator Walters did a one-eighty on electronic health records. In a speech delivered a few weeks after the events at Drexel Memorial, Senator Walters, echoing JFK's sentiments, heralded the future of EHRs as "…the new frontier of medicine that will allow us to explore the human body and push through the limits of science while saving lives and money."

Mumsford also drew comfort from the fact that Charles Richmond was in full agreement. Richmond had displayed great interest and sensitivity. He'd flown to Durham twice. He and Mumsford had dined at Café Parizade in Durham, one of his favorites, and at Bin 54 in Chapel Hill, which was at the very top of his list. Their discussions were long and detailed. Richmond said he had pushed, "and pushed some more," on his broad network of NSA, DOD, CIA and FBI contacts. None of them were behind it; none knew who had done it. He found it hard to believe, but "that's what we have."

The two old friends and partners soon spent a long weekend meeting with teams of investment bankers. All were wildly enthusiastic, not only given the EHR's promise, but the certainty that their investments would have monumental returns. They saw dollar signs in promoting the Drexel EHR as America's EHR and would invest as much as necessary to get there. The future had arrived, and it was bright green.

CHAPTER
42

Carrie drove up the last hill along the rocky granite and dirt road. Her rented Honda Civic had scraped over rocks too many times to count since she turned off the paved two-lane highway. It was a miracle she hadn't gotten a flat or punctured the undercarriage. Now she wondered what she'd find on the other side.

She only had herself to blame. After constant begging, prodding, and cajoling, RT had finally given her some information three days before.

"Alphonse told me he finally heard from Jet," RT said in the Drexel cafeteria. "Didn't say much except he was safe and planned on laying low a while longer. He called from a pay phone. Alphonse caught the area code: 325. That's in Texas. You believe that? I didn't even know there were still pay phones."

"Texas?"

"Yeah, he spent some time in the Southwest. I figured maybe he was visiting someone in in Dallas or Houston. But that area code is from the middle of nowhere: west of Austin, north of San Antonio."

"You're thinking Jet might be with Mason?"

"Could be."

"I wonder if that area code includes the tiny town Mason is from," Carrie said, pulling out her phone. "Castell."

"Great minds think alike, and so do we," RT joked. "I already checked and it is. I also found an old interview where Mason talked about growing up on a ranch outside Castell, along a bend of the Llano River. He said he'd walk down to the river and sit on a big rock to think. The rock stood where the river turned west. After his old man died, that's where he went to get his head straight."

"You've been busy."

"Check out what I found on Google satellite," RT said, showing Carrie a pre-loaded image on his tablet. "Here's Castell, and just to the west, where the river bends, is the highest point in Llano County. Satellite photos aren't the best, but if you look close," he continued, using his right thumb and index finger to zoom in, "you can even see the big rock in the river. Looks like the thing to do is to fly to Austin, rent a car, follow Highway 71 to some county roads, then dirt paths, and then Lord knows what…. It's Texas. But at the end of civilization, all these fancy tools say, there's a house. Maybe that's where Mason grew up, maybe not. Maybe Jet's there. Maybe more."

~

Carrie definitely needed to get away. A chasm had opened up between her and her father after he decided to press ahead with the EHR, despite all that had happened and her impassioned pleas. But oddly, it was something her father had told her years ago that inspired her to head for Texas.

"Don't stumble through life. Live with passion. You'll never be sorry if you give everything you have, every day. I loved your mother with all I had. Her death almost killed me. It still hurts. But I wouldn't trade the passion we had for anything in this world."

Carrie had the same passion, and that was why she was here. Here in the middle of nowhere. The small paved roads she'd driven crossed over the Llano River at least three times. In some places no wider than twenty yards across, it was not a large river, but the crystal-clear water gurgling over limestone rocks into deep pools beckoned to her in the unrelenting Texas heat.

A small flat mountain, more like a mesa, came into view. Even at a distance, she could see huge chunks of granite surrounded by trees and brush. Well beyond the mesa, twenty miles to the south, loomed a much larger pink granite dome. She knew from the photos online that had to be Enchanted Rock. Between the dusty roads and the mesa, there remained miles and miles of short trees, cacti and brush interspersed with herds of cattle and goats.

The closer she got to her destination, the less convinced she was that she was headed anywhere, or that she and Mason had any real connection. Over the past two months, she'd come to the conclusion that her intuition had failed her again.

Finally, she rounded the corner and there it was: a one story, well-kept limestone ranch house set in a neatly fenced large yard that led down to the river. A sweeping porch started at the front of the house and wrapped around the back, towards the river. The metal roof caught her eye, painted a light brown that complemented the limestone and the wood.

Two vehicles were parked in front, a beat-up blue and white Ford 150 pickup truck that had to be from the 1980s, and a generic white van, no different from the ten others she'd seen in the Alamo rental lot at the Austin airport. She pulled around and parked.

The air smelled of dirt and the river. The sun still shone brightly, falling into the western horizon. The temperature had dropped ten degrees already, going from hell to just hot.

Having arrived, Carrie had no idea what to do. She hadn't seen a person in twenty miles, and only two ranch houses, set way back from the road. So many years had passed since Mason had grown up there—*if that was even true*—that there was no way to know if the property was even still in the family. She hesitated. Rural Texas was intimidating. Maybe the owner of the house wouldn't feel charitable towards an outsider showing up unannounced. A large yellow dog came bounding out towards her car. She instinctively reached for the car door handle. But the Labrador mix wasn't barking or aggressive; it nuzzled her hand and slapped her with its wagging tail. She bent over and jostled it, rubbing it behind the ears, and almost forgot where she was, so much so that the loud voice took her by surprise.

"Well, come on up to the porch. Must have been a long day."

Even without seeing him, Carrie knew it was Mason. Before she could say a word, he swept her up in his arms, lifting her off the ground and spinning her around.

"I didn't know…" she started, then stopped. Part of her wanted to cry; part of her demanded an explanation.

"I know, and I'm sorry. Every few days, I'd get a message from one of Alphonse's ladies that RT had been asking about me. I wasn't sure until last week that you were the reason. I was hoping you were."

Now she cried. Real tears, for the first time since her mother died.

"I'm going to need some answers."

"It's a long story," said Mason.

"I've got the time for whatever tale you've cooked up."

They were interrupted by a booming voice. "Well, if it ain't Doc Mumsford. Thought you might show up." The voice was Jet's, but it seemed to be coming from the wrong direction. Not from the house. She craned her neck, looking for him.

"Son, I'll be damned if I could wrangle that big cat out of that hole. RT don't know a thing about fishing. Couldn't get him to keep his knees down. Every time I'd get up close and personal and could feel that catfish, he'd squirt over by RT and get away. Sure didn't want to leave that hole next to the rock. He's a big boy, long as a rake."

"Not to throw shade, but you Texans are messed up," RT called to Mason. "Catching catfish with your bare hands? Some kind of redneck fun, I guess."

Carrie stared, dumbfounded as she saw RT approaching in blue jeans and high-top basketball shoes, no shirt, and soaking wet.

"How did you get here so fast?" Carrie asked.

"I've been here the last few days. You made record time yourself."

"You see, Carrie, RT is one of our team members. Didn't start out that way, but he is now," said Jet. "We're thinking you might be a fine addition too."

"I have no earthly idea what you are talking about," said Carrie.

"In time," said Jet. "Mason, maybe we should take this fine young lady into town for some beer and barbecue."

"Outstanding," replied Mason.

43

"Carrie, you ride in the cab," Jet said, holding the passenger side door of the old pickup open for her. "RT and I will stretch out in the back. I imagine you two have a lot to talk about." He winked at her as she stepped in.

As Mason drove down the bumpy dirt road, Carrie felt a rollercoaster of emotions. She was shocked and relieved, confused and irritated. Why the charade at Drexel? The weeks of silence.

"You've got some explaining to do," she said.

"About what?"

Carrie just stared at him incredulously.

"Oh, that. By now there must have been some press on what happened, right?"

"Nothing. It's weird," replied Carrie.

Mason, who expected the blackout, feigned surprise. "Nothing?"

"Nope."

"I guess there are a few gaps, then," he said and laughed. "Ask me anything."

"Are you really Dr. Mason Fischer?"

Mason laughed. "The one and only."

"Why did you leave so suddenly?"

"I didn't. I stayed in the area for a few days. We monitored the situation through RT and Burgess. When it became clear that the authorities had no interest in finding out what, if anything, had happened to Walters and where Jensen or RT or I were, we figured it was best to vamoose. I headed here, home. Jet and RT joined me. Alphonse stayed to clean up some of the mess."

"Which was?"

"That's complicated."

"No problemo," Carrie said with a smile. "One thing I've learned about this God-forsaken place is that there's lots of dirt, lots of cactus, and, I'd guess, lots of time to hear your big, complicated story."

"I'll do my best," Mason promised. "I've spent the last month trying to piece it together myself. It started more than a year ago when concerns arose about the Drexel EHR. Ultimately, it was decided to put someone on the ground at Drexel. That someone was me."

"Wait, wait, what about all your troubles in Galveston?"

"I can answer that," Jet interrupted, his voice streaming through the open window between the cab and the back of the old pickup. "The idea was to use Mason as bait. We figured if someone wanted to use the EHR as a killing machine, they might like a handy scapegoat—say, a doctor who enjoys killing his patients. Got to say that was some of our finest work, finding some deaths that could be made to fit a nonexistent pattern, creating those 'deleted' email messages raising concerns about him and faking the video feed so it looked like he was in the hospital pulling the plug when he said he was at home. Mason had the harder part, though, convincing Dr. Henderson's girlfriend to believe he liked her. How he gets women to fall for him, I still don't understand."

"Anyway," Mason continued. "Alphonse and Jet were already monitoring the EHR before I arrived. Their web security company had become well known enough that government agencies like the Department of Defense and some non-governmental…"

"But totally legit," Jet added.

"…but totally legit actors were using them for small contract work. Alphonse's operation is one of those that you would never find in a phone book, but it's there. I was called in because they were coming up empty."

"Through no fault of our own," Jet interjected.

"Through no fault of their own. As you saw, whoever we were up against was good."

"Almost as good as us," added Jet.

"Hey," Mason said, "who's telling this story? So at the end of the day, they, the Department of Defense, were convinced something bad was going on but couldn't exactly figure out what. Having a doctor on the inside would help. I didn't see anything for the longest time. But then, do you remember that car crash victim in May?"

"The man who worked at Drexel and skidded off the bridge?" Carrie said. "You said his real name was Cabreja?"

"Yes. He was a friend from Fort Bragg. Special Forces all the way. Unkillable, they used to say."

"You were in the military?" Carrie asked.

"Yes," Mason smiled with a sheepish shrug. "Before he died, he told me something was up. Not what, just something."

"What Mason didn't know was that Cabreja had fallen on hard times after leaving the service. Liked his tequila a little too much," Jet said. "Ended up doing day labor on a project; we think it was called the Cellar. We still don't know what that was—maybe he did, but that secret went with him. Fact is, there was so little info, nothing but stray chatter that died out among undocumented workers that, if it were real, it had to be some kind of black op—maybe NSA, CIA or FBI. Given Cabreja's presence and his dying words, it probably had something to do with Drexel. Cabreja was not part of our operation—at least, I don't think he was—but we're guessing."

"Before he died, I thought all we'd ever have were suspicions," Mason said. "For the longest time, I had no idea that RT was part of the team."

"Truth be told, I didn't know about you or the team," RT said. "All this and y'all were a surprise to me."

"That's the way we like it," Jet explained. "Keep you in the dark, keep you honest, just in case others are watching. But don't feel bad," he added with a Cheshire Cat grin, "we even kept a few things from Mason."

"What about me?" Carrie asked. "Was I part of the plan?"

"I won't lie," Mason said after shooting Jet a playful glance. "Having access to Derrick Mumsford was important. But then it turned out you were so much more, a smart and passionate partner in every sense."

"We told him to cool it with you, no lie. But he wouldn't listen," Jet said. "And thank goodness for that."

For the next twenty minutes on the drive to Castell, Mason covered some nuances, loose ends, and enduring mysteries. Her father had never known about their operation. Burgess only helped at the end, beginning that night in Greensboro. Jensen had disappeared without a trace. So had the guy who was probably running him, a former NSA spook named Hugh Torrence. No one seemed interested in any answers.

"The team. You were going to tell me what Jet was talking about," said Carrie. "And you keep saying you were assigned to come here. By whom?"

"At first, the team was just Alphonse, Jet, and the ladies. Alphonse also guided RT to work at Drexel without telling him what was up in order to have someone on the inside, if necessary."

"And to get him a real job, to start paying for his food," said Jet.

"They were right," said Mason. "RT's a natural. So are you. You did alright back there with your Judo moves on old Jensen."

"That joke is getting old," said Carrie, though she couldn't help but smile. "For someone who's been speaking all this time, you've left a lot out. What does the team do? Who's pulling the strings?"

"Our leader," said Mason, smiling, "was—okay, is—a master of medicine and intrigue named Dr. Thomas Birck."

"You might also say he's a modern-day Lazarus," Jet added.

"Indeed," Mason said, adding to Carrie's confusion. "Dr. Birck took an interest in me when I was in medical school. In addition to being the Dean of Vandy's med school, he was a badass consultant on medical issues for the Department of

Defense. He got me interested by including me in small side projects. Medicine is a great profession, a high calling, but it lacks sizzle. Maybe it's from my football days, but I like taking risks. I was in Galveston when he called me and said he needed me at Drexel. He is not the kind of guy you say no to. Still, I was hedging until Jet called."

"How could he resist?"

"It took a couple of months to set up my backstory in Galveston, and then I was off to Durham. When I got there, they told me Dr. Birck had died."

"We could hide lots of stuff, but not our boy's connection to Birck, which would have been a red flag to certain elements," Jet explained. "Having everyone, including Mason here, believe that Birck was dead would help us sell it and keep Mason safe."

"Jesus," Carrie said.

"It was the right move," Mason said. "One of the happiest days of my life was hearing Tom Birck's voice a few weeks ago. I think he liked being dead."

"So," Mason said, looking at Carrie, "is that enough to earn me some barbecue?"

~

They piled out of the truck. A rooster in a wire cage crowed. They filed into a worn-out general store.

"Hey, dog ass, want to see my rooster do his thing?" yelled an old man in overalls on the porch.

"Maybe later," said Mason. "Don't want to show 'em all the highlights right out of the gate."

The old man ushered them in past racks of ranch supplies, fishing lures, a wall of mounted deer antlers, faded photos of fish caught in the river, and a refrigerator full of beer and soft drinks.

"Mason!" the old man exclaimed. "'Bout time you brung by someone to balance out your sorry looks and personality. Is this little lady Carrie? The one you've been babbling on about?"

Carrie almost melted with joy.

"Carrie, this boy is about as tongue-tied as one of them goats out there in the yard when he talks about you. Fact is, one look is all it takes to see that, for one time in his whole danged life, he's right. Welcome to the Castell General Store." He stuck out his hand. "I'm Kenneth Schultz. German in my genes, Texan everywhere else."

"A pleasure," said Carrie.

"Missy, you have quite a reputation to live up to. How about a beer?" Before anyone could speak, he pulled four icy glasses from a decades-old freezer and four Lone Star longnecks from the refrigerator.

"What's left?" asked Mason.

"I've got brisket, sausage, and some potato salad the missus made this afternoon. And peach cobbler. Everyone in?"

Before he could turn around, Carrie spoke up. "You really do know this man?" She waved her arm at Mason.

"Since he was about this high," said the old man, holding his hand about three feet off the ground. "Got to show you the Mason Fischer room."

"That can wait," said Mason. "Carrie just got in. Save that oddity for another day."

The old man ignored him.

"You've gotta see the room." He made a long sweeping motion with his arm and led her around the corner. He fiddled with his large key ring, unlocking the doorknob and then a deadbolt.

"I love this place. His old man was my best friend. Name was Mason too—or one, I suppose, ha!—but everyone called him Pops, cause he liked to shoot pop cans when he was a kid. Pops was beyond proud of his boy. Kept every scrap, every article, every trophy. Knew it would embarrass the hell out of Mason, so he never showed it to him. When he felt the end coming, he asked me to keep it. Mason was off at U.T., and Pops didn't know if he'd ever come back. If Mason sold the place, this stuff would be lost forever. He made me promise to safeguard it and show it to Mason when the time was right."

Carrie looked back at Mason. He smiled, but his eyes were moist and sad. Maybe the room would provide some of the answers she sought.

"You look through this stuff, and you'll know. Cover of *Sports Illustrated*. How many people have one of them? The boy was something else." He walked back towards the tiny kitchen. "I'll check the barbecue."

It started about as she'd expected. A monument to Mason's successes on the football field: Mason in uniform from junior high to high school to the University of Texas. Headline articles from the *Austin American-Statesman* and the *Dallas Morning News*. Articles from the *Llano Times*— "Local Boy Makes it Big at U.T." and more. It all fit.

What she found next was not at all expected. In one corner of the room hung a collage, painstakingly assembled and labeled. The strong, clear block letters were not the writing of a woman, and the hand that wrote it had a tremor. Unlike most collages, this one had a theme and a timeline. It was a pictorial history. Underneath the collage was an old-fashioned four-drawer file cabinet, begging to be opened. Each drawer was full of neatly organized manila folders, all containing a systematic assortment of articles about football and scholastic achievements.

Carrie leafed through the folders. A few of the folders were particularly worn and dog-eared. She pulled out one that was especially beat up. It smelled of dry dust. The first article was not about Mason but about a young woman.

"Auto Accident Claims Local Woman" read the headline.

Mason's mother, Carrie thought, staring hard for answers that weren't there in the picture of the woman whose sad eyes betrayed her smile.

The same folder contained letters addressed to Mason, written in the same careful block letters. Some a few sentences long, some a few paragraphs, but none of them, evidently, completed and sent. Most started along the same lines:

> *Dear Mason,*
>
> *I've lived my life, and you have yours ahead of you. Tragedy is just that, and my heart goes out to you. If only I could have traded places with her, I would. But I cannot....*

Carrie thought of her own father's anguish when he had to tell her about her mother's unexpected death.

Carrie carefully replaced the letters and the folder and quickly closed the file drawer. She shouldn't have been reading through his private life. After a moment to gather herself, she returned to the others just as Ken Schultz walked up with plates piled high with barbecue and potato salad to the table.

"What did you think about that?" asked Schultz. "Hadn't seen anyone like him around here, before or since. And fearless. Tell you what, though, every time I watched him on the tube when he was at U.T. nailing a big ol' fullback running full steam through the secondary, it gave me a belly-ache. Hell, practically gave me the runnin' fits a time or two. He ended up being all-everything, a kid from Castell. Even today, that boy doesn't look much different from most of the goat-ropers around these parts…cept'n that he ain't carrying an extra thirty pounds in his belly. Did you ever figure the same fella walking around your hospital as fancy as any of those Harvard docs would have been all of this?"

She shook her head, tears welling in her eyes for the second time in twenty minutes, and in twenty years. "I had no idea."

Schultz threw his weather-beaten arm around Carrie's shoulders and erupted into a deep, hearty laugh. "Ain't just you, darling."

"Through all the years, the boy can still hit," said Jet. "Never seen better than the one he laid on Jensen out front of the hospital. Remember?"

"It's still a blur," Carrie said. "I was so scared."

"Not too scared to *hee-yah* the man so he never saw me coming," said Mason.

"Honestly, it was instinct. I don't remember anything until I was in front of the hospital and thought I saw you jumping into Jet's van."

"Truth is, both of you are straight up, and that's all I've got to say about it," said Jet. "Now, I'm going to dig into this Texas barbecue." He broke into a conspiratorial whisper to Carrie. "And let's try not to think about the real thing back in North Carolina."

~

Hours later, in the small front bedroom, Jet flipped the light switch up and down before finally flopping down on the twin bed across the room from where RT lay reading.

"How long you going to stay here, man?" asked RT.

"The closest I ever got to Texas was when I was at O.U. Them Okies hate Texans. Ain't no love for Texans in Carolina either. Not since Mack Brown left the Tar Heels for the Longhorns. Course maybe since the Mack Attack is back at UNC, they ain't so pissed about his leaving. My home's in Carolina. I'll be moving along in a day or two. How about you?"

"Me too. Somebody's got to keep an eye on those people at Drexel."

"You do that. I'm sure we'll be getting together before you know it. Misery never sleeps."

~

By midnight, all was calm. Mason and Carrie sat on the long porch facing the Llano River. Light danced over the water as it bounded over rocks and back into the streambed. The night offered a natural symphony: the hoot of an owl, a far-away cry of a distressed rabbit, the yip of a coyote. The moon had yet to rise, making the stars all the more brilliant in the clear summer sky.

"I've never seen stars like this," said Carrie.

"No real city lights for nearly a hundred miles. I used to sit out here at night, just like this, and try to identify the con-stellations. I'm still no good at it."

"You're a hard guy to get to know, Mason Fischer. About the time I think I get it, you show me another wrinkle. Tell me about those years that Dr. Burgess and my father said you couldn't be found."

"It's a really long story."

"Of course."

"It would take a month to get through it."

"Start talking. I want to know about those years."

Mason looked at Carrie and knew he could give her—and give himself—the great gift: trust. "This wasn't my first foray out of medicine."

"You mean with electronic medical records?"

"No, government-type work."

For the next hour, Mason detailed his long relationship with Thomas Birck, beginning with a Christmas phone call when he interviewed at Vanderbilt to their many conversations about having a purpose in life and Birck's disclosure about his sub-specialty: small, precise investigations.

"When he told me about that," Mason said, "I knew he had shared something with me that only a handful of others knew. When someone trusts you like that, it's impossible to refuse them."

Mason confided in Carrie that he'd had several missions—*projects* he called them—before Drexel. He described them all. They had included "a research project at NASA where faked data could have killed the Space Station crew and a secret and utterly crazy attempt at a research lab in Galveston to cross the highly lethal Ebola with the easily transmissible smallpox."

Carrie gazed towards the river as Mason spoke, wishing he had told her earlier, but at the same time being glad he had not.

"Did any of these make the news?"

"Never. Just like the business with Jensen. You'll never see a word about it in print. National security, you know."

"I don't know whether to be relieved or mystified. Did you know what you were getting into this time?"

"It's my life. And I love it," he said, squeezing her hand, "but I also see that I've only been living half a life. Meeting you at Drexel was the best thing that ever happened to me."

"Smooth move, but not so fast. You're not getting anywhere with me until you fess up to what's next on your calendar."

"I seriously doubt your father wants me at Drexel. Last I heard, he thought I was the one trying to kill him in the ER."

"It was Jensen. RT told me. My father knows."

Mason nodded. "Still…maybe it's time for a move for me."

"And the team?"

"I told Jet that if something else came up where they needed a doctor to call me. Anytime. He and Alphonse will keep working with the DOD. I imagine they'll get a crack at whatever the Department thinks is the greatest threat. Seems like a calling that I've fallen into, too. I was thinking you might be of a like mind."

"They'll be back in Greensboro?"

"Greensboro?" Mason laughed. "As much of a deal as they made about that, about saving the community, it was just part of the job. The NSA, or whoever it was, torched the house they worked out of and that was that. I don't know where they'll go next."

"I'm thinking of going back to Galveston, starting over with a medical practice." He looked at her intently. "But, as usual with my life, my decisions aren't mine alone to make."

"One more question," Carrie said.

"Promise, just one?"

"After taking into account the woman's prerogative… absolutely. Tell me about that plaque on the wall inside."

"My pop loved Theodore Roosevelt. The quote on that plaque was one of his favorites. He told it to me over and over when I was a kid. When I was down, or discouraged, he'd recite it to me. Must have read it to me a hundred times. He made this plaque and gave it to me when I was in college, after a special person, my girlfriend, died. It was only a year later that he passed away. Heart attack. That's why I ended up choosing cardiology."

Without a trace of irony, Mason began to recite the quote.

"'It is not the critic who counts; not the man who points out how the strong man stumbles, or where the doer of deeds could have done them better. The credit belongs to the man who is actually in the arena, whose face is marred by dust and sweat and blood; who strives valiantly; who errs, who comes short again and again, because there is no effort without error and shortcoming; but who does actually strive to do the deeds; who knows great enthusiasms, the great devotions; who spends himself in a worthy cause; who at the best knows in the end the triumph of high achievement, and who at the worst, if he fails, at least fails while daring greatly, so that his place shall never be with those cold and timid souls who neither know victory nor defeat.'"

"Sounds like the life you found, Mason Fischer."

"It can be your life, too. Why don't you join our little band of spies?" Mason grinned mischievously, grabbed Carrie by the hands, and pulled her to her feet. "Time to go fishing."

"Oh, no. I'm not going out there."

"Oh yes, you are."

"It's pitch black. There could be mountain lions, coyotes, rattlesnakes, or almost anything out there and I wouldn't see it."

"Makes it more exciting," he responded, his eyes twinkling. "Here," he said, handing her an elbow-length leather glove.

"What's this for?"

"So you'll be ready when that big catfish grabs your arm in his mouth."

"Dr. Fischer, I hope you know by now that I am always ready."

"Our arena awaits."

ACKNOWLEDGMENTS

A decade (or two) has passed since I decided I could write a medical thriller. Turns out it was a lot more difficult than I imagined. *Coded to Kill* could have never become a reality without the generous advice and expertise of many smart friends.

First and foremost, many thanks go to my co-author, J. Peder Zane, who helped me develop the characters, shape the plot and sharpen every sentence. Peder is talented and thoughtful and has amazing perseverance. He is always a joy to work with, as long as the topic doesn't involve his beloved Buckeyes.

Our agent extraordinaire, Jonathan Bronitsky, stepped outside his nonfiction comfort zone to champion this book, providing the kind of encouragement and guidance every writer needs but usually only hopes for.

Our editor, David Bernstein, provided superb feedback, and the team at Post Hill House Press improved the book in every way.

So many friends and colleagues read various iterations of *Coded to Kill*; it's hard to know where to start. What they all shared in common was their knowledge, their encouragement, and their exceeding kindness when they pointed out areas that could "use a little work." Larry Klein and Andrew Rosenberg are physicians who are also experts in the ways of computers, networks, and especially cybersecurity. Rose Glenn, a fabulous communications guru, read through the highs and lows of the manuscript, and she and her colleague Sally Liaw offered invaluable advice. Angela Rego spent countless hours editing—finding errors, inconsistencies, and repeatedly suggesting just the right word. Beth Johnson brought her expertise in writing and organizing to the novel. Among the many others who helped along the way, David Des Rosiers, Eve Robinson, Laurel Choate, Mitch Hoffman, James Varney, Kendall Conger, Suzanne Pederson, and Janine Steel Zane deserve special thanks.

My greatest thanks go to my wife, Susan, and our five children, who not only helped shape the plot and the characters—they put up with my obsession to write a novel.

Ann Arbor, January 2023

ABOUT THE AUTHOR

Marschall S. Runge, M.D., Ph.D., is the executive vice president for Medical Affairs at the University of Michigan, dean of the Medical School, and CEO of Michigan Medicine. He earned his doctorate in molecular biology at Vanderbilt University and his medical degree from Johns Hopkins School of Medicine, where he also completed a residency in internal medicine. He was a cardiology fellow at the Massachusetts General Hospital. He is the author of over 250 publications and holds five patents for novel approaches to health care. As a Texas native who spent fifteen years in North Carolina and an avid thriller reader, Runge has experienced so many you-can't-make-this-up events that his transition to fiction was inevitable.